LATIN AMERICAN CRIME

THIRTEEN STORIES

SELECTED BY

DANIEL GALERA

CAROL BENSIMON
BRAZIL

RODRIGO BLANCO CALDERÓN
VENEZUELA

BERNARDO CARVALHO
BRAZIL

ANDRÉS RESSIA COLINO
URUGUAY

MARIANA ENRIQUEZ
ARGENTINA

RODRIGO HASBÚN
BOLIVIA

JORGE ENRIQUE LAGE
CUBA

SANTIAGO RONCAGLIOLO
PERU

RODRIGO REY ROSA
GUATEMALA

ANDRÉS FELIPE SOLANO
COLOMBIA

JOCA REINERS TERRON
BRAZIL

JUAN PABLO VILLALOBOS
MEXICO

ALEJANDRO ZAMBRA
CHILE

INTERNS & VOLUNTEERS: Charlotte Bhaskar, Amanda Nolen, Victor Inzunza, Elizabeth
Layman, Elizabeth Kurata, Joseph Grantham, Alastair Boone, Berenice Freedome, Aubrey
Young. ALSO HELPING: Andi Winnette, Annie Wyman, Ian Delaney, Casey Jarman, Sam
Riley, Clara Sankey, Sunra Thompson, Brian Christian, Ruby Perez. WEBSITE: Chris Monks.
SUPPORT: Jordan Karnes. ART DIRECTOR: Dan McKinley. COPY EDITOR: Will Georgantas.
PUBLISHER: Laura Howard. MANAGING EDITOR: Daniel Gumbiner. EXECUTIVE EDITOR:
Jordan Bass. EDITOR: Dave Eggers.

INTERIOR ILLUSTRATIONS: Ciro Hernandez.
COVER ILLUSTRATIONS & LETTERING: Sunra Thompson.

Printed in Michigan at Thomson-Shore.

This project was created with the help of RT/features.
Thanks to Rodrigo Teixeira, Lourenço Sant' Anna,
Camila Buralli, and Daniel Galera.

RT/features
ENTERTAINMENT

DEAR MCSWEENEY'S,

I'm not certain you care about soccer, but there's a World Cup happening later this year, and I can hardly think about anything else. I daydream about it in my idle moments, on the bus, walking home, doing laundry. I talk to my ten-month-old son about it, and he smiles. (But then again, he smiles at everything.) The World Cup gives me a reason to carry on when all else seems bleak—and I'm only exaggerating a little bit. Naturally, I intend to watch as many matches as my schedule allows.

Not long ago, a friend sent me a link to a video of Diego Maradona's famous "Goal of the Century," widely considered the best individual goal in the history of the tournament, scored at the 1986 World Cup in Mexico. Argentina versus England. I saw it live, of course. I was nine years old. It remains a startling piece of improvisation, one that transcends sport: a ten-and-a-half-second dash past, through, and around four tentative, flailing English defenders and one helpless goalkeeper. I've seen it more than a hundred times, played it over in my head a thousand more. And every time I'm amazed. Maradona tilts and turns, pauses, changes direction, sprints, and, most improbably of all, finishes. The Argentine announcer calling the game for audiences back home famously ended his description of this sporting marvel with a question: "Diego, ¿de qué planeta viniste?"

Diego, what planet are you from?

If you've seen the goal, you know this is an entirely fair question.

But that's not why I'm writing. This new video, the version my friend sent, was the same clip, but slowed down, and set to tango. Nothing to it; the kind of music video mash-up a twelve-year-old could make on their cell phone these days. But I'm a sucker for this sort of thing, so I watched it. Then I watched it again. And then again—as entranced as I was when I was a nine-year-old, sitting before our old, giant wooden-console television set. There was a sadness to it that I hadn't recognized before. Because, let's be honest, the English defending is egregious, almost slapstick. Even in real time, there's a hint of slow motion to it, a throwback to the age when soccer players smoked cigarettes at halftime and managers limited their tactical discussions to shouts of "Come on, lads!" But when the video is *actually* slowed down, and then set to tango, it feels even more ridiculous: these poor Englishmen whirling and falling over, as if perform- ing a cruelly choreographed shambles dance. The defenders melt away gently, making room for the Argentine genius. The subtle accordion riffs highlight the inevitability of it all. You can see that the defenders were never going to stop him—even when one sticks out an arm, Maradona glides past, as if he's hardly noticed it was there. And there's another thing: here is the recklessness of a man who believes in himself and believes that he can score when he wants. He is selfish. He never considers passing, no matter how many defenders toss themselves in his path. That was part of his greatness.

It would also be his downfall.

This is where the sadness comes in. In that moment, on June 22, 1986, Maradona became my hero. I'd even say he was the first person I identified in that way, with that language. A hero. He was mine and everyone's. Children were named in his honor. A church was founded in his name. A cult appeared, you might say. He was young then, in his prime, but this is what I wanted to write to you about: his fall from grace a scant eight years later would mark, for me, an important shift toward adulthood. That's what I thought about as I watched the Goal of the Century set to tango. Those dense minor chords, the weaving melody veering toward a kind of gloom, more like resignation—you are watching a near miracle, but you're also watching a man at his peak, a man whose talent would flame out, whose demons would catch up to him, even when the English defenders could not.

Let's not make too much of this, *McSweeney's*. It's just the mood I'm in. But yes, the roots of Maradona's downfall were always there. This was, after all, the same man who scored the famous "Hand of God" goal: a 5´5˝ Argentine pretending to head the ball over a 6´ English goalkeeper. This happened in the same tournament, the same match, in fact. And we celebrated that too. How sly. How clever. How audacious. But imagine if he'd been caught, if he'd been given a red card, and suspended. How stupid, we'd say. How selfish. How self-destructive.

Maradona was all those things.

That day in 1986, I asked my old man if the Hand of God was cheating, and I remember very clearly how he thought for a moment before answering. "Yes," he said carefully. "But it doesn't matter, because his second goal was so beautiful, it's worth two points."

Sincerely,

DANIEL ALARCÓN
SAN FRANCISCO, CA

DEAR MCSWEENEY'S,
Let's Kill Carlo is a game we used to play at the dinner table when I was young. We'd be there making fun of each other and drinking, the adults with their wine, us kids with our *agua fresca*—there was a strict no-alcohol policy for anyone under twelve—when someone would say, "There was an earthquake in Oaxaca last week." Or, "Did you hear about the plane crash in Colombia?" Or, "Apparently some reactor exploded in Russia." Immediately, the rest of us would chime in, "Let's kill Carlo!" That's how the game would start. Now, Carlo, in case you were wondering, was my brother.

Let's back up a bit here.

In 1973, my mom—I'll call her Maria, since that's actually her name—graduated from high school in Mexico City and enrolled in college. She had three months of vacation before her and also some savings, so she signed up for an Italian summer course in Perugia. One day, while she was there, she walked into a grocery store and instantly fell in love with the man handling the fruit. A few weeks later, she had moved in with the *fruttivendolo*, Elio, who happened to be a medical student. She would end up spending half a decade in Italy.

Maria also decided to go ahead with the degree she had intended to pursue back in Mexico. She'd study by herself all semester long, and then fly home to take her exams and see her family. Every time she went home, her grandmother would make the same scene. It played out like a *telenovela*:

ABUELA: Stop living in sin! I'll pay for the wedding!

MARIA: I already told you, Elio can't leave the country!

ABUELA: Why is that, again?

MARIA: Because military service is mandatory for all men in Italy. Unless you're studying medicine; then you're exempt, but they won't give you a passport.

ABUELA: Right… But can't we have the wedding anyway? At my house?

And that, *McSweeney's*, is exactly what they did. Maria and Elio got married at grandma's house by proxy. My mom's uncle stood in for the groom, holding a letter of attorney signed by Elio, who celebrated all by himself back in Perugia. Years later, a picture of that wedding still hung on our wall. It didn't bother

my father or me—after all, it's just my mom in a pretty dress, holding a bunch of flowers.

The trouble was that medical students were only exempt from military service while they were students. Upon graduation they were still expected to put in a year, usually stationed far from home. Unless you were a *capofamiglia*, "a head of the family." When Elio's last semester rolled around, he and Maria started panicking. A year apart was out of the question. But so was having a baby. They couldn't even afford new winter coats, and whatever extra money they made went toward airfare to Mexico. Elio was in his finals when Maria had to leave for yet another round of her own exams.

Now, you may not know this, *McSweeney's*, but because we Mexicans are not really used to laws being enforced, we tend to view them as negotiable. This begins to explain why, upon returning to Mexico, Maria asked to borrow a baby. It was Carlos, the newborn boy of the *señora* who took care of her grandma. "Take him to the park," said the *señora*, assuming that my mother wanted to get some practice caring for a newborn. But of course, Maria never made it to the park. Instead, she pushed the stroller right over to the *registro civil*. Too nervous to come up with a name, she just Italianized "Carlos" and attached her husband's surname to the end of it. And that's how, without ever being born, my half-brother Carlo Moretti came into existence.

By dinnertime, the baby was home and Maria was on a plane to Perugia—a mother in name only. The fake birth certificate worked like a charm, and Elio got a permanent exemption from service. Carlos with an *s* never knew about this ingenious, utterly illegal exploitation of his weeks-old self, and neither did his mom. In fact, after Elio and Maria split up five years later and Maria moved back to Mexico, no one gave Carlo Moretti another thought. At least not until the day Elio phoned our place. He and Maria had kept in touch; to me, he was like a distant uncle who calls on birthdays. But this time he had shocking news: Carlo had come of age, and now he was being called up for military service.

That morning eighteen years earlier, Maria had been worried only about her immediate future. It never crossed her mind that she could—that indeed she *should*—have made Carlo a Carla. But now it was too late, and the army was inquiring about Carlo's whereabouts. First letters, then calls, then visits. All Elio could say was that he had no idea. But they weren't buying it; people have been known to try all sorts of things to avoid service, and having your father lie for you was about as common as saying you had flat feet. Elio then tried arguing that, for all he knew, Carlo might be dead. "In that case," they said, "where's the death certificate?"

It was in a collaborative effort to answer this very question, *McSweeney's*, that we played Let's Kill Carlo for the first time. Rather seriously. We were brainstorming plausible deaths so that Elio, without having to produce a cadaver, could have a solid story to tell the soldiers at his door. I was seven years old, and I proposed a scuba-diving accident—body never found. People clapped. I was awfully good at Let's Kill Carlo. And it really was a special game. It felt purposeful and inclusive. Visitors, it turned out, were always eager to point out the potential ways a person could disappear off the face of the Earth. I remember how one time my cousin's new girlfriend suggested spontaneous combustion. This idea was quickly dismissed, but we were smitten with her. Let's Kill Carlo became something of a litmus test: if a guest was too proper to play, we knew they'd never be one of us.

When I was nine, my mom and I went to Italy. It was my first trip to Europe, and alongside postcard memories of tiny Fiats, gelato, and couples petrified mid-embrace in volcanic ash, one image stands out. We're in a bleak office. My feet dangle from a chair while Maria and Elio explain the Carlo predicament to two lawyers. The *avvocati* leap out of their chairs, deploying an impressive range of gestures. "*Porca madonna! Il santo esercito!*" they yell.

I don't remember what followed this choreography of disapproval, but I know that after a couple of years of paperwork, the *avvocati* managed to conjure up what Elio needed: a death certificate. That's why we haven't played Let's Kill Carlo lately—there's no use for it anymore. Anyway, I'm not sure we could enjoy it these days. It would be all too easy to come up with possibilities in Mexico, where tens of thousands have disappeared in the past few years. It would be too macabre even for us, especially considering that the families of the disappeared often receive nothing from the authorities: no investigation, and definitely not a death certificate.

LAIA JUFRESA
MADRID, SPAIN

DEAR MCSWEENEY'S,
Was on the corner of Conti and Saint Claude, smoking, waiting for the 88 to come and take me to Piety Street. The 88, like most of the public transportation in New Orleans, is quite temperamental. So I was there, not clinging to high hopes or anything, smoking, when I heard, "Hey, hey." I looked around but didn't see anybody. Kept watching the smoke moving toward Canal and then one more time, "Hey, hey." I looked around again and out of the corner of my eye I see a guy lying on the sidewalk in what looked like a comfortable but very elaborate position (one arm behind his neck, crossed legs). There was also a woman and her child waiting for the bus, partially blocking my view; perhaps that's why I hadn't seen the guy before. I nodded *whassup* in his direction. I thought he was going to ask for a cigarette.

"You waiting for the 88?" he said.

"Yes."

"Could you wake me up when it comes?"

"Sure."

He went back to napping and I went back to smoking. Some five or ten minutes later a guy walked by and looked hard at the man on the ground. It was nearly dusk. He leaned in closer, almost bending over his body.

"Larry?" he said.

The guy on the ground opened his eyes, blinked, and looked at the other man.

"Yes?"

"Oh, I'm sorry," the standing guy said. "I thought you were someone else."

"But my name is Larry," the guy on the ground said. The other man raised his hands, apologetically, and kept walking.

Larry put his head back down, but didn't close his eyes this time. Kept staring at the street, or at the wheels crossing his line of sight at street level. The 88 came a few minutes later. I looked in Larry's direction, but he didn't need to be woken up: he was squatting, watching others board the bus. The lady and her daughter got on the bus first. Then I got on the bus. The driver glanced at Larry, who was still looking at the bus, with no particular intent. So the driver closed the doors and the bus leapt forward. I got one last look at Larry: he was on his feet now, staring in the opposite direction.

YURI HERRERA
NEW ORLEANS, LA

10

DEAR MCSWEENEY'S,

Two weeks ago I received a telephone
call from my friend Gaya, who recently
moved to Minneapolis. She has a nerve-
wrecked Chihuahua called President,
who was diagnosed with terminal cancer
by a holistic veterinarian. President has
always behaved as if on the verge of a
nervous breakdown, so that has nothing
to do with the illness. The holistic
veterinarian suggested massage therapy,
mud cataplasms, and a better diet. I am
not sure which—the diagnosis or the
cure—seems more unlikely. He also
interrogated Gaya about her own stress
management and somehow implied that
the dog's cancer could be related to her
general attitude toward life.

In my opinion, Gaya's attitude
toward life is fine. She is in fact the most
practical, intelligent, and inventive
person I know. She is also generous,
good-hearted, and manages to live
according to principles while still being
spontaneous. I'll give you an example,
McSweeney's, because it would be frivolous
of me to say such good things about
someone without offering some kind
of proof—even if praise, nowadays, is
questioned less often than criticism,
when it should be the other way around.

I just looked up *praise* and found
forty-two decent synonyms. So here is
proof for my acclamation, extolment, and
exultation of Gaya's virtues.

When Gaya was a teenager she had
a boyfriend called Chema. They were
both junkies and lived under a bridge
in Mexico City. One day, they overdosed
and were taken to a hospital in an ambulance. When Gaya woke up, Chema was
still asleep—if that form of tortured bliss
can ever be called sleep. She was afraid
of breaking her parents' hearts should
they find her there, wearing a little
white robe, so she got dressed, kissed
Chema on the forehead, and ran away.
Years went by, she got clean, finished
high school, married a good man, and
found President—the dog who has been
diagnosed with cancer. When she was
twenty-six she was accepted into a PhD
program at Harvard. Shortly afterward,
she got divorced and decided to find
Chema again. He didn't have a Facebook
page or anything of the sort but, through
a chain of people, she eventually found
him. He was working in a supermarket
on the outskirts of Mexico City. They
got married on a rainy summer day. She
sent me a picture of that day, in which
she's wearing a crown of daisies and blue
jeans. I'm not sure if she looks happy.
This is all true, *McSweeney's*; so much so
that I prudently asked her permission to
tell you this story. She agreed.

When the summer ended, she took
Chema back with her to Cambridge.
After a few weeks—although maybe it
was days—she realized it wasn't going
to work out between them, because
he played too many video games. She
phoned Umberto, an anthropologist
friend we have in common, and asked
his advice. But Umberto doesn't give
advice, which is exactly why he is our
friend. The only thing he said was that
he was in the middle of reading *In Search*

of Lost Time and was finally enjoying it after many years of failed attempts. Then he hung up. That evening, in the middle of an argument, Gaya told Chema that if they were going to live together for the rest of their lives, he had to read *In Search of Lost Time*.

I'm sure that, with the exception of Colm Tóibín, Ruben Gallo, my friend Umberto, and perhaps Mr. Edmund White, nobody alive has read *In Search of Lost Time*. I have certainly never read more than a few pages, dear *McSweeney's*, and I don't know that Gaya has either. I'm also sure that she never meant what she said that evening. But Chema acquiesced and she was loath to take her words back—she didn't want to seem inconsistent or untrustworthy. During the following months, Chema went to the library every day and read Proust.

Gaya finished her PhD and they moved to Minneapolis. She got a good job, bought a house and a tiny doghouse. Then, six months ago, Chema and Gaya separated. Gaya told me back then in an email that he had continued reading *In Search of Lost Time* every day, but he had never progressed beyond the first volume. When she had asked him why, he'd told her that every time he finished it, he just turned back to the first page and began all over again, because he felt he hadn't understood everything yet. He always found new meanings within the sentences, and learned words he'd overlooked. Her email ended enigmatically: "He's a genius, Valeria, there's no other explanation."

Today, after getting a haircut twice—two consecutive unsuccessful bobs—I walked down Saint Nicholas Avenue and called Gaya on FaceTime. I showed her my hair—the ends on both sides arching conspicuously upward—and she said I looked like an upside-down croissant. Then I asked about President's health. I'm happy to report that the holistic veterinarian was right: President's terminal cancer went away with the mud cataplasms and change of diet. There was no massage therapy, though, because it seemed to make President even more nervous.

Yours,

VALERIA LUISELLI
HARLEM, NY

DEAR MCSWEENEY'S,

Why are the immigration agents at Newark Airport such dicks? Okay, not all of them, of course, but boy oh boy, definitely some of them. For years I've wanted to write something about how immigration agents harass Mexicans who have to go through passport control and customs at Newark and other airports, even when they are merely in transit, flying back from Europe to Mexico, for example, and simply changing planes in the U.S. For years, I've collected anecdotes about the nasty treatment my Mexican friends have received, always vowing to write about it someday, but in the end I've always decided against doing so, because, after all, as my friends are always the first to point out, what they've endured at those airports is nothing compared to what so many undocumented Mexicans endure when trying to cross the border, and especially compared to what Central Americans endure when trying to cross Mexico on their long journeys toward the United States—journeys that all too often, especially on the Mexican side but also on the U.S. side, end not only in deportations but also in kidnappings, torture, rape, and death. Some seventy thousand Central Americans are said to lie buried in anonymous graves along the Migrant Trail, in what must be one of the world's most underreported human tragedies. *McSweeney's*, if you haven't yet, I urge you to read *The Beast*, recently published in English by Verso, a firsthand narrative account by the outrageously courageous and gifted Salvadoran journalist Oscar Martínez of the harrowing journeys made by Central Americans across Mexico. (He was just twenty-five when he wrote it, a young George Orwell, that *cabrón*!) What my friends have put up with at Newark and other airports are just moments of inconvenience compared to what undocumented immigrants endure in this country every day, I sure do understand that. Many of the incidents my friends have told me about over the years are even funny—good stories about dumbass gringo meanness to share in the cantina. No big deal, not worth writing about, until suddenly it's your own life that an immigration agent fucks up, which is what recently happened to

J. and me, and then, well, it becomes pretty hard to keep quiet about it.

As you may know, *McSweeney's*, for the last fifteen years or so, and especially over the last seven years, I've mostly lived in Mexico City, but I do spend at least one semester a year in New York, from where I commute to a teaching job in Connecticut. But in 2010 I spent several months in a writer-scholar residency in Berlin. A woman I'd been seeing in Mexico City, M., came to visit me there. I was headed back to Mexico as soon as the residency was over, and I asked her to bring some books back for me. M. had to change planes at Newark. "Ahh, you're Mexican," the immigration agent said, looking at her passport, like he'd already caught her doing something wrong. "Why, if you were only in Berlin for ten days, do you have two bags?" he asked. She had a small suitcase packed with clothing and books, hers and mine, and a knapsack that also held some books. M. answered that she didn't think that was so many bags for a ten-day trip. The agent sent her over to a side counter, the equivalent of a penalty box for international airline travelers, to undergo a more thorough inspection. M. was nervous because she had only forty-five minutes to make her flight, and had to get to another terminal, and she didn't know her way around this airport. She was met by another agent, a large man, she recalls, a *jetón*—a man with a big, unfriendly face—who was wearing latex gloves. The *jetón* poked through everything in her bags, even inside the sack holding her dirty laundry. But it was the books she was carrying, about ten in all, in English and Spanish, that made the agent especially suspicious. He pulled them all out and stacked them on the counter. I'd given her a few fat paperbacks, including the third and fourth volumes of *In Search of Lost Time*, and I forget what else, in delusionary hope of not having to fly back to Mexico in a couple months' time with the usual packed library drop boxes for luggage. The immigration *jetón* asked her, in a sarcastic tone, why she was traveling with so many books. M. is a pretty young woman, raven haired, dark skinned, who studied at the Tec de Monterrey, which is like Mexico's MIT, and who at that time was employed by a reforestation NGO. She answered that she liked to read, which was certainly true. Then he asked her if she'd really read all of these books, and if she could tell him what each book was about. He picked up each book and slowly leafed through it, nearly one page at a time. M. tried to explain that she was worried about missing her connection. "*Le valio madre*," she told me, which literally means, "It mattered mother to him," a Mexican way of saying that he could have cared less. He seemed to be taking a deliberately long time poring over every book, like an envious and greedy collector. The *jetón* said that he needed to examine each book carefully, "In case one of them held an illegal substance." Finally he let her go, and she ran through the airport, and just caught her flight, but the memory of that man's *jetón* face, and of his rude sarcasm and hostility, of the way he tried to make her feel guilty of something just for being a Mexican with a lot of books in her bags, still burns her up.

Look, it could have been much worse, at least he didn't ask to look inside her clothes or even inside her body, because that happens too, when they take you into the "naked room." But why would a young woman flying home to Mexico from Europe, and only switching planes in the U.S., arouse such suspicion? Believe me, this kind of thing happens to Mexican travelers—and to travelers from other countries too, I have no doubt—all the time, not only when they are trying to come into the country with legitimate visas but even when they are merely passing through an airport on their way to someplace else. This is just one of many such stories I could tell.

Even I've had incidents, coming into this country with my U.S. passport. Some of them have actually been pretty funny, like that time some years ago when I arrived at JFK, I think it was, on a morning TACA flight from El Salvador, and at customs the immigration agent looked at my passport, skeptically hooted "Goldman!?" and said, "Get over there!," sending me off to the penalty box. Just last year I was refused entrance at passport control and sent to wait, without any explanation, in what seemed to be a kind of courtroom in the airport until, an hour or so later, it was over, and I was told by the official who handed my passport back that they'd had their suspicions that it wasn't an authentic document. The official told me that I should be grateful, that it is their vigilance at borders and airports that protects our country from terrorists. I am willing to concede that point.

* * *

I now live with J., a Mexican woman who has a U.S. tourist visa. So that she could experience New York City and the U.S., and improve her English, we decided to spend more than a semester up here this year. We arrived in New York in the fall and in January we went home to Mexico to spend a week at a beach and so that J. could spend time with her family. We returned to New York, via Newark Airport, a few weeks later, just before the start of my teaching semester. Our plan was to do some travel—to New Orleans to visit our Mexican friend Yuri during spring break, and, when the semester is over, around the U.S. a bit—and then go back to Mexico at the beginning of July. At Newark, I, of course, went through the passport line for U.S. citizens and legal residents, arrived at the luggage carousel well before J. did, and collected our bags. About an hour passed, and J. didn't appear. Nearly another hour passed. I'd been standing by that luggage carousel for almost two hours, feeling pretty helpless. J.'s smartphone was turned off. What else could I do but wait? By then all our flight's luggage had been claimed, but for a lonely three or four

suitcases that an airport worker had stacked side by side next to the carousel; luggage, I understood, that belonged to passengers from our flight who'd been detained by the immigration authorities, as J. clearly had, and who possibly might not be allowed into the country—as J. clearly might not. Holy shit!

I told myself not to worry, that nothing could really go wrong. J. wasn't breaking any laws. She wasn't doing anything illegal in the U.S. She was what she said she was, and what her visa allowed her to be: a tourist. She was taking English classes at an ESL school, the tuition she paid contributing to the salaries of the people working there. She was spending money in clothing stores and the like. She'd never been in a winter climate before, and so had needed to outfit herself as if for an arctic expedition. We were going to restaurants, to shows, movies, museums, and concerts, buying MetroCards and taking taxis. The U.S., like any other country, allows tourists into its borders in order to make money off them, and there's nothing wrong with that. Why give out tourist visas if you're not going to let tourists be tourists? Don't worry, I thought; they're just asking her some questions, maybe they're suspicious of the books in her knapsack— she's a reader, too—but everything is going to turn out fine. Despite all that, I was a nervous wreck. What if they didn't let J. in? Our apartment in Mexico had been sublet until July. She had nowhere to go. And I was stuck up here until May, the end of the semester.

At that moment J. was being detained and interrogated by immigration officials upstairs. They had decided that she must not be telling the truth. They had decided that she must be working illegally. How could she prove that she was not doing what they accused her of, illegally working? How could she prove that? J. was not doing anything illegal, but they were determined to treat her as if she was—all this I found out later. Finally I left our luggage next to the cluster of pariah bags and went back upstairs to see if I could find something out. A scattered group of individual travelers was standing around in the area facing the long passage down which people exit from passport control. All of the others waiting there, I noticed, seemed worried, and some were outright frantic. All were facing the possibility of being separated, then and there, from the person they had been traveling with; in many cases, I learned after talking to them a bit, from their romantic partners. A uniformed immigration agent approached us, lifting his arms as if shooing off flies. He was a burly, blue-eyed, cheerfully swaggering Cossack sort of guy. He looked, also, like the kind of fellow who in movies would play a lifeguard who is secretly a serial killer, or else a sociopathic platoon sergeant. We were all trying, individually, to talk to him, but he only responded with shouts of, "Get back! How many times do I have to tell you, get back!" Everybody obediently stepped backward. It turned out that he had come from the very

room that people were being detained in. I finally got his attention, and asked about J. He knew exactly whom I was inquiring about. He grinned, though not in a nice way, and barked, "What are you, fifty years older than her?"

Ha. Older, yeah—but fifty years? Not even close. Funny guy. But what business is it of his, anyway? Later I thought, I can't believe my taxes help to pay that guy's salary. He said he was going to go check on what was happening and that he'd get back to me. If he'd brought back some information, all would have been forgiven; let him crack all the jokes he wanted about my age. But I never saw him again.

About a half hour later J. finally came out. She was wan and quiet. It wasn't until we were in the taxi that she told me that they had given her only five more weeks, until March 8. What were we going to do?

Here is what we finally did. I had to hire an immigration lawyer. For nearly two thousand dollars, we can petition for a tourist visa extension. If she gets it, wonderful. What a great and generous nation! If she doesn't, she'll have to leave immediately, and won't be allowed into the country again. In the lawyer's office the lawyer told me that some of those immigration agents actually enjoy fucking up people's lives for no good reason.

That sounds like just a line, but she spoke it with the authority of a lawyer who has been fighting in these trenches for a long time. I don't think of myself as especially naïve, but I was really struck by that. I sort of took it personally. Could there really be people who enjoy fucking up other people's lives for no good reason? Could there really be somebody out there who would enjoy fucking up my and J.'s lives for no good reason? It's certainly not true of all immigration agents, but I don't doubt it's true of my friend, the jokey Cossack.

If U.S. immigration authorities succeed in separating me from my love for a period of months, and impose a period of hardship on her that there will be little I can do to alleviate, and expel her from this country as if she has done something criminal when she has done nothing wrong at all, what will I do? I expect that my feelings of futility and helplessness will be overwhelming, to say nothing of my anger. To be a U.S. citizen, a taxpayer in good standing, forced to stand by and watch his love be separated from him for no good or legal reason, because of the mean-spirited capriciousness of a U.S. immigration agent—I've been thinking about that a lot. Lately, I've been obsessing over the lives of immigration agents. They leap and climb through my dreams like antic squirrels. I've been trying to understand them and their culture. I've been imagining it all as if it was one of those cable TV shows, something like *The Wire*, though I have to admit I've never seen *The Wire* or any episode of any other cable TV show other than a few episodes of *Girls*, with J., on her computer, and six years ago, with Aura, most of the first season of *The Sopranos*. Where do immigration agents live? How do they come and go from the airport? I've been imagining myself as a character who finds a way to get a job as a Newark Airport immigration agent in order to identify the agent responsible for separating him from his love, or else who finds a way to follow that immigration agent to his home. But please understand, I don't want any violence in this show. That's not what I'm after at all. *McSweeney's*, let's say my character finally does find him—then what do you think he should say or do? How does this end?

FRANCISCO GOLDMAN
BROOKLYN, NY

INTRODUCTION

by DANIEL GALERA

t used to be simple to talk about Latin American fiction. One would
mention magical realism, slums and urban violence, the struggle against
dictatorships, pre-Columbian cultures, the colonial legacy; the colorful,
sensual frenzy above the Tropic of Capricorn and the cold, existential gloom
below it; Borges, Cortázar, Rulfo, García Marquez, Rosa, Llosa. And more
recently, one could try to sum things up with Bolaño. It would all feel relatively straightforward.

But it's not so simple anymore. In the last couple of decades, and especially in the last few years, the panorama has changed. On the one hand,
you have globalization, widespread democracy (or something like it), the
occasional rise of a workers' party to national power, new technologies, new
weapons, new drugs, new oil reserves, swarms of brand-new middle classes
taking over shopping centers, buying cars and cell phones at exploitative
prices—all while wealth and poverty continue their tortured dance.

On the other hand, there's a new generation of readers and writers eager to put the stereotypes of their cultures and literatures behind them. Translation of literary works between Portuguese and Spanish, and between those two languages and others, has increased in a book market fueled by economic and educational progress. Social, political, and economic change, plus our old friend the Internet, have helped foster the so-called "anxiety of influence": when everything is available as a reference and pretty much everything has already been made, unmade, and remade by canonical and contemporary authors (sometimes the ones you go drink with), what the hell should you do?

The good news is that a lot of new Latin American authors find the situation rather stimulating, and are dealing with it in interesting ways. Their voices are suffused with wildly diverse influences—from old scripture to last week's memes and pop songs, from the fast-changing realities of their backyards, neighborhoods, and home countries to the places to which they travel and the ones they read about on their smartphones. They're finding new ways to depict tradition and history through the lens of the hyperconnected present moment. Some pay homage to classics in one page, only to defy them in the next. Some sound distinctly Latin American (or Brazilian, Mexican, Peruvian…), while others avoid this at all costs, or simply don't care. Some go to great lengths to sound foreign. There's a lot of noise. There's trash and redundancy. There's also genius. Don't trust anyone claiming to pinpoint exactly what's going on. Like I said, it's not so simple anymore. As readers, we're all trying to figure it out, and have some fun in the process.

This issue of *McSweeney's* sprang from a desire to bring together a collection of stories that would offer a comprehensive sample of new Latin American fiction. To tie it all together, we selected a single target—thirteen writers from ten different countries were asked to write a contemporary crime story set in their home country. The choice of that broad and beat-up genre was intentional—we wanted to see how each writer would adapt the themes and tropes of outlaw life to suit their own style and sensibility, and how they'd show us their surroundings through it. Beyond that restriction, our vision was an inclusive one: some authors here are well established, and have been translated into English and other languages; others are newcomers, even in their local literary scenes. They were encouraged to do what they liked with the concept. Some stuck to the rules, and others got wild.

The resulting stories, as you'll see, have a bit of everything. Latin American life emerges in characters and plots that range from the funny and farcical to the violent and disturbing. You'll read about corrupt politicians and inexpert detectives, satanic altars and stolen ambulances, the middle class and the nouveau riche, crooked cops and reclusive graphic designers. Some stories revolve around corpses, while others only point toward potential brutality. Every author, however, has managed to use the architecture of the crime story to express their own mix of personal, political, and societal anxieties. The usual suspects have all materialized—murder and love, comedy and tragedy, hope and hopelessness—but so too has a glimpse of the complex world these writers live within today. Have a great trip.

THE FACE

by **SANTIAGO RONCAGLIOLO**

Translated by Natasha Wimmer

"Is it her or isn't it?"

"I don't know, sir. It could be anybody."

Assistant Prosecutor Félix Chacaltana frowned. Over the course of his career, he had come across all kinds of bodies: familiar and unfamiliar, many of them undocumented, some of them in an advanced state of decomposition. Sometimes they were missing bits, nothing big, fingers and such. Occasionally something had been stuffed into the mouth, or another orifice. Regulations required that every body be identified with the help of a relative or friend of the victim. But in order to be recognized, a body had to have a face. And this one didn't.

"I hope it's not," said Officer Basurto, shaking his head with concern. "She was a fine singer, sir."

"'Is,' officer. Make that present tense. Until the death is certified in writing, the lady is officially alive."

"Then who's this?"

The assistant prosecutor shrugged. There was no room to stand up inside the trailer; the two officials were sitting across from the dead body, around a little camp table, like a couple of day trippers. They took another look at the bloody mess, the shapeless muddle of hair, skin, and bones. A few hours ago, that red blob had been a face.

"What was she hit with?" asked the cop. "A stone?"

"I don't think so. A stone is hard to handle. And the victim would have tried to defend herself. To do this right, you need a hammer."

Chacaltana imagined the claw end of the hammer sinking into flesh, puncturing an eyeball, smashing bones in the skull. But his mind returned rapidly to his main problem: the proper procedure for identifying the body. He couldn't remember any item in the regulations for cases like this. And if the body wasn't identified, he wouldn't be able to complete the appropriate forms. He hated to leave administrative procedures half finished.

"Maybe there's an ID in one of her pockets?" he asked.

"*Pues*, that outfit doesn't have pockets, sir," said Basurto with a laugh. He didn't know a thing about procedures, but he was clearly an authority on folkloric attire.

Assistant Prosecutor Chacaltana contemplated the victim's majestic outfit: the pink-and-green-flowered bodice, the full skirt, the yellow kerchief fastened at the shoulders. The murderer had taken the trouble to set her Andean hat on her head after he'd killed her. Bashed-in face aside, she looked very presentable.

"People need to carry their IDs," scolded the assistant prosecutor. "I always have mine with me, to make things easier for the authorities in case I'm the victim of a homicide. Premeditated or not."

"Mm," agreed the officer, and the two were silent for a minute, looking out the window at the concert grounds littered with empty bottles and cigarette butts. In the distance the stage was still standing, but it looked naked without lights, musicians, or instruments. The assistant prosecutor was reminded of something.

"Women hide things beneath their clothing sometimes. What if that's where she kept her ID?"

"Could be."

"Why don't you take a look?"

"Me?"

"That's right. You're a cop, aren't you?"

"Petty officer third-class, sir."

"All right, then. Look and see."

"You want me to feel up a dead woman?"

The two of them turned toward the subject in question, as if she had overheard them making unsavory remarks. She had a serene look about her, and the assistant prosecutor was on the verge of offering her an apology.

"I want you to do your duty," he muttered.

"Sir, with all due respect to you as a professional and a human being, allow me to remind you that the deceased individual here present, as well as bearing a physical resemblance to Señora Casilda Martínez Vilcas, is also wearing Señora Casilda Martínez Vilcas's clothes, and was found in Señora Casilda Martínez Vilcas's trailer, three hundred yards from where Señora Casilda Martínez Vilcas gave a concert last night. Can't we deduce that she is therefore Señora Casilda Martínez Vilcas?"

"It's your job to investigate, not deduce, officer. What if the killer wants to confuse us? What if Señora Martínez Vilcas is alive?"

"I hope she is, sir. She was a good woman. And a fine singer."

"'Is,' Petty Officer. And now search her."

Basurto resigned himself to the task. He tried not to look the deceased in the eyes, or rather in the place where her eyes had been, and slid his hands slowly down her wide gauzy sleeves into her bodice. He rummaged around in there for quite a while, testing the ramparts, and then he exclaimed:

"Ah hah!"

Withdrawing his hands, he turned to Assistant Prosecutor Chacaltana with triumph in his eyes.

"Look, sir: a hundred-sol note. Now we can get ourselves some lunch."

*   *   *

The terrible death of Casilda Martínez Vilcas shook all of Peru. The story spread that she had been raped and murdered by savage thieves; Lima is a violent place, and not even the Princesita de Huancayo was safe from harm. Thousands of weeping fans attended her funeral, many of them children. Industry figures remembered her as a woman with a heart of gold. Street vendors began selling a series of Princesita-themed temporary tattoos, which depicted her with little angel wings on her back. A Catholic association in Huaraz petitioned the Vatican to name her a saint.

Pictures of the singer—always in the typical dress of the Central Andes, where she was from—were all over the front pages of the tabloids. Her sad songs of love and suffering played constantly on the radio. Assistant Prosecutor Chacaltana had never heard the songs before, but now they engraved themselves onto his memory. He was especially struck by the *huayno* "The Liar," whose chorus went like this: "You lowdown cheat / you did me wrong / now turn your face away."

The only person who didn't seem moved was Petty Officer Third-Class Basurto, whose pitiful investigation wasn't up to the standards of the profession. He had managed to verify the identity of the body with the help of the victim's husband—there was no doubt that she was Casilda Martínez Vilcas. But otherwise, there had been no progress. The assistant prosecutor was constantly on the phone to the station, demanding reports so that he could set the proper proceedings in motion. But either Basurto wasn't in, or he had nothing to report. Chacaltana was for the most part a mild and retiring person, but the man's ineptitude drove him wild.

"What do you mean you haven't filed anything, Basurto?"

"That's right, sir. Things are stable for now."

"*Pues*, they shouldn't be, officer. They need to move along."

"You're in a big hurry, sir," replied Basurto with evident annoyance. "A little respect, if you don't mind, for the authority I represent."

The assistant prosecutor got more details from the tabloids than he did through official channels. The Huancayo Teachers' Union and the Ministry of Culture had dedicated tributes to an artist gone before her time, but Basurto wouldn't give her even half an hour a day. It took the man two weeks to deliver the witness statements to Chacaltana's office. There were only three, full of contradictions, omissions, and mistakes. And not a single one of them had been signed by the witness.

"Basurto, these reports are worthless!" Chacaltana said to him over the phone that evening, beside himself.

"You're too hung up on details, sir."

"These aren't details! The witness has to sign! If not, how do I know you didn't write these reports yourself?"

"There's no call to think the worst of people," the policeman said, offended. "How could I make them up?"

"It's a hypothesis."

"I'm no hypnothogist. And I'm not a liar either, sir. I'm an honest cop."

"You don't understand..."

"Are you telling me I'm stupid now?"

"Basurto, that's not..."

"Listen, Señor Assistant Prosecutor. Want witnesses? Find them yourself."

And the officer hung up. Chacaltana sat there with the receiver in his hand. He didn't know whether he should apologize or whether he was due an apology himself. Basurto was clearly telling the truth: he couldn't have made up the reports. A task like that required brains that the petty officer plainly didn't have. But he had left Chacaltana in an impossible position. He couldn't accept paperwork that was blatantly incorrect. Nor, however, could he demand that the officer do work that was beyond his abilities.

The assistant prosecutor turned up the volume on the radio. A music program was on, and at that very moment the announcer was talking about the Princesita de Huancayo. In a hushed, solemn voice, he said that Peru was still mourning the death of one of its most beloved performers, the soul of the Andes, killed by dirty thieves. Then he put on a song, and Assistant

Prosecutor Chacaltana heard those lyrics again, the words that were still buzzing in his head:

"You lowdown cheat / you did me wrong / now turn your face away."

"Good morning. I'm Félix Chacaltana and I represent the Public Prosecutor's Office. I'm here to follow up on an administrative matter."

"Wha?"

The man who opened the door was fat and had a big mouth, like a giant frog. He must have just woken up, because it took his bleary eyes a few seconds to focus on Chacaltana's face. Chacaltana wanted to lend the situation a certain formality, so he explained:

"I'm an assistant prosecutor."

"*Uy, chucha*... I don't know anything, boss, yeah?"

There was a calm, reassuring smile on Chacaltana's face, but it did no good. His host's dark face turned a yellowish shade, and the man's eyes opened wide at last, glancing nervously all around. The assistant prosecutor read out the personal information from his witness statement.

"Are you Señor Elmer Cachay, age thirty-six, of Indian ethnicity, cousin of Señora Casilda Martínez Vilcas?"

The man mumbled yes, as faintly as possible. Then he was silent. The assistant prosecutor asked:

"May I come in?"

"Why?"

"It's in regards to your statement to the police, regarding the passing of your cousin. I've found some irregularities that require my attention..."

"*Uy, chucha*," repeated Cachay. His eyes kept moving back and forth, like a pendulum.

But he let the assistant prosecutor in.

The little house in the neighborhood of Ate-Vitarte looked half finished. The living room, where Chacaltana took a seat, was fully built, at least, and even had bars on the windows. But unpainted cement stairs led up to what looked like a second floor of naked bricks and metal rods where walls should have been. Chacaltana chose to sit with his back to the stairs, at a table with a plastic tablecloth. Cachay sat across from him.

"I understand that you worked as…" Chacaltana checked his papers to keep the titles straight, "a guitarist, composer, manager, driver, security chief, press agent, and beer concessionaire at the concerts of the deceased."

"Who?"

"Your cousin."

"Uh. I also sell Princesita de Huancayo notebooks and pencil cases. Casilda rules the schools. Her concerts are full of teenagers."

"I see." Chacaltana had put on his glasses and was taking notes in a graph-paper notebook, armed with an old fountain pen. He wondered whether this was the proper way to proceed. Strictly speaking, what he was doing was outside the scope of his responsibilities. "And with all those duties, how is it that you had already left the grounds when the lady died? Did you leave her alone in the trailer?"

"*Uy, chucha…*" repeated the man, scratching his head. On the wall behind him hung a picture of the Princesita de Huancayo with a llama, which seemed to nuzzle Cachay's hair. "A beer for you, boss?"

The assistant prosecutor peered at him over his glasses and replied:

"It's ten in the morning."

"Some pisco?"

Without waiting for a reply, the man unscrewed a flask that was sitting on the table. He took a quick swallow and screwed it shut. Now he seemed more confused than he'd been a minute before. The assistant prosecutor tried to continue:

"Señor Cachay, I've checked your record. You've served sentences for extortion, narcotics trafficking, counterfeiting, and document fraud. I'm surprised to see you employed as a security chief."

"Yes, *pues*," said the other man. "There's no work, is the thing, boss."

"I'm not your boss. But these issues with your statement are a problem. It could be very serious for you. You know how it is. Sometimes the police lock up the first suspect they come across. And, to be frank, you're a pretty likely suspect. I say that with all due respect, Señor Cachay. I would like to protect you. But you've got to help me help you."

He didn't say it in a harsh way. He was just stating the facts. But the other man clammed up. Time dragged heavily. On the clock on the wall, the second hand beat out a long funeral march.

"Look, boss," Cachay announced at last. "I can tell you what I know, but I don't have anything to do with the body, all right?"

"I would appreciate it if you would use more respectful language in referring to Señora Martínez Vilcas, may she rest in peace."

"Peace isn't the word for where she'll rest," Cachay interrupted him brusquely.

"What do you mean by that?"

His host sighed. As he was collecting his thoughts, his reddened eyes turned upward, as if reading the truth in the sky.

"You know what, boss? It's expensive to run a touring group. You have to pay for hotels, venues, sound and lights, transportation. And our fans aren't rich people. They can't afford expensive tickets. So the box office just barely covers costs. The profit is in selling add-ons."

"Add-ons?"

"Beer, cigarettes, sandwiches…"

"I see. School notebooks, pencil cases…"

"Princesita de Huancayo T-shirts…"

"Autographed photos…"

"Cocaine…"

The assistant prosecutor froze. It took him a few seconds to be sure he had heard correctly. He thought about the temporary tattoos showing the Princesita dressed as an angel. And about the Catholic association that wanted to canonize her.

"Was Señora Casilda aware that she was engaged in narcotics trafficking?"

"Aware? She was happy. She loved blow!" said Cachay, laughing, but he stopped when he saw that Chacaltana was unamused. "The seats of her trailer were full of the stuff. The group travels all over Peru, so we sell along the way. We bring shipments from the jungle and make deliveries on the coast. I take care of the micro-sales at concerts, sometimes, but the real head of the business is Ajipanca. Casilda's husband. He makes the big sales. During the concerts, too."

"And could that have gotten her killed?"

Cachay swallowed some more pisco and shrugged.

"All I know is that there were some suppliers who weren't happy. Ajipanca stiffed them, I think, but it's not the kind of thing you ask about. The night of the concert, the suppliers were there. And after the concert they were still there, not looking very friendly. Ajipanca told me: 'Close up and get everybody out of here. I've got a deal to do.' And I did what he said. I can't tell you anything else, because that's all I know."

Ajipanca was the nickname of Teddy Quispe Malpica, age fifty, ethnicity mixed race, occupation husband of the victim. The subject in question had personally identified the body by means of various birthmarks, and his sorrow had seemed genuine, or at least that's what Petty Officer Basurto's report said. The report, however, was only two paragraphs long, and it ended the same way as all of the witness statements: "Subject not present at the crime scene at the time of the incident."

On the way to see Ajipanca, Chacaltana stopped for an herbal tonic at a cart in Barrios Altos. The vendor had his radio on. On the news, a mother said that the Princesita de Huancayo had performed a miracle: she had cured her daughter. The girl had polio, but when she heard "Old Friend of Mine," she had risen from her wheelchair. The cart's customers all remarked on the goodness of Casilda Martínez Vilcas. They called her "the voice of the people." The assistant prosecutor continued along his way.

When the Princesita's husband opened the door, the assistant prosecutor understood how he'd gotten his nickname: his face was wrinkled and curved—almost twisted—like an aji panca chile. A bland name like Teddy didn't suit him at all. To one side of that face, pressed to an ear, was a cell phone, which the man raised a little in order to direct an inquiring look at his visitor. Chacaltana explained the purpose of his visit.

"Señor Quispe Malpica? I'm here from the assistant prosecutor's office regarding your statement about the night of your wife's demise."

When he heard this, Ajipanca's black eyes opened wide, and he looked hopeful:

"Have you found the motherfucker who did it?"

"We're working on it, sir."

The man nodded, not looking particularly sorry, and resumed his phone conversation as he headed back inside. Chacaltana took this as an invitation and followed him.

Casilda Martínez Vilcas's house was better furnished than her cousin's in Ate-Vitarte, though the decor was a little over the top for the assistant prosecutor's taste: pink cushions, electric-blue rugs, and an ample collection of porcelain figurines. Cupids, traditional singers, little animals. Quispe Malpica was still on the phone, giving orders to someone:

"Just let people leave their offerings right there on the grave. And we'll give them something to take home, some little token. We still have the glossies we used to promote *When Life Lets You Down*... Uh-huh... Uh-huh... But don't let them leave just anything, all right? No live chickens or pigs. We'll end up needing a farm. Better for them to leave cash, *pues*."

For ten minutes, the conversation revolved around funeral offerings and their possible exchange value. When he hung up, Quispe Malpica remembered that he'd left an assistant prosecutor forgotten on the sofa. He turned to him.

"Sorry about that. The people love their Princesita de Huancayo. They're flocking to visit her remains. At least my wife will go out surrounded by her people, her kin. Right?"

"I suppose so," conceded the assistant prosecutor.

"How can I help you?"

"I just want you to confirm some details of your statement to the police... And I'd like to ask you to sign it."

"Whatever you say."

Unlike the evasive Elmer Cachay, Quispe Malpica had the confident air of a businessman, a man used to dealing with people. The assistant prosecutor took out his notebook and began his inquiries.

"You identified your wife's body. Is that right?"

The businessman's chile-pepper face grew even more twisted. His gaze turned sour.

"She didn't have a nose," he said curtly. "Nothing. They beat her to a pulp, sir... With a hammer, can you believe it?"

The assistant prosecutor shook his head. He was assailed by the memory of that shattered face. Quispe exhaled sharply.

"The bastards. How could they do that to her?"

Chacaltana saw a chance to continue his questioning. He felt for the man, but he couldn't let that distract him from the proceedings.

"It's strange that you weren't present at the scene—it's strange that no one was, really. Did she return to her trailer alone, after the concert? Was she planning to sleep there, maybe?"

"Señor Assistant Prosecutor," replied Quispe Malpica with an indulgent smile, as if addressing an illiterate, "Casilda was a very spiritual woman, very religious. Sometimes she asked to be left alone in the strangest places, to spend the night praying and thanking the Lord for everything He'd done for her and for us."

The assistant prosecutor noted down this answer, and then spent a while looking through his notebook before asking:

"So it didn't have anything to do with the twenty kilos of cocaine you had in the trailer?"

Now Quispe's face stretched into a pale grimace, like a banana. His gaze turned cold. He was silent. Chacaltana said:

"Señora Casilda—may she rest in peace—her cousin..."

"That jackass Elmer..."

"Señor Elmer Cachay will testify in court that you sent him home that night because of a problem with the shipment. He says that there was trouble between you and other... well, other..."

Criminals? Traffickers? Chacaltana didn't want to presume anything. Finally he settled on a word:

"Suppliers."

The businessman's phone started to ring, to the tones of "The Sadness in My Heart." He muted it, but it kept vibrating. Quispe looked ready to come after the assistant prosecutor with a drill.

"The... suppliers," he began, weighing his words. "They took care of business and they left. Peacefully, as always."

"There was no altercation?"

"We all have business disagreements, sometimes. But it's in everyone's interest to get along."

"But you sent away the whole concert team so that you could meet alone with the gentlemen in question."

"I sent those men away, too. And then I left."

"Without your wife?"

Suddenly, Quispe's face and body sagged. He had turned into a Teddy after all, vulnerable and afraid. He set his phone on the table the way he might've set down a gun. When he spoke, it was in a broken voice:

"Casilda and I weren't... We were married, but she..."

The man paused for a few seconds. Gathering strength, he declared:

"I loved her, sir. I loved her with all my heart. I really did. But then she got into all that shit and everything changed. First it gave her extra energy on stage, but before long she was staying up partying all night. The hangovers were terrible. Toward the end, the parties lasted for days. And the people who came just kept getting stranger. They did strange things. It's been five months since I stayed around for all that. And three since I slept with Casilda."

"So why didn't the two of you just stop dealing?"

At the mention of dealing, Quispe started. He squirmed uncomfortably on his pink cushion. Chacaltana reminded him:

"Your business affairs don't concern me, Señor Quispe. I'm here to investigate a murder."

The man resumed his mournful look.

"We had to keep dealing. The more the better. There's a lot of family to support, on my side and Casilda's: cousins, in-laws, stepkids, aunts and uncles. Every day new relatives show up looking for work. You can't tell them no, *pues*—if you can give them a job, you have to give them a job. What will they do, otherwise? Some of those pricks make messes no matter where they go. You have to deal with all their shit. But that's life."

"Was there a party that night in Señora Casilda's trailer? Is that why you sent everyone home and left?"

"I guess so. I didn't want to know anything about what was going on, either. I left because I was told to go."

"Who told you to go?"

"Mercy. Casilda's niece. She was her personal assistant, too. She organized the parties, invited the guests, and told us when to leave. She was the one who told me to go that night. She always stayed until my wife finally decided to go to bed, and then she kicked everyone else out, too. That's why Casilda was all alone the next morning, when the cleaning people found the body."

Niece was an excellent word to describe Mercy Gálvez Pinchi, age twenty-one, 5´2´´. She was so small and young looking that it was as if she'd been born for the role. Her gentle ways and soft voice were in striking contrast to the coarseness of her male relatives. Even in her own apartment, she looked as if she were afraid of breaking something. She moved as lightly as a ghost.

And it was the right place to be a ghost, because Mercy Gálvez Pinchi's house was like a shrine to the Princesita de Huancayo. Posters of the singer covered the walls and ceiling. Promotional objects stamped with the dead woman's face were piled on all the tables. Even the furniture was upholstered in memories of her songs, the assistant prosecutor realized, as Mercy led him past an armchair embroidered with the lyrics to "The Day You Left Me."

"Can I offer you a tea, Señor Assistant Prosecutor?" asked the young woman, marking the first time that day that Félix Chacaltana had been called "Assistant Prosecutor," and not "boss" or "sir." Chacaltana accepted, and she turned to put water on to boil in an electric kettle. Her long black braid hung stiffly, like a second backbone. Surveying the girl's temple to the Princesita de Huancayo, the assistant prosecutor commented:

"I see that you admire Señora Casilda, your aunt…"

Mercy turned to look at him. Her eyes were as round as dinner plates, and she spoke slowly, as if explaining something very obvious.

"All of Peru admires her! But I don't call her Casilda. To me, she's the Princesita de Huancayo from the minute she gets up till the time she goes to bed."

The assistant prosecutor noticed that the girl was speaking in the present tense. Sometimes, he thought, it takes us a while to get used to someone being gone. We keep talking about them as if they were still alive.

"She was quite a singer," he agreed, accepting a cup of tea. "She touched people's hearts."

"She's the people's singer," said the girl in the same breathy voice, still using the present tense. Behind her, Casilda Martínez Vilcas watched attentively from a publicity poster. Even the assistant prosecutor's teacup was part of a Princesita de Huancayo tea set, adorned with Andean patterns and the face of the dead woman. The assistant prosecutor set it back on its saucer and decided that it was time to get down to business.

"Señorita Gálvez Pinchi…"

"Mercy, please."

"Mercy. I understand that on the night of the last concert you stayed with Señora Casilda until the end, even after her husband had left the grounds. Is that correct?"

"Of course. No one knows how to take care of the Princesita like me. She needs me. I have to help her out of her stage outfit, remove her makeup, put on her bathrobe, massage her feet after all the dancing she does, and pray with her, because she always thanks Our Lord for a successful concert. Then I apply her avocado mask to keep her skin fresh and stay with her until she falls asleep, in case she needs anything."

The girl recited all her duties without faltering, proudly. The assistant prosecutor had begun to feel uncomfortable. He wondered how to speak the word *cocaine* in front of such a sweet young woman.

"Listen, Mercy," he began, as kindly as he could, "you don't have to hide anything from me. Elmer Cachay and Teddy Quispe have already confessed to their illicit activities... And they've also told me about the... parties."

"What did you say?"

The girl's voice was calm, as if she really hadn't heard him. The assistant prosecutor cleared his throat and explained, his eyes on the floor.

"I've been informed of Señora Casilda's tendencies where controlled substances and extramarital relations are concerned."

The expression in Mercy's docile black eyes didn't change. Until now, Chacaltana had thought she was looking at him; now he realized that she was actually staring at some point in space, slightly to the right of his head.

"What you're saying is ridiculous. The Princesita is an honest woman with the biggest heart in the world. Everybody knows it. Turn on the TV and you'll see how they're all talking about her. They love her because she's good."

"Then what happened that night? The night of the concert? What happened when you were left alone with her?"

On Mercy Gálvez Pinchi's face there appeared the last thing the assistant prosecutor expected to see: a smile.

"I told you already. I did my work: I helped her out of her stage outfit, removed her makeup, put on her bathrobe, massaged her feet, and prayed with her, because she always thanks Our Lord for a successful concert. Then I had to apply the avocado mask to keep her skin fresh and stay with her until she fell asleep. That night she wanted to sleep in her concert outfit, and I dressed her in it. Even the hat. She looked beautiful."

"And were you still there when she was killed?"

"What?"

"I'm sorry to be blunt. You understand that some of my questions may sound..."

"She's not dead."

"Pardon me?"

"I told you already. Turn on the television. Turn on the radio. Everybody is talking about the Princesita. My uncles told you all those lies because they're jealous of her. The Casilda they're describing isn't the real Casilda. The real Princesita is on TV. All the time."

Assistant Prosecutor Chacaltana scrutinized her face for signs of irony or a clue that this was poetic license, a manner of speaking. But he was greeted with the same flat look. It was she who spoke, asking:

"More tea?"

The assistant prosecutor shook his head. He had hardly touched his cup. He tried to continue with his line of inquiry, though Mercy's replies had thrown him.

"You never saw your aunt engage in... excesses? Or shady business?"

"It would be impossible," she answered simply. "It would be a contradiction of the most important part of her: her music. It would make her a liar. Do you know what she sang about liars?"

"Turn your face away," murmured Chacaltana, half singing the words.

Mercy rewarded him with a beatific look, as if he'd sprinkled her with holy water.

"You know it! It's the Princesita's best song. And she's true to her fans and true to her songs. Do you see now? How could she—of all people—be two-faced? It can't be."

Chacaltana let his gaze wander over the posters on the walls. He felt watched by an army of Princesitas de Huancayo. All with the same face. In the pictures, at least, she had a face.

"May I use your bathroom, please?"

"At the end of the hall, on the left."

The hallway was very short and the apartment had just one bedroom. The assistant prosecutor calculated that it would take him only a few minutes to search it.

"Do you know what you could do for me, Mercy? You could make me a cup of coffee. Do you have coffee?"

"I'll have to brew it. But there is some."

She went into the little kitchen and the assistant prosecutor began his search. The hallway and even the bathroom had their full quota of pictures and posters of the Princesita de Huancayo. Trying not to look the singer in the eye, which was almost impossible, Chacaltana went through the medicine cabinet, the wastepaper basket, the toilet tank. Then he went into the bedroom, where he felt the bed, lifted the rug a little, and opened the drawers.

In the second-to-last one he found what he was looking for.

A hammer. Mercy hadn't even washed it. Most of the handle was stained dark red, but there were also other marks, especially on the head: some greenish and some of an indefinable color.

He went out and found Mercy in the kitchen. Before he spoke to her, he was careful to position himself between the woman and her knives.

"Mercy, do you keep a hammer in your room?"

She was brewing coffee. She didn't hesitate for a second.

"It isn't a hammer. It's an arm of God. It's for wiping out lies and evil."

"Of course… um, do you mind if I make a call?"

She shrugged. Without moving from where he stood, the assistant prosecutor dialed Basurto's number.

"Good afternoon, Petty Officer."

"Why are you calling, sir? Did you find a punctuation mistake in one of my reports?"

"No, it's… I need you to come by the house of one of the witnesses: Mercy Gálvez Pinchi."

When she heard her name, she gave him a friendly smile. He tried to smile back.

"Sir, I have things to do. Right now I'm on the taxi-driver case."

Chacaltana sighed deeply. He counted mentally to ten before he answered, so that his voice would be steady.

"Basurto, it's important. Make it quick, please."

"All right, but first I'm going to grab a sandwich. I haven't had my lunch yet, *pues*."

"The sooner the better, Basurto."

"Do you want me to bring anything?"

A computer, thought the assistant prosecutor. So I can teach you how to write a real report.

But he just repeated:

"The sooner the better, Basurto."

When he hung up, Mercy had set a steaming cup of coffee in front of him, this one commemorating the Princesita's greatest-hits album. The two returned to the living room, but this time he sat in the chair by the door, the one closest to the knives and the hammer.

"I hope you're not in a hurry," he said to his hostess.

"Only if the Princesita calls. You know I have to be ready for her twenty-four hours a day."

"Of course, that makes sense."

As they were waiting for Basurto, she put on one of her idolized aunt's CDs. Every CD she owned was by the Princesita, she told the assistant prosecutor. The first strains of "Here's to You, Cholita" sounded from the speakers.

"She dedicated this song to me once at a concert," said Mercy proudly.

"That was very good of her," answered the assistant prosecutor politely.

"Oh yes," the girl said. "No one could ever be as good as she is."

THE DIRTY KID

by **MARIANA ENRIQUEZ**

Translated by Joel Streicker

My family thinks I'm crazy because I choose to live in the family house in Constitución, my paternal grandparents' house, a hulk of stone and green-painted iron doors on Virreyes Street, with Art Deco details and old mosaics on the floor so worn out that, had it occurred to me to wax them, I could have set up a skating rink. But I had always been in love with that house, and, as a girl, when they first rented it to a law firm, I remember how much it upset me, how much I missed those rooms with tall windows and the interior patio that seemed like a secret garden, how frustrated I was when I went by the door and could no longer freely enter. I didn't miss my grandfather much, a quiet man who scarcely smiled and never played. I didn't even cry much when he died. I cried a lot more when, after his death, we lost the house.

After the lawyers a dental office took over. Then, finally, it was rented to a travel magazine, which closed in less than two years. The house was beautiful and comfortable, and in notably good condition for its age; but now no one, or very few people, wanted to move to the neighborhood. The travel magazine had only set up shop because the rent, back then, had been very cheap. Not even that had saved them from bankruptcy, although it certainly didn't help that their offices were robbed a few months after they moved in. The thieves took all the computers, a microwave, even a heavy photocopier.

Constitución is where the trains from the south enter the city. It was the neighborhood where the Buenos Aires aristocracy lived in the nineteenth century—that's why these houses, like my family's, exist. In 1887, the aristocrats fled to the north of the city, trying to escape an epidemic of yellow fever raging in the south. Few, almost none, returned. Some of the mansions were converted into hotels or old-age homes; over time, rich merchants like my grandfather were able to buy up the unoccupied ones, with their gargoyles and bronze door knockers. But the neighborhood has been marked by flight, abandonment, undesirability. On the other side of the station, in Barracas, the old houses have been reduced to rubble.

And it's worse all the time.

But if you know how to handle yourself, if you understand the dynamics, the schedules, it's not that dangerous. Or not *as* dangerous. It's a question of not being afraid, of making a few key friends, of greeting the neighbors even though they're criminals—especially if they're criminals. Of walking with your head up, paying attention. I know that Friday nights, if I approach Plaza Garay, I may get trapped in a fight between various combatants: the small-time drug dealers of Ceballos Street, the brain-dead addicts who attack one another with bottles, the drunken transvestites determined to defend their stretch of pavement. I also know that if I come home on the avenue, I'm more exposed to a mugging than if I return down Solís Street, despite the fact that the avenue is very well lit. You have to know the neighborhood to learn such strategies. I was mugged twice on the avenue; both times kids came running by and snatched my bag and threw me to the ground. The first time I filed a report with the police. The second time I knew it was useless, because I had learned that the police had given them permission. The kids were allowed to claim victims on the avenue as far as the freeway overpass—three liberated blocks—in exchange for certain favors.

I like the neighborhood. No one understands why. But it makes me feel precise, daring, sharp. There aren't many places like Constitución left in the city, which, except for the slums on the outskirts, has grown far richer and friendlier—it's intense and enormous, still, but easy to live in. Constitución isn't easy or friendly, but it's beautiful, with all its old buildings that stand, now, like abandoned temples, occupied by infidels who don't know that praises to the gods were once heard within those walls.

A lot of people live in the street here. Not as many as in Plaza Congreso, which is a couple of kilometers from my door; that's a real encampment, right in front of the legislative buildings, neatly ignored but at the same time so visible that, each night, squads of volunteers flock in to give the people food, check the kids' health, and hand out blankets in the winter and cold water in the summer. In Constitución the street people are left on their own—organized help seldom reaches them. In front of my house, on a corner alongside the boarded-up grocery store, its doors and windows blocked with bricks, live a young woman and her son. She's pregnant, a few months along, although you never know with the addicted mothers in the neighborhood, skinny as they are. The son must be about five years old. He doesn't go to school and spends the day on the subway, asking for money in exchange for prayer cards of San Expedito. I know this because, one night, when I was coming back from downtown, I saw him in my subway car. He has a very unsettling method: after offering the prayer cards to the passengers, he forces them to shake his hand, a brief and filthy clasp, and sometimes he gives them a kiss on the cheek. The passengers contain their shame and disgust: the kid is dirty and he stinks. No one was compassionate enough to take him out of the subway, bring him home, give him a bath, call a social worker. People shook his hand, kissed him, and bought the prayer cards. He was scowling. When he talks, his voice is hoarse; he usually has a cold, and sometimes he smokes with the other kids in the subway station.

That night we walked together from the subway station to my house. He didn't talk to me, but we walked together. I asked him a few silly questions, his age, his name, but he didn't answer me. He wasn't a sweet or affectionate kid. When I got to the door of my house, though, he said good-bye.

"Good-bye, neighbor," he said to me.

"Good-bye, neighbor," I replied.

The dirty kid and his mother sleep on three mattresses that are so worn-out that, stacked up, they're the same height as a single box spring. The mother keeps their few clothes in black garbage bags and has a backpack full of other things that I can never make out. She never leaves the corner, where she begs for money in a mournful and monotonous voice. I don't like the mother. Not just because she smokes crack and the ashes burn her pregnant belly, or because I never saw her treat her son, the dirty kid, with any kindness. It's something else.

I was telling this to my friend Lala while she cut my hair in her house— it was Monday, during a three-day weekend. Lala is a hairdresser, but she hasn't worked in a salon in a long time; she doesn't like bosses, she says. She earns more money and has more peace of mind in her apartment. She has less hot water, however, because the water heater works terribly. Sometimes, when she's washing my hair after dyeing it, I get a stream of cold water on my head that makes me shout in surprise. Then she rolls her eyes and explains that all the plumbers cheat her—they overcharge her, they never come back. I believe her.

"That woman is a monster, girl," she yells, while almost burning my scalp with her ancient hair dryer and smoothing my hair with her thick fingers. Lala decided to be a woman, and Brazilian, many years ago; she was born a man, in Uruguay. Now she's the best transvestite hairdresser in the neighborhood. She no longer works as a prostitute; just the same, she's so used to faking a Portuguese accent (very useful for seducing men on the street) that sometimes she speaks Portuguese on the phone or, when she's upset, raises her arms toward the ceiling and demands vengeance or pity from Pomba Gira, her personal exú, for whom she has a small altar set up in the corner of her living room, right next to the computer, which is always on and perpetually set up for instant messaging.

"A monster?" I say. "Really?"

"She gives me the shivers, *mami*. She's, like, I don't know, damned."

"What makes you say that?"

"I'm not saying anything. But here in the neighborhood, they say she'll do anything for money—that she goes to witches' covens, even."

"Ay, Lala, what are you talking about? There aren't any witches here."

She gave my hair a pull that seemed intentional, but then said she was sorry. It was intentional.

"What do you know about what *really* happens around here, *mamita*? You live here, but you're from another world."

She's a little bit right, but it bothers me to hear it like that. It bothers me that she, so directly, puts me in my place—the middle-class woman who thinks she's defiant because she decided to live in the most dangerous neighborhood in Buenos Aires. I sigh.

"You're right, Lala. But I mean, she lives in front of my house. She's always there, on the mattress. She doesn't even move."

"You work a lot. You don't know what she does, and you don't monitor her at night either. The people in this neighborhood, *mami*, are really... How would you say... Before you know it, they attack you?"

"Stealthy?"

"Yes. You've got a great vocabulary—doesn't she, Sarita? She's classy."

Sarita has been waiting for Lala to finish with my hair for about fifteen minutes, but waiting doesn't bother her. She flips through a magazine. Sarita is a young transvestite who works as a prostitute on Solís Street. She's very beautiful.

"Tell her, Sarita. Tell her what you told me."

But Sarita puckers her lips like a silent-movie diva and has no desire to tell me anything. So much the better. I don't want to listen to neighborhood horror stories anyway. They're all far-fetched and credible at the same time, but for the most part they don't scare me, at least during the day. At night, when I try to finish up the work I'm behind on, sometimes I'll remember one of them. Then I check to make sure the door to the street is well locked and also the one to the balcony, and sometimes I go to the window to watch the corner where the dirty kid and his mother are totally quiet, like the nameless dead.

2

One night, after dinner, the doorbell rang. Strange: almost no one visits me at that hour. Except Lala, on nights when she feels lonely, and we stay up together listening to sad *rancheras* and drinking whiskey. When I looked out the window to see who it was—no one opens the door straight off in this neighborhood if the bell rings around midnight—I saw that it was the dirty kid. I ran to look for the keys and I let him in. He had been crying; you could tell by the clear tracks that the tears had made on his filthy face. He came in running, but he stopped before he got to the dining room door, as if he needed my permission. Or as if he was scared to keep going forward.

"What happened to you?" I asked him.

"My mom didn't come back," he said. His voice was less harsh, but it still didn't sound like a five-year-old's.

"She left you alone?"

Yes, he nodded.

"Are you scared?"

"I'm hungry," he answered. He was also scared, but he was already hardened enough not to acknowledge that to a stranger, much less one who had a house, a beautiful and enormous house, right in front of the piece of ground where he lived.

"All right," I told him. "Come in."

He was barefoot. The last time I had seen him, he'd had on some pretty new gym shoes. Had he taken them off because of the heat? Or had someone stolen them during the night? I didn't want to ask. I had him sit in a chair in the kitchen and I popped some rice and chicken into the oven. While he waited, I spread cheese on a slice of sourdough bread. He ate while looking me in the eye, very serious and calm. He was hungry but not starving.

"Where did your mom go?"

He shrugged.

"Does she go off a lot?"

He shrugged again. I wanted to shake him; immediately, I was ashamed of myself. He needed me to help him. He had no reason to satiate my morbid curiosity, but something about his silence angered me. I wanted him to be a friendly and enchanting little boy, not this sullen and dirty kid who ate his rice and chicken slowly, savoring each mouthful, and belched after finishing his glass of Coca-Cola. I had nothing to give him for dessert, but I knew that the ice cream shop on the avenue would be open; in summer, it stayed open until after midnight. I asked him if he wanted to go and he said yes, with a smile that changed his face completely. He had small teeth; one of them, a lower tooth, was about to fall out.

I was a little scared to go out so late, especially on the avenue, but the ice cream shop was neutral territory, muggings and fights seldom took place there. Instead of bringing my purse, I put a little money in my pants pocket. In the street, the dirty kid gave me his hand. We crossed the street, and I noticed that the mattress he slept on with his mother was still empty. The backpack wasn't there, either.

We had to walk three blocks to the ice cream shop and I chose Ceballos Street, which could be quiet and peaceful on some nights. Certain transvestites—the least statuesque, the plumpest, the oldest—chose Ceballos Street to work on. I regretted not having gym shoes to put on the dirty kid: there were usually pieces of glass and broken bottles on the sidewalk, and I didn't want him to get hurt. But he walked barefoot with great assurance; he was used to it.

That night, the three blocks were almost devoid of transvestites, but they were full of altars. They were celebrating the Eighth of January, the day of Gauchito Gil: a saint mainly popular in Corrientes province, but venerated throughout the country, especially in poor neighborhoods. Antonio Gil, it is said, was murdered for being an army deserter at the end of the nineteenth century. A policeman tortured him, hung him from a tree by his feet, and was about to cut off his head when the deserting gauchito said, "If you want your son to be cured, you have to pray to me." Then the policeman decapitated him.

As it happened, the policeman's son was very sick. The man learned this when he returned home; when he prayed to Gil, the child was cured. So the policeman returned to the body and took Antonio Gil down from the tree, buried him, and, in the place where he'd been killed, erected a sanctuary, which still exists today, and which, every summer, receives almost a million visitors. I found myself telling the story of the miraculous gauchito to the dirty kid, and we stopped in front of one of the altars. There was the plaster saint, with his sky-blue shirt and his red handkerchief around his neck—a red headband, too—and a cross on his back, also red. There were several red cloths and a small red flag: the color of blood, a reminder of injustice. But somehow it wasn't morbid or sinister. The gauchito brings luck, cures, he helps and doesn't ask much in return, just that people pay homage to him and sometimes offer a bit of alcohol, or make the pilgrimage to the sanctuary of Mercedes, in Corrientes, with its 120-degree heat. Devotees arrive there on foot, by bus, on horseback, from everywhere, even Patagonia. The candles all around made the dirty kid blink in the half darkness. I lit one that had gone out and then used the flame to light a cigarette.

The dirty kid seemed uneasy. "Let's go to the ice cream shop," I said to him. But that wasn't it.

"The gauchito is good," he said. "But the other one isn't."

He said it in a low voice, looking at the candles. "What other one?" I asked.

"The skeleton," he told me. "There are skeletons back there."

Back there. In the neighborhood, "back there" was a reference to the southern side of the station, beyond the platforms, where the rails and their embankments fade into the distance. Altars for saints less benevolent than

Gauchito Gil turn up there. I know that Lala takes her offerings to Pomba Gira—her colorful dishes and her supermarket-bought chickens, because she can't bring herself to kill a hen—to the embankments. She does this during the day, because it can be dangerous at night. She's told me that there are altars for San La Muerte, Death, *back there*, the little skeleton saint with his red and black candles.

But even Death's not a bad saint, I said to the dirty kid, who looked at me with wide eyes, as if I were telling him something completely nuts. He's a saint who can do bad things if people ask him to, but most people don't ask for awful things—they ask for protection.

"Your mom takes you back there?" I asked him.

"Yes, but sometimes I go by myself," he answered. And then he tugged on my arm so that we would keep going to the ice cream shop. It was very hot. The sidewalk in front of the ice cream shop was sticky—so many cones that had dripped. I thought about the dirty kid's bare feet, now with all this new filth. He ran inside and ordered, with his old person's voice, a large cone with custard crème and chocolate chips. I didn't order anything. The heat had taken away my appetite, and I didn't know what I should do with the kid if his mother didn't appear. Take him to the police station? To a hospital? Make him stay at my house until she returned? Was there something like Social Services in this city? There was a number to call during the winter, if someone who lived in the street was getting too cold, but I didn't know of much more. I realized, while the dirty kid licked the ice cream off his fingers, how little other people mattered to me, how natural these sad lives seemed.

When he finished the ice cream, the dirty kid got up from the stool and walked toward the corner where he lived with his mother. I followed him. The street was very dark, the lights had gone out, which often happened on very hot nights. I was able to make him out by the lights of passing cars; every few feet he was also lit up, he and his now completely black feet, by the candles of the improvised altars. We got to the corner without him giving me his hand.

His mother was on the mattress. Like all addicts, she had no notion of the temperature and was wearing a thick sweatshirt with the hood on, as if it were raining. Her belly, enormous, was naked—her too-short shirt couldn't cover it. The dirty kid said hello and sat down on the mattress. She didn't say anything.

She was furious. She approached me growling, there's no other way to describe the sound. It reminded me of my dog when it broke its hip and was crazy with the pain.

"Where'd you take him, bitch? What do you want to do to him, huh? Huh? Don't even think about touching my son!"

She was so close that I could see each one of her teeth, how her gums bled, her lips burned by the pipe, the smell of tar on her breath.

"I bought him an ice cream cone!" I shouted, and then I backed up when I saw she had a broken bottle in her hand.

"Get out of here or I'll slice you up, bitch!" The dirty kid looked at the ground, as if he weren't thinking about anything, as if he didn't know us, neither his mother nor me. I was angry with him, then. The ungrateful little snot, I thought, and I took off running. I went into my house as fast as I could, although my hands were shaking and it was difficult for me to find the key. I turned on all the lights; the electricity hadn't gone off on my block, luckily. I was afraid the mother would send someone after me. I didn't know what might be going through her head. I didn't know what friends she had on the block. I didn't know anything about her. After a while I went up to the second floor and spied on her from the balcony. She was lying down, faceup, smoking a cigarette. The dirty kid seemed to be asleep next to her. I went to bed with a book and a glass of water, but I couldn't manage to read or even watch TV. The heat seemed more intense with the fan on, just stirring the hot air and muting the noise from the street.

In the morning I forced myself to eat breakfast before going to work. The heat was now suffocating, and the sun had just barely come up. When I closed the door the first thing I noted was the absence of the mattress on the corner in front. There was nothing left of the dirty kid and his mother.

They hadn't even left behind a bag or a stain or a cigarette butt. Nothing. As if they had never been there.

The body appeared a week after they vanished. When I came home from work, with my feet swollen from the heat, dreaming about the coolness of my house with its high ceilings and large rooms that not even the most hellish summer heat could spoil completely, I found the block in a frenzy, with three patrol cars in the middle of the street and crime-scene tape holding back a crowd. I recognized Lala easily, with her white-heeled shoes and golden bun; she was so nervous that she had forgotten to put the fake eyelashes on her left eye.

"What happened?"

"They found a child."

"Dead?"

"Get this: decapitated! Do you have cable, honey?"

Lala's connection had been cut months ago because she hadn't paid the bill. We went to my house and lay down on the bed to watch the news, the ceiling fan spinning dangerously and the balcony window open in case we heard something noteworthy from the street. I brought in a pitcher of cold orange juice and Lala ruled over the remote. It was strange to see our neighborhood on TV, but we both knew the dynamic well: no one was going to talk during the first days, not about the truth, at least. First, silence, in case someone involved in the crime deserved loyalty. Even if it was a horrible crime against a kid. First, closed mouths. The stories would begin in a few weeks. For now it was TV's moment.

Around eight, Lala and I shifted over to pizza and beer, and then to whiskey—I opened a bottle my father had given me. Information was sparse: a dead kid had appeared in an unused parking lot on Solís Street. Decapitated. The head had been placed next to the body.

At ten, it was reported that the top of the head had been scraped clean to the bone and that no hair had been found in the area. Also, the eyelids had been sewn shut and the tongue chewed on, perhaps by the dead kid himself or perhaps—and this caused Lala to scream—by the teeth of another person.

The news programs continued giving information far into the night, rotating journalists with live coverage from the street. The police, as usual, weren't saying anything on camera, but they constantly supplied information to the press.

By midnight, no one had claimed the body. It was also known that the boy had been tortured: the torso was covered with cigarette burns. A sexual assault was suspected, and was confirmed around two in the morning, when a preliminary report from the forensics experts was leaked.

And still, at that hour, no one had claimed the body. Not a family member. Not the mother or father or brothers or aunts and uncles or cousins or neighbors or acquaintances. No one.

The decapitated kid, the TV said, was between five and seven years old. It was difficult to determine because, when alive, he had been malnourished.

"I'd like to see him," I said to Lala.

"Don't be crazy, no one's going to show you a decapitated kid! What do you want to see him for? You're so morbid. You were always a little monster, the morbid countess of the palace on Virreyes Street."

"It's just… Lala, I think I know him."

"Who do you know, the child?"

I told her yes and started to cry. I was drunk but I was also certain that the dirty kid was now the decapitated kid. I told Lala about my encounter with him that night when he rang my doorbell. Why didn't I take care of him? Why didn't I find out how to take him away from his mother? Why didn't I at least give him a bath? I have a big old beautiful bathtub that I hardly use. Why didn't I at least wash off his filth? And, I don't know, buy him a rubber duckie and those little wands to make bubbles? I could have easily done it. Yes, it was late, but there are little stores in the city that never close, that sell gym shoes, even; I could have bought him a pair. How could I have let him walk around barefoot, at night, on these dark streets? I shouldn't have let him go back to his mother. When she threatened me with the bottle, I should have called the police. They could have put her in jail and I could have kept the kid, or helped him get adopted by a family that would love him. But no. I got angry at him because he was ungrateful, because he didn't defend me from his mother! I got angry at a terrified kid, the son of an addict, a five-year-old kid who lives in the street! Who lived in the street, because now he was dead, decapitated!

Lala helped me vomit in the toilet, and then went to buy some pills for my headache. I was drunk and scared but I was also sure it was him, the dirty kid, raped and decapitated in a parking lot.

"Why did they do this to him, Lala?" I asked, curled up in her strong arms, once again in bed, the two of us slowly smoking our early-morning cigarettes.

"Princess, I don't know if it's your kid they killed, but when it opens, let's go to the district attorney's office so you can get some peace of mind."

"You'll go with me."

"Of course."

"But why, Lala, why did they do something like this?"

Lala put out her cigarette on a plate beside the bed and served herself another glass of whiskey. She mixed it with Coca-Cola, and stirred the ice with her finger.

"I don't think it's your kid. The one they killed... They were merciless. It was a message for someone."

"A narco's revenge."

"Only big-time drug dealers kill like that."

We fell silent. I was afraid. Were there narcos in Constitución? Like the ones who shocked me when I read about Mexico—ten headless bodies hanging from a bridge, six heads tossed from a car onto the steps of the legislature, a common grave with seventy-three bodies, some decapitated, others without arms? Lala smoked in silence and set the alarm. I decided to skip work in order to go straight to the district attorney's office.

*　　*　　*

In the morning, with a headache still, I made coffee. Lala asked to use the bathroom, and a minute later I heard the shower and knew that she was going to be in there for at least an hour. I turned on the TV again. The newspaper didn't have any new information, and the Internet, in times like this, was a roiling pot of rumors and madness.

The morning newscast was saying that a woman had appeared to claim the decapitated kid. A woman named Nora, who had come to the morgue with a newborn baby in her arms and several family members. When I heard "newborn baby" my heart leapt in my chest. It was definitely the dirty kid, then. The mother hadn't gone to look for the body before because—what a frightening coincidence—the night of the crime had been the night of the birth. It made sense. The dirty kid had stayed alone while the mother was giving birth and then... Then what? If it were a message, if it were revenge, it couldn't be directed at that poor woman who slept in front of my house so many nights, that addicted girl who probably wasn't much older than twenty. Maybe the father: that's it, the father. Who could the dirty kid's father be? But then the cameras went berserk, the journalists were running in, they all threw themselves on the woman who was leaving the district attorney's office and shouted, "Nora, Nora, who do you think did this to Nachito?"

"His name was Nacho," I whispered.

And suddenly there was Nora on the screen, a close-up of her grief and her screams, and it wasn't the dirty boy's mother. It was a completely different woman. A woman about thirty years old, already gray-haired, dark-skinned, and very fat, surely the kilos she'd gained during the pregnancy. Almost the opposite of the dirty boy's mother.

You couldn't understand what she was screaming. She was falling. Someone was holding her up from behind, a sister, for sure. I changed the channel, but they all had on this screaming woman, until a policeman stepped in between the microphones and the mother and a patrol car arrived to take her away. There were a lot of new details. I sat on the toilet lid and related them to Lala while she shaved, fixed her makeup, gathered her hair in a tidy bun.

"His name is Ignacio. Nachito. The family had reported him missing on Sunday, but when they saw what was happening on TV they didn't think it was their son because this kid, Nachito, disappeared in Castelar. They're from Castelar."

"But that's so far away, how did he wind up here! Ay, Princess, this is all so frightening. I'm canceling all my appointments, I've already decided. You can't cut hair after all this."

"His belly button is also sewed up."

"Who, the child's?"

"Yes. It seems they tore off his ears."

"Sweetie, in this neighborhood no one is ever going to sleep again, I'm telling you. We might be criminals here, but this is satanic."

"That's what they're saying. That it's satanic. No, not satanic. They say it was a sacrifice, an offering, to San La Muerte."

"Pomba Gira, save us! María Padhila, save us!"

"Last night I told you that the kid told me about San La Muerte. It's not him, Lala, but he knew."

Lala kneeled in front of me and fixed her enormous dark eyes on my face.

"You, Princess, are not going to say anything about this. Nothing. Not to the district attorney or anyone else. Last night I was anxious to let you go talk to the judge. Now, nothing, no way—we're silent as the grave, if you'll pardon the expression."

I listened to her. She was right. I had nothing to say, nothing to tell. Just a nighttime walk with a street kid who had disappeared, as street kids commonly do. Their parents move out of the neighborhood and take them along. They join a band of child thieves or windshield cleaners on the avenues, or find work as drug mules; the mules have to change neighborhoods constantly. They make a camp in a subway station. The street kids never stay in one place; they may last for a while, but they always leave. They escape from their parents, or a distant uncle takes pity on them and brings them to the south, to a house on a dirt street, to share a room with five siblings—but at least they have a roof over their heads. It's not unusual, not at all, for a mother and son to disappear like that. The parking lot where the decapitated kid had appeared wasn't on the route that the dirty kid and I had taken that night. And all that about San La Muerte? Coincidence. Lala was saying that the neighborhood was full of devotees of San La Muerte, all the Paraguayan immigrants and the people from Corrientes were loyal to the little saint, but that didn't make them killers. Lala was a devotee of Pomba Gira, who has the look of a demon woman, with horns and a trident—did that make her a satanic murderer?

Of course not.

"I want you to stay with me for a few days, Lala."

"Obviously, Princess. I'll prepare my bedchamber myself."

Lala loved my house. She liked to put music on real loud and go down the steps slowly, with her turban and her cigarette, a black femme fatale. "I am Josephine Baker," she would say, and then lament being the only transvestite in Constitución who had the slightest idea who Josephine Baker was. "You can't imagine how stupid these new girls are, ignorant and empty as tubes. It gets worse all the time. Everything's lost."

It was difficult for me to walk around the neighborhood after that. Nachito's murder had produced a narcotic-like effect on that part of Constitución; fights weren't heard at night, and the dealers moved a few blocks south. There were too many police guarding the place where they had found the body. Which, the newspapers and investigators were now saying, hadn't been the scene of the crime at all. Someone had simply deposited him, already dead, in the old parking lot.

On the corner where the dirty kid and his mother used to sleep, the neighbors made an altar to the Little Decapitated Boy, as they called him. And they put up a photo, which said JUSTICE FOR NACHITO on it. Despite these apparent good intentions, the investigators didn't entirely believe in the neighborhood's shock. On the contrary, they thought that, maybe, they were covering for someone. That's why the district attorney had insisted that so many neighbors be questioned.

I was among those called in to give a statement. I didn't tell Lala, so she wouldn't agonize over it. She hadn't received the notification. It was a very short interview, and I didn't say anything that could be of value to them.

"That night I slept deeply."

"No, I didn't hear anything."

"There are several street kids in the neighborhood, yes."

They showed me Nachito's photo. I denied ever having seen him. I wasn't lying. He was completely different from the neighborhood kids: a little fat boy with dimples and well-combed hair. I had never seen a kid like that in Constitución—he was smiling!

"No, I never saw black-magic altars in the street or in any house. Just for Gauchito Gil. On Ceballos Street."

Did I know that Gauchito Gil had been decapitated? "Yes, the whole country knows that. I don't think this has anything to do with Gauchito, do you?"

"No, of course, you don't have to answer anything I ask you. Well, anyway, I don't think so, but I don't know anything about rituals."

"I work as a graphic designer. For a newspaper. For the Women and Fashion supplement. Why do I live in Constitución? It's my family's house, a beautiful old building—you can see it when you come by the neighborhood."

"Of course I'll let you know if I hear anything. Of course, you're welcome. Yes, it's difficult for me to sleep, just like everybody else. We're all really afraid."

They clearly didn't suspect me, but they had to talk with all the neighbors. I took the bus home to avoid the five blocks I would've had to walk had I taken the subway.

Since the crime, I preferred not to use the subway. I didn't want to run into the dirty kid. At the same time, I wanted, in an obsessive, sick way, to see him again. Despite the evidence—including photos of the cadaver, which a newspaper had published on the front page, selling out several editions as a result—I kept believing that the dirty kid was the one who was dead.

Or who would be the next to die. It wasn't a rational idea. I explained it to Lala in the beauty shop the afternoon I decided to dye the ends of my hair pink, a job that took hours. No one flipped through magazines or painted nails or sent text messages while waiting their turn now. No one talked about anything except the Little Decapitated Boy. The time for prudent silence had ended, but I still hadn't heard anyone name a suspect in anything more than a general way. That day Sarita said that, in her town, in Chaco, something similar had happened, but with a girl.

"They found her with her head by her side, also, and totally raped, poor little soul. She was all covered in shit."

"Sarita, please, I beg you," said Lala.

"But that's how it was, what do you want me to say? This was done by witches."

"The police think it's narcos," I said.

"The country's full of witch-narcos," said Sarita. "You don't know what it's like there in Chaco. They have rituals to ask for protection. That's why they cut off the head and put it on the left side. They believe that if they make these offerings, the police won't catch them, because the heads have power. They're not just narcos, they also sell women."

"But do you think there are any here in Constitución?"

"They're everywhere," said Sarita.

That night I dreamed about the dirty kid. I was going out on the balcony and he was in the middle of the street. I waved at him to move, because a truck was coming, and fast. But the dirty kid kept looking up, watching me on the balcony, smiling, his teeth dirty and tiny. Then the truck ran him over and I couldn't avoid seeing how the wheels ripped open his stomach like it was a soccer ball and dragged his intestines down the street, as far as the corner. Nonetheless, the dirty kid's head remained in the middle of the street, still smiling and with its eyes open. I woke up sweating, trembling. From the street a drowsy cumbia was sounding. Little by little, the sounds of the neighborhood returned: the fights of drunks, the music, the motorcycles with disengaged mufflers, a favorite trick of teenagers. Secrecy had been imposed on the investigation, which suggested that the authorities were totally disoriented. I visited my mother several times. When she asked me to move in with her, at least for a while, I said no. She accused me of being crazy, and we got into a shouting match the likes of which we'd never had before.

That night I got home late because, after work, I went to a birthday party for a coworker. It was one of the last nights of summer. I returned on the bus and got out before it reached my stop so that I could walk around the neighborhood by myself. I felt like I knew how to handle myself again. If you know how to handle yourself, Constitución is pretty easy. I was smoking. Then I saw her.

The dirty kid's mother had always been skinny, even when she was pregnant. From behind, no one would have guessed she had a belly. It's a typical build for addicts: the hips remain narrow as if refusing to cede space to the baby, the body doesn't produce fat, the thighs don't widen. At nine months the legs are two weak little sticks supporting a basketball. Now, without the belly, the woman seemed more like a teenager than ever. She was leaning against a tree, trying to light her crack pipe under a street lamp. She seemed unconcerned with the police—who were still circulating through the neighborhood—or the other addicts or anything else.

I approached her slowly; when she saw me, there was immediate recognition in her eyes. Immediate! Her eyes narrowed to slits: she wanted to run away, but something stopped her. A weariness, perhaps. Those seconds of doubt were enough for me to block her way, step in front of her, oblige her to speak. I pushed her against the tree and I held her there. She didn't have enough strength to resist.

"Where is your son?"

"What son? Let me go."

We were both talking softly.

"Your son. You know what I'm talking about."

The mother of the dirty kid opened her mouth and her breath—smelling of hunger, sweet and rotten like a piece of fruit left out in the sun, mixed with the medicinal odor of the drug and that permanent stink of burning—nauseated me; addicts smell like burning rubber, toxic factories, polluted water, chemical death.

"I don't have any children."

I pressed her harder against the tree, I grabbed her neck. I don't know if she felt pain, but I dug my fingernails into her. It didn't matter, she wasn't going to remember anything within a few hours. I wasn't afraid of the police, either. They weren't going to bother too much over a fight between women.

"You're going to tell me the truth. Until a little while ago you were pregnant."

The mother of the dirty kid tried to burn me with the lighter, the thin hand moving the flame near my hair. The bitch wanted to burn me. I squeezed her wrist so hard that the lighter fell on the sidewalk. She stopped resisting.

"I DON'T HAVE ANY CHILDREN!" she shouted at me, and her voice, so sick and coarse, woke me up. What was I doing? Strangling a dying teenager in front of my house? Maybe my mother was right. Maybe I had to move. Maybe, as she'd told me, I had a fixation with the house because it let me live in isolation, because no one visited me here, because I was depressed and had made up romantic stories about a neighborhood that, in truth, was a piece of shit, a piece of shit, a piece of shit. That's what my mother had shouted and I'd sworn I would never talk to her again but now, with the neck of the young addict in my hands, I thought that she might have a point.

I wasn't the princess in the castle, but rather a crazy woman locked in the tower.

The addicted kid tore herself out of my hands and began to run, slowly: she was half choking. But when she reached the middle of the block, just where the main street lamp illuminated her, she turned around. She was laughing and the light revealed her bleeding gums.

"I gave him to them!" she shouted at me. The shout was for me, she was looking into my eyes, with that horrible recognition.

And then she stroked her empty belly with both hands and said, loudly and clearly: "And I also gave this one to them. I promised them both."

I ran after her, but she was fast. Or she had suddenly become fast, I don't know. She crossed Plaza Garay like a cat and I managed to follow her, but when the traffic took off down the avenue she succeeded in crossing back over among the cars and I didn't. I could no longer breathe. My legs were shaking. Someone approached and asked me if the girl had robbed me and I said yes, in the hope that they would pursue her. But no: they only asked me if I was all right, if I wanted to take a taxi, if I could tell them what had been stolen.

A taxi, yes, I said. I stopped one and I asked him to take me to my house, only five blocks away. The driver didn't complain; he was used to short trips in this neighborhood. Or maybe he didn't want to grumble. It was late. It must have been his last fare before returning home.

Inside, I didn't feel the relief of the house's cool rooms, its wooden staircase, its interior patio, its old tiles, its high ceilings. I turned on the light and the lamp blinked: it's going to go out, I thought, I'm going to remain in the dark. But finally it stabilized, giving off its yellowish, old, low-watt light. I sat on the floor with my back against the front door. I was waiting for the soft knocking of the dirty kid's sticky hand, or the noise of his head rolling down the stairs. I was waiting for the dirty kid who was going to ask me, again, to let him in.

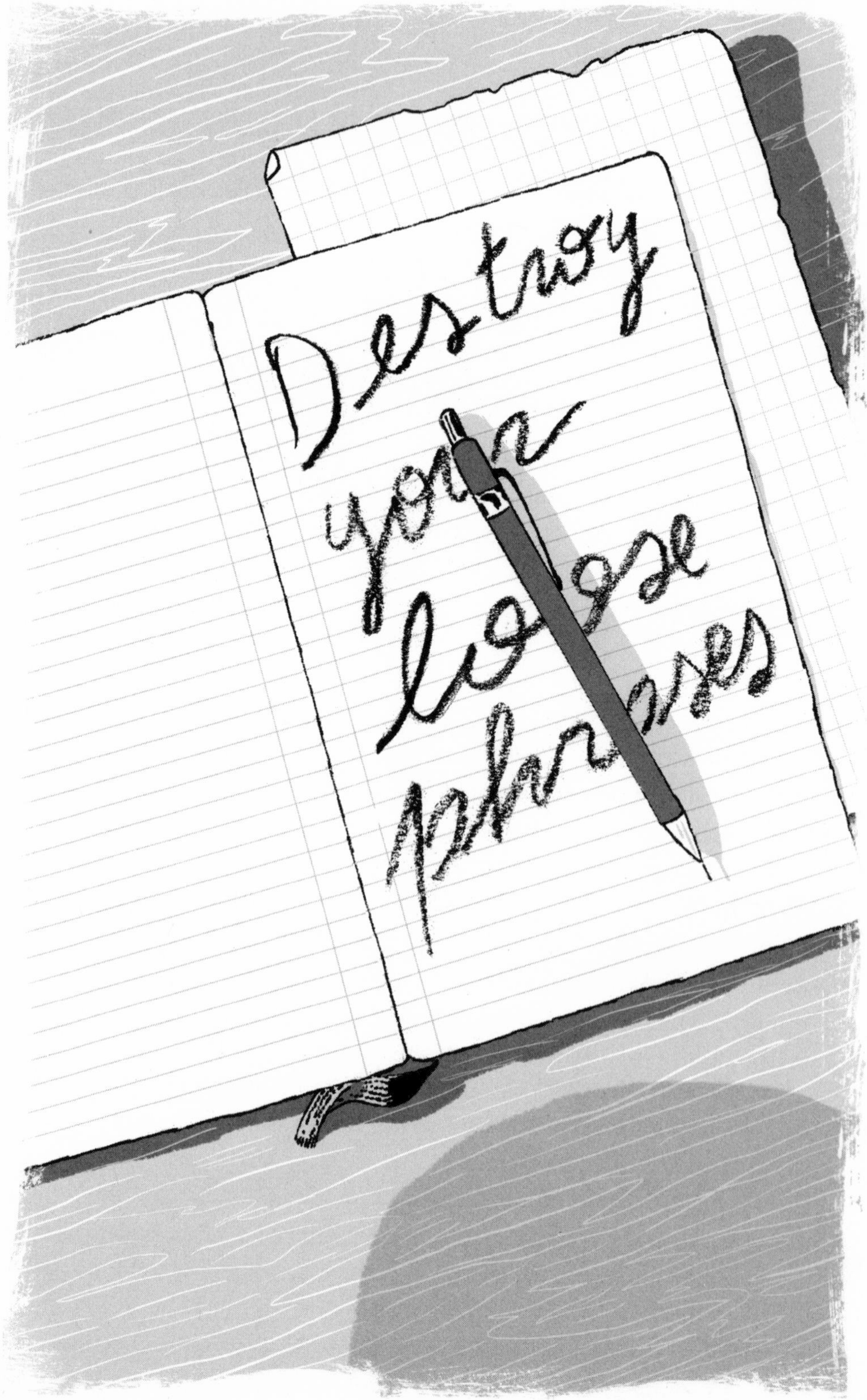
Destroy your loose phrases

BITCHES

by JORGE ENRIQUE LAGE

Translated by Anna Kushner

"I don't know what I'm doing in this place," Amy Winehouse told me. "It's true that I get depressed, that I'm a little anorexic, a little bulimic. I'm not completely well, but I don't think any Cuban woman is."

A nurse passed in front of us, pushing a small cart. Amy Winehouse tapped her temple with her index finger.

"Do you know anyone who doesn't have any problems up here?" she said with a smile.

My answer was to smile as well. I was thinking of how many women she must have known. And above all, what kinds of women.

"Look," she said. "This is my mom."

She showed me a photo. A young, happy *mulata* was posing in the doorway of a wooden house. Next to her, hugging her waist, was a boy.

"My house, out in Baracoa," Amy said, and she used her long, red-painted fingernail to caress the boy in the photo. "This is me. I was seven years old."

I looked more closely and yes, without a doubt, it was her, twenty years and far fewer hormones ago. I looked and that image was engraved into my memory. Shortly afterward, it would come back to my eyes, like a flash, when the young, happy *mulata* showed up at the door of my house, twenty years older herself and with eyes worn out from crying.

I asked her if she had gone to the police. She nodded.

"They said they were going to take care of it. They assured me that they would do everything they could… but three days have passed already and I haven't heard a thing. I'm desperate. I went back to the precinct today, I asked them again, I talked to other officers, I talked to higher-ups, and they all told me not to worry, that my son was a responsible adult, that maybe he had gone to the U.S., that I would probably hear from him soon…"

I offered her a glass of water. She kept going in between sobs:

"He wouldn't go anywhere, I'm sure of it… I came because he called me, he wanted me to come visit him, he wanted us to talk, he felt very alone… He even told me that he might go back to Baracoa with me, because he couldn't stand Havana anymore…"

"You must have told the police this, I suppose," I said.

"Yes, all of it, all of it. I gave them his name, his description, some old photos I have… But today they didn't seem interested in the case anymore. They treated me like a hysterical mother inventing some tragedy."

She looked at me pleadingly, perhaps trying to discover if I was of the same opinion. I thought the greatest tragedy was how logical her trepidation sounded.

"At the hospital, they suggested I come see you—they gave me your address," she said. "The last day he was there, they saw him talking to you a lot… Were you friends?"

"Well, actually…"

"If you know anything, please, anything that could help me find my boy… I'd be eternally grateful."

What could I tell her? To get back on the same train on which she'd arrived? To return to the other end of the island to contemplate the ocean of our disappeared?

I asked myself what Autistic Man would have said in such a situation.

"If only you'd seen me the day I got to Havana," Amy Winehouse told me. "This splendid body was something else. I looked like a broomstick dressed in men's clothing."

She still hadn't shaken off the dust of Guantánamo province when she met the love of her life. The guy took her to live with him, she said, set her up with every comfort he could provide in a little room near the Malecón. There, they dreamt up schemes and lived nestled together on a permanent honeymoon.

"We couldn't get married, of course," Amy said, "but he was my husband. One day, he gave me a short dress, shoes, a purse filled with all kinds of makeup… And a very lovely wig. That night, I dressed up for him, and we went out. We met up with some foreigners he already knew. One of them took me to a hotel and, after sleeping with me, gave me eighty dollars. It was incredible. Eighty dollars! I had never in my life held so much money in my hands. I had never felt so good. My husband and I celebrated in style. We ate, we fucked, we drank rum… Two days later, I was at it again. This time, I made a hundred euros. I felt like I could touch the clouds with my hands. I began to dress up three or four times a week. Money rained down on us. My husband bought me the best clothes, the most expensive shoes. 'I'm going to make a diva out of you, *mami*,' he would whisper in my ear. And I would say, 'I love you, *papi*, I love you.' We kept fucking like animals, but now instead of rum, we poured liters and liters of whiskey on each other. I was already taking the hormones he got for me, one bottle after another. Really good hormones, by the way, made in England. I looked at myself in the mirror and thought I looked lovely, divine. I thought I was living in a dream. Until he disappeared.

"I spent a week without hearing a word from him, crying and shaking in fear. At last, he called me. He was in Miami. He had left on one of those illegal speedboats. He told me, 'I'm sorry, *mami*, I couldn't say anything to you or it would mess up my game.' I yelled, kicked, scratched the walls, and then he calmed me down, saying that as soon as he could, he would come get me, and then we would be together again in the States. I remember that when I hung up the phone, I fell on the bed and didn't have the strength to get back up. I stretched my arm out, grabbed a bottle, and drank until I lost my senses. I wanted to die. I wanted the alcohol to kill me. Seriously, I was a mess. But afterward, after the most horrible hangover of my life, I told myself that I had to move on. I had to continue on my path. Because I hadn't come to the capital to fall apart like one of those old buildings, but rather, to succeed... Listen, I'm not boring you with my story, right?"

"Of course not," I told her politely.

She lit a cigarette and looked pensive as she stared at the sky through one of the large windows of the psychiatric hospital. I sensed that her tale would have a little bit of nausea, a little bit of hell, a little bit of the pop music that you can't hear on the radio.

Amy Winehouse, *guajira Guantanamera*, I thought stupidly.

I found Autistic Man in one of El Vedado's new cafés. El Lateral. He was seated near the bar, watching a Premier League soccer match on TV. It took him a few seconds to recognize me.

"London, London," he said. "The ball rolls over to us, but we don't know how to kick it. What is to be done? Lenin's question. The ones who sit in a café trying to decide whether to do this or that have no future. It's historical circumstances that decide."

Autistic Man owes that nickname to a particular conjunction: his lack of facial expressions and his strange way of speaking. He was often saying things only he understood, as if he were talking to himself, or stuck inside himself: a private language.

The match ended. Tottenham and Arsenal had tied at two goals each.

"Do you remember everything I told you about that Winehouse girl?" I got straight to the point. "Well, I think something happened. Her mom came to see me. Come with me to ask around and I'll tell you on the way."

Autistic Man looked at me with his face devoid of expression and said, "It's always the same thing in this country. You, me, and a dead woman."

"The first decision I made was to get a tattoo," Amy Winehouse told me. "I think it was a way of gaining more control over my own body. I had my husband's name etched between my tits, above my heart, and next to it, I got a black tear as a symbol of my sadness over being far away from him. I felt my pain lightening, like it was being burned away by the pain of the needle on my skin. I liked that. I became addicted to that pain. I'm like that: I get hooked very easily. I kept getting tattoos, one after another. I don't know how many I got. I lost count."

I was trying to count the visible ones, the ones she displayed on her arms and legs: human figures, very feminine figures. Pinup cartoons, some with their big tits hanging out. Old-school icons: Betty Boop, Jessica Rabbit...

Amy Winehouse dried away a few tears, then quickly rubbed her eyes, dug around in her purse, took out some contact lenses, and put them in. Now her eyes were green. They glittered above a puddle of runny eyeliner.

"I gave myself a new look with these eyes and this hair, which is my own, you know? Not a wig," she said, pointing to the Afro rising from her head. "I had to go out and conquer the night, struggle for money... but when you're alone, everything is more difficult. I was new on the streets, and Centro Habana's old transvestites started to view me as a threat. They didn't want me on their turf. They protected their corners, their poorly lit parks, their filthy nooks and crannies, as if I was going to take them away... They were envious of me! I was all glamorous and they looked like clowns in heels. When I passed close to a group of them, I heard things like, 'Look who's here, the hairy one who fell off the stage, ha, ha.' Envious bitches... Oh, but they didn't know who they were messing with. One night, I answered their provocations. 'Do you want me to cut off your prick and stick it up your ass?' I asked one of them.

"From there, things went from bad to worse. The first one I came to blows with ended up with her bald head in a gutter. I emptied the little bottle of rum I always carried in my purse into another one's nose. I took a few beatings myself, but I didn't care. I started earning respect through those fights, which many times ended at the police station..."

The other streetwalkers were always let out after a few hours. But Amy was often kept in jail for the day. Sometimes they didn't arrest the other women at all, putting only her in a patrol car, handcuffed. And it was almost always the same car, with the same two guys.

"One day that patrol car stopped in front of me," she said. "I was walking, I was alone, I wasn't doing anything. One of the cops got out and ordered me into the car. 'What's the problem now, dude?' I asked him. 'Am I breaking the law?' He smiles and points at the back door. I get in. We take off. The one driving asks me my name. 'Amy,' I answer. 'We're going for a ride, Amy,' he says to me. When the patrol car went up Zanja Street, I thought they were taking me back to the station. But they weren't."

On the way to the police station at Zanja and Dragones, Autistic Man covered his ears with his headphones. He seemed determined to increase his isolation.

"What are you listening to? I mean, if you're listening to something."

"Jazz," he answered.

"Since when do you like jazz?"

We entered the old building and went to the front desk.

"Good morning. How can I help you?" the young officer asked me.

"I'd like to talk to two of your patrolmen, but I don't have their squad-car number."

"Do you know their names?"

I hesitated. The names I had were surely fake.

"Chinese shadows," Autistic Man said. "At the end of the day, under every onion-skin layer is another onion-skin layer, and a few fetuses, nationalist demons…"

"Shut up," I whispered. The young policeman was beginning to look worried. "Look, what happened is that…"

"Is there a problem, *compañero*? Do you want to file an abuse complaint? Undue use of force? Is that it?"

"No… Not exactly. I…" I noticed that several blue uniforms were coming toward the desk to listen to me and Autistic Man. "I understand that, several times, they stopped a young transvestite who's missing now. Her mother came here a few days ago to file a complaint. I want to write something about it."

"About the kid who left on a speedboat for the United States?" said a man behind us. When I turned around, I saw the rank on his shoulders—a major. "Poor woman. Her son had problems, you know? With alcohol, with drugs… Are you a journalist?"

"No. I just want to write a story."

"A story, how about that! You know, imagination is the best thing there is!" He patted me affectionately on the shoulder and turned toward a smiling, gray-haired officer, recently arrived. "Isn't that right, Santiesteban?"

When we left, Autistic Man said, "This caustic landscape is the new era, with its many posts. Many crashes and many replacement parts… But at least we remain innocent."

At no point had he removed his headphones.

"They'd already had their eye on me, they were hunting me down," Amy Winehouse told me. "There were two of them, strong black guys. I remember it as if it were this morning. First they wanted to know where I was from. I told them I'd been born in Baracoa, but that I'd lived in Havana for many years. 'That's strange,' one of them said, 'you haven't lost the accent.' 'Or your manly voice,' said the one driving, the younger one. 'Don't mess with her, buddy,' the other one said to him. 'Maybe she was kept at home, like a good girl, until she decided to go out and take up prostitution. That's why we hadn't seen her before.'

"I told them that their mothers were bigger whores, that they hadn't caught me doing any of that, that they had no proof. They said it was true, that until now they had only caught me attacking other whores, but that they'd always let me go despite the fact that they could have charged me with disruption of public order and pre-criminal dangerousness. The one in the passenger seat stretched his hand behind him, squeezed my thigh, and said, 'So you don't charge? You do it for free?' I kept quiet, looking out the window. He went on, 'Hey, calm down, if I understand you right, you need the money to pay for food, clothes, that whole sexy rocker look...' and I started to remember all of those American movies in which the police always tell you that you have the right to remain silent, because everything you say will be used against you. I was scared to death, but at the same time, I was getting turned on.

"The driver added, 'And for rent, too, Lieutenant,' and the lieutenant took his sweaty hand off of me and said yes, rents were sky-high, that's why they had a duty to help me, and then they promised that they were going to make a deal with a friend, Angelón, to see if he could lend me the empty room he had in his apartment. I wouldn't have to pay this Angelón anything. I told them, 'No, thank you,' although the offer was tempting. It was already night by then. They stopped the patrol car on the darkest corner they found. The driver opened my door and, when I was getting out, lifted my dress brusquely and stroked the bulge between my legs.

"I tried to slap him and he dodged it, laughing like he was retarded. 'Faggots!' I yelled. 'The two of you are a couple of faggots. I'm going to file a complaint!' And the lieutenant said, 'Go ahead, go to the station and see if they believe you. This is Sergeant Yasmani, also known as El Micha, and I'm Lieutenant Alexander, better known as the Jackal. You copy?'

"I got away as quickly as I could. I wish I could have run in those damned high heels. A block later, when they drove past me, the sergeant slowed down, popped his head out the window, and said, 'Don't feel bad about what I said, *mami.* You have a very pretty voice. You should be a singer.'"

The apartment was in Chinatown. A dog started to bark when we rang the doorbell. *"Shut up, Minister!"* a voice yelled, and then an immensely fat, shirtless man who looked like a Buddha showed up at the door.

"Yes, his mother came around looking for him the other day…" Angelón said when we explained the reason for our visit. "I'll tell you the same thing I told her. In my opinion, her son… or her daughter, went off to Miami, running after that husband she had. She talked about that every once in a while."

The apartment was small but luxurious. A flat screen that looked large enough for a movie theater was showing a Telesur special about Hugo Chávez. Minister, a robust German shepherd, tried to sniff me from the corner where he was chained up.

"Why did she come to live here?" I asked.

"Why not? The room is comfortable, and I rent it cheaply."

"I've done a count of empty heads and chopped-off heads," Autistic Man said. "Without a doubt, there are more chopped-off heads. Although they get all mixed up in eternity."

I held back the impulse to interrupt him. This is why I asked him to come, I reasoned. Because of the things he says. Next to him, I feel rational and effective. Next to him, I am a guy who's fully in touch with reality.

"Did she prostitute herself?"

"I couldn't tell you for sure…" Angelón said, looking at the notebook I had taken out to make it seem like I was taking notes. "She almost always went out at night and came back at dawn, drunk, and sometimes even a little out of it… I don't know. As if she were drugged."

"Did she ever come here with drugs? Did you see her do drugs here?"

"I didn't search her, brother, nor was I watching her every move… Look, I don't have anything against transvestites. Some are decent people, they work at their shows and those things. But you could see from a mile away that this one had problems. All those tattoos, with a real criminal vibe… I don't know if it was prostitution, but I'm sure he was tied up in something bad. If I accepted him as a tenant, it's because I'm an angel. I like helping people."

"In other words, nobody came here to be with her," I clarified. "Foreigners, for example."

"No, of course not." Angelón's face was becoming stern. "In this house, everything is legal. I pay my taxes."

"Do you have friends in the police department?"

He looked at me for a few seconds, hesitating, before his face relaxed.

"You're saying it because of the dog, aren't you?"

I looked at Minister, who was barking again, furious. "Of course," I said. "Why else would I think that?"

"You have a good eye. Yes, he's a police dog. He used to work in the municipal canine brigade. Now he's retired. I adopted him, but I'm regretting it. He's a very spoiled dog—all he eats is meat, if you can believe it… I'm coming, Minister, stop being such a pain!"

As Minister's barks bounced off the walls, I watched Angelón take a fibrous strip out of a freezer that I imagined was full of the choicest cuts. He defrosted it in the microwave and then started flipping it around in a frying pan.

"I have to feed him often, he's always hungry," he complained. "I think it's the anxiety, the change in his lifestyle. At this rate, he's going to end up wider than I am."

In the blink of an eye, the fillet went from the kitchen to the German shepherd's teeth.

Autistic Man gave me back my notebook. He had taken it without my noticing. He'd written: DESTROY YOUR LOOSE PHRASES.

"Listen, that little article you're writing…" Angelón said as we were leaving. "Do you think that I could read it?"

*   *   *

"Two nights later, they stopped me again," Amy Winehouse told me. "Since there were people around, Yasmani went through the motions of asking me for my ID card before sticking me into the patrol car. When we took off, I asked them how long they would be following me for, because I like to stick close to men but I don't like men sticking close to me.

"'And do you like it when men stick it in you? You like that, don't you?' Alexander said, being funny. 'Jerk-off,' I said to him. 'You don't know me.' Then he said it was true, that he didn't know me, but even so, he was helping me. Because they had spoken with Angelón and he had offered to let me stay at his house for free for as long as I liked. 'And what if I don't want to?' I asked them, and Alexander said to me, 'Girl, do you want to be deported back to Guantánamo? Not that there's anything wrong with the East, look, I'm from Holguín, and the sergeant is from Bayamo, but you like Havana a whole lot, isn't that right?'

"I was thinking. We were close to the train station. Yasmani went down a lonely alley and stopped the car, cutting the engine. I asked them if they were serious about the free room. Alexander put his face up close to mine and said, 'Us Easterners, we're here to help each other.' Yasmani had already taken out his prick... It was hard... It was enormous... Oh, I don't know if I should tell you this..."

She told me everything. Even if she didn't have much trust in therapy, she knew that the first thing, the most important thing, the most difficult thing, was *opening up*.

She spread her ass and sat on top of Alexander's erection. He had moved into the backseat. She began to move up and down on top of the lieutenant while Yasmani pulled her by the neck until he sunk his prick into her mouth. Afterward, the sergeant lay her facedown and fucked her while he slapped her ass and said, 'Qué rico, whore, yeah, like that...' The two policemen both ejaculated inside of her several times. She ejaculated on the floor of the squad car. She ended up all crumpled up and with her hair a mess.

"I felt like shit," Amy said. "I often feel like that, like shit from head to toe. But I can't deny that I'd had fantasies about that before... Big black guys, guys with uniforms... In any event, I don't want to remember the whole thing. They threw me on the street with Angelón's address written on a piece of paper. And before they left, they put a packet in my purse for me to take to him. It was a little sack of weed."

"Marijuana?" I asked.

"Keep it down. We're in a hospital."

The patrol car came out of nowhere. The two agents got out and motioned to us. It was them.

"Are you the one who went to the station to ask about us?" El Micha asked.

"I have some slippers made from plastic that's too hard," Autistic Man said. "When I go at top speed, it's painful."

These things came out of his head like echoes, like the words to splintered songs, like the remains of an untranslatable threat...

"How did you find me?" I asked.

"Don't worry," the Jackal said. "We're police." They both smiled, but without losing their stern masks. "What's this about?"

I repeated what they already expected.

El Micha asked his colleague:

"Wasn't that the transvestite with the crazy tattoos and the out-of-this-world hairstyle?"

"Yeah, now I remember," the Jackal said. "What an Afro. It looked like he had a wasps' nest on top of his head."

"And he looked like a real woman, he would've fooled anyone," El Micha added. "A big *mulata* with green eyes, tall, pretty. Although a little unkempt."

"We found ourselves obliged to stop him a couple of times and give him a warning," the Jackal said, getting serious. "Prostitution is against the law."

"Besides, he was acting with deliberate and unjustifiable violence," El Micha recited. "All under the influence of alcohol and other damaging substances."

"I would say that he was a kid under some bad influences, lots of foreign influences. A young man who was on the wrong path, despite all the possibilities afforded to him by socialism," the Jackal summarized. "It's been a while since we've seen him around the neighborhood. I hope he changed his lifestyle."

"Can we give you a ride somewhere?" El Micha asked me at the car door, inviting me to enter. I looked at Autistic Man: he had his eyes closed and was saying, "No, no, no," moving his head from side to side ceaselessly.

That's the only jazz playing in his ears now, I thought.

"After I moved, everything ended up being easier," Amy Winehouse told me. "Angelón was in the business, of course. The first night he saw me dressed to go out, he said to me, 'Don't go out on the streets now, my love, a few friends are coming over.' It was two Italians. We had some drinks, smoked some weed, and then I took them both to bed. The next morning, Angelón gave me two hundred euros, asking if that seemed okay to me. I leapt on his belly and covered his face with kisses. That was just the beginning. We decided I would set the number of nights per month, and he would take care of bringing the customers to the house. I decorated my room to my taste, and Spaniards, Canadians, Frenchmen, Germans, Swiss, Russians came through there... My favorite were the British, with those nice English accents, but I spoiled all of them, and made them all feel like kings. Who doesn't like money?

"Angelón was very happy. He made the apartment look new. He bought an enormous flat-screen TV, and he told me the freezer would always be full of meat for me, because I had to eat well. He also took care of keeping the house supplied with the best alcohol, for me and for the customers. Me? What can I say? I felt like someone else. Especially after getting silicone in my tits, a very expensive operation on the black market. A dream made reality. I only remembered my days on the streets when I went to check in with Yasmani and Alexander."

"Check in" meant to serve as a go-between. Attend night meetings with the two policemen, who would hand over packages meant for Angelón. She was supposed to be the courier, in order to not raise any suspicions. Before long the bags of weed got mixed up with bags of cocaine.

"At first, I was curious," she said. "I thought that using nose powder, as they say, was going to be something difficult and uncomfortable. But it wasn't. When you have a bill that's rolled up real tight, preferably a hundred-dollar bill, you can take all of those white lines as if they were nothing—as if instead of powder, you were breathing pure air."

She shivered, remembering it.

"Sooner or later, everything is going to change," Autistic Man was saying. "I just hope that the bourgeoisie has time to remember my carbuncles…"

Our lack of good ideas had forced us to take up posts on the street corner, to watch over the building's entrance.

We watched a fifty-year-old woman pulling on the leash of a German shepherd with a muzzle. She went up the stairs and came back down a few minutes later, without the dog, headed toward a grimy corner store across the street.

We went after her.

"Excuse me, miss; was that your German shepherd you had?"

"I wish," the woman said, smiling cheekily. She was going to be a talker. "But no, it's my neighbor's dog, a police dog he was given recently. His name is Minister."

"They should call him Prime Minister," I said. "He's a beautiful animal."

"Isn't that right? I adore him. That's why I ask my neighbor to let me take him out for a walk every once in a while. I like walking next to him. This neighborhood is full of stray dogs that just bark and bark and are very aggressive, and raging combat dogs, the kind that kids raise to be fighters… But you should see them, as soon as Minister passes by, they all stick their tails between their legs, lower their snouts, and go hide. It's like they realize that he's one of those herd leaders... what do you call them?"

"Alpha males."

"That's it, an alpha male. Big, strong, imposes authority, fierce when necessary. My neighbor says that he doesn't even worry about locking his door anymore, because he knows that Minister would jump at the throat of the first person to go inside... Do you buy purebred dogs, to breed them or something like that? You'll have to talk to the owner, Ángel Chang, on the first floor. I live in the apartment just across from his..."

"No, what I'm looking for is something to rent, some small, cheap room. But I hear there's a lot of clandestine business around here, pimps and prostitutes."

It was as if the woman's demeanor had received an electric charge. She maintained the smile, but her lips grew tight.

"Oh, I don't know anything about that," she said.

"I was a star," Amy Winehouse told me. "I was the most exclusive thing in Havana. You can't imagine how many perverted rich men came and went in that house, in my bed. They'd come back for a repeat dose. I'm not even talking about the ones who showed up with masks on. I don't know, maybe they were celebrities, diplomats, important businessmen..."

They went to fuck her, or for her to fuck them. They went to go on sadomasochistic benders, to smack her and tie her up, or for her to smack them, tie them up, and whip their backs. Some went to take pictures: Amy modeling latex and fetish outfits, Amy in all kinds of positions, with vibrators, masturbating, on all fours, a savage explosion of silicone and Caribbean hair and tattoos, in black and white and in color. She was the lead in home videos, films that Angelón screened in the small porno movie theater he set up in the living room, that big screen where Amy showed up looking at the spectator with an expression that had an aura of dripping semen... An expression that revealed fullness but, at the same time, darkness, because in those marathon sessions, filmed or not, she could barely remember more than a few loose moments, random details. All the nights started to mix together in her head into one long, single night, full of cuts and lagoons of unconsciousness. The only things she remembered clearly were the endless lines of cocaine and the thirst that made her drink constantly. She drank and drugged herself when she was with her customers, drank and drugged herself alone, and there came a point at which even the money that she made in bed, her original fuel, started to disappear behind the fog that dirtied her green contact lenses.

"I lied to you, when I said I didn't know what I was doing here," she said. "I was lying to myself. Now you know the reason. I'm not one of those good girls. I have a self-destructive impulse that I'd always kept under control. But control, like love, is a losing game. One I wish I'd never played."

We were leaving Chinatown when the patrolmen showed up again. The back door opened, like an invitation.

"No," I told them. "No, thank you."

"Yes," they told me. "Today you're coming in."

I resisted, I tried to escape. Vain instincts. I ended up pushed headfirst into the patrol car, my hands handcuffed behind my back. A group of people were watching without an ounce of shock. I saw Autistic Man run away. I suddenly understood it was the last time I'd see him.

This is it, I told myself. There's no going back. This is the black hole of Cuban reality. This is the wide-open space where we are lost and alone.

"Why do you have to be that way, writer?" El Micha protested. "All we want is to help you, take you to your house..."

The patrol car took the street bordering the Malecón.

The Jackal said, "We picked up Amy here once, remember? She looked like a dishrag. Standing there on top of the seawall, stumbling, drunk..."

"Of course I remember," El Micha confirmed. "She was urinating there, standing up. She had taken her prick out and was pointing at the sea with her stream... I'm sure she was thinking of her husband, up there in the

North. Or maybe she just wanted to give herself a hand job."

"She was a crazy woman, a sick person… Her head was full of crap."

Through the car window I saw corners full of trash, beggars, signs for new businesses hanging on crumbling balconies and walls cracked by salt spray. The parade of ruins was beginning to seem interminable.

"Now you're so quiet," the Jackal said to me. "Yet we know that you like going around asking questions, talking to people…"

"We've even seen you talking to yourself," El Micha added. "You see? We're watching you, and you haven't even noticed…"

"What's wrong? Do you need company? Because we could give you a dog. A trained German shepherd. Let's see, what would you name him?"

They both laughed.

We left Centro Habana behind us. We stopped.

"Be careful," the Jackal warned me when he opened my handcuffs. "The streets are really bad, there are a lot of criminals. Anyone could deliver a blow to your face much worse than the one my friend is going to give you now."

Then El Micha punched me.

I spit blood on the curb and watched the patrol car drive off.

"I made a decision," Amy Winehouse told me. "Recently, I woke up and decided that it was enough. As always, I had no idea what had happened the day before; I saw in the mirror how skinny I was getting, I saw the crusted blood under my nose, I felt the taste of vomit in my throat and I told myself: You're killing yourself, Amy, you have to stop, you have to get help… And then, without saying anything to Angelón, I went to the clinic. From there, they sent me to this hospital, where they say the best specialists are. I called my mother, crying, and I told her that I was thinking of going to a weekly appointment at the psychiatric clinic because of problems with depression and an eating disorder. What could I say to her? That her beautiful boy was an alcoholic and a drug-addicted whore? Although to be honest with you, I don't think any treatment is going to work on me. The poison I have inside me is stronger than I am, I already know that, but I also think that it's stronger than all those therapies, stronger than the whole Ministry of Public Health. Last week, I sat down in a group where everyone had to share their experiences. I didn't say anything. Can you imagine? If I opened my mouth, they would have had me committed, they would have given me pills to shut me up... No, I'm not crazy yet. While I was there I realized something: when you come from where I come from, when you come with the wrong story, in a place like this, there's nothing they can teach you."

"So why did you come to talk to me?" I asked her.

Amy Winehouse lit another cigarette. "I'm not sure. I saw you looking around and it seemed like you were different from everyone else. Like you'd seen things the rest of them couldn't or didn't want to see. That's why. Do you think I'm crazy, or do you believe me?"

"Believing or not believing isn't important now," I told her, just to say something.

She nodded. We were silent for a few minutes.

"But I still haven't told you everything," she said.

Lieutenant Colonel Santiesteban remembered me very well. He took me to his office and listened closely to my story: police brutality, kidnapping, aggression, etc. He wrote down the patrol car's registration number, got up to make a couple of phone calls, and then said:

"It's odd. The ones who show up here with this kind of complaint are always dissidents. They think that all of us Ministry of the Interior officers are thugs. They don't understand that we're in service to the people. They contort everything. They exaggerate, they make things up..."

"Excuse me, have you listened to a word I said?"

"Of course. But I'm going to ask you to put those same words in writing. I find it odd that you haven't already done so, to be honest. You independent journalists..."

"I already told you that I'm not a journalist," I interrupted him. "This doesn't have anything to do with journalism."

"Well, it has to do with writing counterrevolutionary things. Isn't that right?"

Lieutenant Colonel Santiesteban's eyes were shining. He was smiling. So was I. I thought of the voices, of the echoes that Autistic Man transcribed in my fake notebook. Where could he be now?

I got up and left.

"It was two months ago," Amy Winehouse told me. "I was supposed to meet Yasmani and Alexander but I told Angelón no, that I was not, absolutely was not, going—that he shouldn't count on me anymore to bring that shit, that I had already signed up for a rehab program and I didn't even want to touch any drugs. I told him that it was all the same to me to go to jail or go back to Guantánamo, because maybe that was just what I needed, a change, and that if they didn't like it, it was their problem—that for all I cared, the three of them could go to hell. He was speechless. I shut myself up in my room, slammed the door, got dressed, and then went out for a walk. I went down to the Malecón. I needed to relax, to breathe in a little ocean breeze. I ended up passing by the street where I'd lived with my husband. And there, suddenly, when I was most distracted, a shadow jumped on me from the darkness. The only thing I managed to see was a hand holding a gun. After that, everything went black. I fell into a kind of limbo. I remember feeling a piercing pain, the feeling of being gagged without being able to scream... I remember laughter and a voice saying, 'Let's see if she really likes tattoos,' or something like that. I don't remember anything else. It was all a mixed-up nightmare.

"When I opened my eyes, the next day, I was in my bed again. My body was sore and full of bruises. I got in the shower and, after I got out and looked at myself in the mirror, I realized what they had done to me, what they had tattooed on me, what anyone would see anytime I was naked: PNR.

Policía Nacional Revolucionaria. There were those three capital letters, fresh and bloody... PNR on each ass cheek, on each thigh... PNR on my tits, around my nipples... a long line of PNR, PNR, PNR that went down to my pubic area and went down to the tip of my... of my penis..."

With shaking hands, Amy Winehouse pulled up her shirt a little to show me. Then she leaned back and wiped away her tears. For a moment their eloquence overshadowed the acronym emblazoned all over her skin.

I waited on the corner until I saw Angelón leave. Alone.

I went up to the apartment.

I had the story with me: my failed attempt to delve into Amy's deep, choked-up voice. Too many clichés revolving around a too-simple subject.

I slipped the pages under the door. Two stapled copies, with similar dedications: one for him, and the other for the police.

I heard the very loud barking.

Why not? I told myself, and raised my hand to the knob.

I opened the door slowly. The German shepherd was growling in front of me. He dropped the half-chewed pages to better show me his fangs.

I stared at the animal as I knelt down in front of him. I looked at him as no one ever had. I looked at him not so much in a threatening way as in a crazy or even an inhumane way. Autistic Man had taught me that look. It had its moments.

Instead of attacking me, Minister lowered his head with a soft moan.

"Good boy," I whispered. "Now I'm going to search your home a little... But I'm sure you're hungry."

I went to the freezer and found it practically empty. There was just one piece of meat left, which I defrosted in the microwave under Minister's anxious watch. Then I skewered it with a knife and saw it all at once:

In the piece of meat, thick and badly cut, was an islet of an animal's skin.

And on the skin were traces of ink, part of a drawing of a pinup doll.

Big tits, an enormous ass, long and sumptuous legs. The fatal look she revered, and to which she perhaps aspired.

I felt a wave of dizziness, an immense tiredness. I let myself fall to the floor.

"I bet you can eat it raw," I said to the dog.

He ate it, of course. With the tattoo and everything. Later, he cleaned his snout with this tongue and came to lie down next to me, heavy and satisfied. It seemed like deep down he was scared of me. I patted his back and his belly and, surprised, felt two rows of nipples.

There weren't genitals anywhere to contradict that discovery.

The German shepherd started to fall asleep. Minister was a bitch.

"Is everyone blind?" I asked her, closing my eyes as well.

Out on the street, a police siren wailed. I don't know why, but I immediately knew that it wasn't the PNR. It was a State Security patrol car.

But I didn't go to confirm it. I stayed on the floor.

"They called me just today," Amy Winehouse told me, calmer, inspecting the remains of her makeup in a small mirror. "I talked to Alexander just today and he asked me to forgive him. He sounded sincere. He was almost begging me on the phone. He told me that it had all started as a joke and that they went too far, they let themselves get carried away... In short, they were very sorry about what they did to me and they wanted to give me something to make up for it. A sign of friendship, for everything we'd struggled for together. Enough money to go to the U.S. or wherever I felt like. And we set up a meeting for tonight."

"So you believe him," I said. "You're going to see them again."

"Why not? It's not like they're monsters, animals... Look, I heard about this famous method they call the Twelve Steps here. It seems like that's too many. I don't even know if I have enough strength left to stand in a pair of heels. But maybe what I have to do is take just one step, one step *outside*. The definitive step. Escape, disappear..."

In a back room, a group of people were starting to set up chairs.

"I'm not going in," Amy Winehouse told me. "I already had my last session. Thanks for your patience. Thanks for listening to me."

We said good-bye. She blew a kiss at me before starting down the hallway. The same hallway the nurse was coming back down, pushing her little cart, accompanied by Autistic Man.

"Your pills," she told me, and she waited in front of me to confirm that I was swallowing them. The water tasted like the disposable plastic cup.

When the nurse left, Autistic Man looked at me with his face devoid of expression and said something I didn't understand, as always. Then, in just a few moments, I couldn't see him anymore: he had disappeared into thin air.

It doesn't matter, I thought. I'll find him again.

ARTIST'S RENDITION

by ALEJANDRO ZAMBRA

Translated by Megan McDowell

Yasna fired the gun into her father's chest and then suffocated him with a pillow. He was a gym teacher, and she wasn't anything, she was no one. But she's something now: now she's someone who has killed, someone who sits in jail waiting for her shitty food and remembering her father's blood, dark and thick. She doesn't write about that, though. She only writes love letters.

Only love letters, as if that were nothing.

But it isn't true that she killed her father. That crime never happened. Nor does she write love letters, she never has, maybe because she knows almost nothing about love, and what she does know, she doesn't like. What she does know is monstrous. The one doing the writing is someone else, someone urgently recalling her, not because he misses her or wants to see her but simply because he was commissioned, a few months ago now, to write a detective story. Preferably one set in Chile. And right away he thought of her, of Yasna, of that crime that was never committed, and although he had dozens of other stories to choose from, some of them more docile, easier to turn into detective stories, he thought that Yasna's story deserved to be told, or at least that he would be able to tell it.

He took a few notes at the time, but then he had to focus on other obligations. Now he has only one day left to write it.

The innocent part of the story, the least useful part, the part he won't include, and that he doesn't even fully remember—since his job consists, also, of forgetting, or rather of pretending that he remembers what he has forgotten—begins in the summertime, toward the end of the eighties, when both of them were fourteen years old. He wasn't even interested in literature yet; back then the only thing that held his interest was chasing women, with timidity but also persistence. But it's excessive to call them women—they weren't women yet, just as he was not yet a man. Although Yasna was several times more a woman than he was a man.

Yasna lived a few blocks away. She spent her afternoons in the messy front yard of her house, surrounded by roses, rue shrubs, and foxtails, sitting on a stool, a block of drawing paper on her lap.

"What are you drawing?" he asked her one afternoon from the other side of the fence, momentarily emboldened, and she smiled, not because she wanted to smile, but out of reflex. In reply she held up the block, and from a distance it seemed to him that there was a face sketched on the paper. He didn't know if it was a man's or a woman's, but he thought he could tell it was a face.

They didn't become friends, but they went on talking every once in a while. Two months later she invited him to her birthday party, and he, breathing happiness, going for broke, bought her a globe in the bookstore on the plaza. The night of the party he ran into Danilo, who was smoking a joint with another friend on the corner—they had a ton of weed, they'd started growing it a while ago, but they still hadn't made up their minds to sell it. Danilo offered him the joint, and he took four or five deep drags, and straight away he felt the dulling effect that he knew well, though he didn't smoke with any real frequency. "What've you got there?" Danilo asked him, and he'd been waiting for that question, hiding the bag precisely so they would ask him: "The world," he replied with glee. They carefully undid the cellophane wrapping and spent some time searching for countries. Danilo wanted to find Sweden, but couldn't; "Look how big that country is," he said, pointing to the Soviet Union. They finished the joint before parting ways.

Yasna seemed to be the only one taking the party seriously. She wore a blue dress down to her knees; her eyes were lined, her eyelashes curled and darkened, and there was a shadow of shy sky blue on her eyelids. The music came from a cassette tape played end to end, one that was no longer in fashion, or that was only in fashion for the more or less fifteen guests crammed into the living room. They were clearly all good friends, they'd change partners in the middle of the songs, which they sang along to enthusiastically, though they knew absolutely no English.

He felt out of place, but Yasna looked over at him every two minutes, every five minutes, and the rhythm of those glances competed with the lethargy from the weed. After gulping down two tall glasses of Kem Piña, he sat down at the dining room table as a new cassette started to play, Duran Duran this time. *No-no-notorious.* They danced to it strangely, as if it were a polka, or one of those old ballroom dances. It all seemed ridiculous to him, but he wouldn't have said no to joining in, he would have danced well, he thought suddenly, with an inexplicable drop of resentment, and then he focused on the chips, on the shoestring potatoes, the cheese cut up into uneven cubes, the nuts, and a few dozen multicolored crunchy balls that struck him, who knows why, as interesting.

He doesn't remember the details, except for the sudden lash of hunger, the wound of hunger: the munchies. He made an effort to eat at a normal speed, but when Yasna came in with the tortilla chips and an immense bowl of guacamole, he lost control. Tortilla chips and guacamole had only recently been introduced in Chile, he had never tried them before, he didn't even know that was what they were called, but after trying one he couldn't stop, even though he knew everyone was watching him; it seemed like they were taking turns looking at him. He had bits of avocado on his fingers, and tomato and grease from the chips; his mouth hurt, he felt half-chewed bits of food stuck in his molars, he extricated them tenaciously with his tongue. He ate the entire bowl almost by himself, it was scandalous. And still he wanted to go on eating.

Just then the door to the kitchen opened and a white light hit him right in the face. A man looked out; he was fairly fat but brawny, his parted hair divided into two identical halves combed back with gel. It was Yasna's father. Beside him was someone younger, very similar in appearance, you might say good-looking if it weren't for the scar from a cleft lip, though perhaps that imperfection made him more attractive. Here ends, perhaps, the innocent part of the story: when they grab him tightly by the arm and he tries desperately to go on eating, and a few moments later, after a long and confused series of hard looks and clipped sentences, of scraping and dragging, when he feels a kick in his right thigh followed by dozens of kicks on his ass, his shins, his back. He's on the floor, enduring the pain, with Yasna's sobbing and some unintelligible shouts in the background; he wants to defend himself, but he barely manages to shield his groin. It's the second man who is beating him, the one Yasna will later call *the assistant*. Yasna's father stands there and watches, laughing the way bad guys laugh in lousy movies and sometimes also in real life.

Although none of this, in essence, interests him for his story, he tries to remember if it was cold that night (no), if there was a moon (waning), if it was Friday or Saturday (it was Saturday), if anyone tried, in all the confusion, to defend him (no). He puts his clothes on over his pajamas, because it's the middle of winter and much too cold, and as he drives to the service station to buy kerosene, he thinks with confidence, with optimism, that he has all morning to work on his notes and in the afternoon he will write nonstop, for four or five hours, and then he'll even have enough time, in the evening, to go with a friend to try out the new Peruvian restaurant that opened up near his house. He fills the gas cans and now he's at the Esso market, drinking coffee, chewing on a ham-and-cheese sandwich, and thumbing through the newspaper he got for free for buying a coffee and a ham-and-cheese sandwich. What they want from him is simply a blood-soaked Latin American story, he thinks, and in the margins of the news he jots down a series of decisions that take shape harmoniously, naturally, like the promise of a peaceful day at work: the father will be named Feliciano and she will be Joana; the assistant and Danilo are no good, nor is the marijuana, maybe a hard drug instead, and though he doesn't really want to make Feliciano into a drug trafficker—too hackneyed—he does think it's necessary to move the protagonists down in class, because the middle class—and he thinks this without irony—is a problem if one wants to write Latin American litera-ture. He needs a Santiago slum where it's not unusual to see teenagers in the plazas cracked out or huffing paint thinner.

Nor will it work for Feliciano to be a gym teacher. He imagines him unemployed instead, humiliated and jobless at the start of the eighties; or later, surviving in the work programs of the dictatorship, endlessly sweeping the same bit of sidewalk, or turned into a snitch who informs on suspicious activity in the neighborhood, or maybe even knifing someone to the ground. Or maybe as a cop, one who comes home late and shouts for his food, and who has no qualms about threatening his daughter at night with the same billy club he used to beat back protesters at noon.

He has some doubts at this point, but they're nothing serious. Nothing is that serious, he thinks: it's just a ten-page story, fifteen pages tops, he doesn't have to waste time on the backstory. Two or three resonant phrases, a few well-placed adjectives will fix any problems. He parks, takes the gas cans out of the trunk, and then, while he fills the heater's tank, he imagines Joana splashing kerosene all over the house, with her father inside—too sensationalist, he thinks, he prefers a gun, maybe because he remembers that there *was* a gun in Yasna's house, that when she said she was going to kill her father she mentioned the gun in the house.

There was a gun, of course there was, but it was only an air rifle, which had lain idle for years in the closet. It was a testament to the time when the man used to go to the country with his friends to hunt partridge and rabbit. Only once, one spring Sunday, coming back from church when she was seven years old, did Yasna see her father fire it. He was in the yard, downing a beer and taking aim with a steady hand at the kites in the sky over the park. He hit the bull's-eye four times: the owners couldn't understand what was happening. Yasna thought about those parents and children from other neighborhoods watching their kites founder and crash, so disconcerted, but she didn't say anything. Later she asked him if you could kill someone with that rifle, and he answered that no, it was only good for hunting. "Though if you got the guy in the head from close up," amended her father after a while, "you'd fuck him up pretty good."

After the party, the writer—who at that time didn't even dream of becoming a writer, though he dreamed about many other things, almost all of them better than being a writer—was terribly scared and didn't make any effort to see Yasna again. He avoided the street that led to her house, all the streets that led to her house, and he didn't go to church, either, since he knew that she went to church, and in any case this didn't take a lot of effort because by then he had stopped believing in God.

Six years passed before their paths crossed again. He saw her by chance, in the city center. Yasna's hair was straighter and longer; she was wearing the two-piece suit they'd given her at work. He was wearing a plaid flannel shirt and combat boots, his hair disheveled, as if he wanted to exemplify the fashion of the times—or the part of fashion that corresponded to him, a literature student. By then he could be called a writer, he had written some stories. Whether they were good or bad was not important—a writer is someone who writes, a little or a lot, but who writes, just as a murderer is someone who kills, whether they've claimed one person or many. And it isn't fair to say that she was nothing, then, that she was no one, because she was a cashier at a bank. She didn't like the work but she also didn't think—nor does she think now—that there existed any job that she would like.

While they drank Nescafé at a diner they talked about the beating, and she tried to explain what had happened, but she said she wasn't very clear on that herself. Then she talked about her childhood, especially about her mother's death in a car crash, she'd barely gotten to know her, and she talked to him about the assistant, which was how her father had first introduced the man to her while they were varnishing some wicker chairs in the yard, although some days later he told her, as if it weren't important, that actually the assistant was the son of a friend who had died, that he didn't have anywhere to go and so he'd be living with them for a while. The assistant was twenty-four years old then, he came home late at night, he slept most of the morning, he didn't work or study, but sometimes he babysat the little girl, mostly on Tuesdays, when Yasna's father got home at midnight after practicing with his basketball team, and Saturdays, when her father had games and then went out with his teammates to drink a few beers. The writer didn't understand why she was telling him all this, as if he didn't know (and maybe he didn't, although, by that point, since he was already a writer, he should have known) that this was the way people get to know each other, by telling each other things that aren't relevant. By letting their words fly happily, irresponsibly, until they reach dangerous territories.

Although the conversation wasn't over, he asked her if she had a phone, if there was some way they could see each other again, because right now he had a party to go to. She shrugged her shoulders, and maybe she was waiting for him to invite her to that party, although in any case she couldn't go, but he didn't invite her, and then she didn't want to give him her number anymore. She also forbade him from showing up at her house, even though the assistant no longer lived there.

"Then how will we see each other?" he asked again, and she, again, shrugged her shoulders.

But she'd mentioned the name of the bank where she worked, which had only three branches, so he was able to track her down a few weeks later, and they began a routine of lunches, almost always at a fried-chicken place on Calle Bandera, other times at a joint on Teatinos, and also, when one of them had more money, at Naturista. He went on hoping for something more to happen, but she was elusive, she told him about a boyfriend who was so generous and understanding he seemed clearly invented. Sometimes, for long stretches, he watched her talk but didn't listen to her. He looked most of all at her mouth, her teeth, perfect except for the stains from cigarette smoke on the front ones. He would do this until she raised or lowered her voice, or maybe let slip some unexpected bit of information, as she did one time with a sentence that, although he hadn't the slightest idea what she'd been talking about, brought him back to the present, though she didn't say it in the tone of a confession: on the contrary, she said it as if it were a joke, as if it were possible for a sentence like that one to be a joke. "I wasn't happy in my childhood," was what she said, and he didn't understand what he should have understood, what anyone today would understand, but hearing her say it still shook him, or at least it woke him up.

Did she really use that word, so formal, so literary: *childhood*? Maybe she said "when I was a kid," or "when I was little." Whatever she'd said, one would have had to tell the entire story, years ago, cultivating a sense of mystery, taking care with one's dramatic effects, building up gradual, shocking emotion. Good writers and also the bad ones knew how to do this, it didn't seem immoral to them, they even enjoyed it, to the extent that depicting a story always brings a certain kind of pleasure. But what would that mystery be good for now, what kind of pleasure could be gained when the sentence that says it all has already been let loose? Because there are some phrases that have won their freedom: phrases we have learned how to hear, to read, to write. Fifteen, thirty years back, good writers, and bad ones too, would have trusted in a sentence like that to awaken a mystery that they would reveal only at the end, with a scene of the father asleep and the assistant in the bedroom touching the nipples of a ten-year-old girl, who is surprised but, as if it were a game of Monkey See, Monkey Do, puts her own hand under the assistant's shirt and, with utter innocence, touches his nipple back.

Another scene, two days later. The father is at basketball practice and the assistant calls her into his room, closes the door, takes off her clothes, and leaves her locked in there. The girl doesn't resist, she stays there, she searches among his clothes, which are still in bags as if, though he's lived there for months now, he had just arrived or were about to leave—the girl tries on shirts and some enormous blue jeans, and she's dying to look at herself in the mirror, but there's no mirror in the assistant's room, so she turns on a little black-and-white TV on the nightstand, and there's a drama on that isn't the one she watches, but the knob spins all the way around and she ends up getting sucked into the plot anyway, and that's where she is when she hears voices in the living room. The assistant appears with two other guys and he takes the clothes she's found off her, threatens her with the bottle of Escudo beer he has in his left hand, she cries and the guys all laugh, drunk, on the floor. One of them says, "But she doesn't have any tits or pubes, man," and the other replies, "But she's got two holes."

The assistant doesn't let them touch her, though. "She's all mine," he says, and throws them out. Then he puts on some grotesque music, Pachuco, maybe, and orders her to dance. She's crying on the floor like she would during a tantrum. "I'm sorry," he consoles her later, while he runs his hand over the girl's naked back, her still shapeless ass, her white toothpick legs. That day in his room he puts two fingers inside her and pauses, he caresses her and insults her with words she has never heard before. Then he begins, with the brutal efficiency of a pedagogue, to show her the correct way to suck it, and when she makes a dangerous, involuntary movement, he warns her that if she bites it he'll kill her. "Next time you're gonna have to swallow," he tells her afterward, with that high voice some Chilean men have when they're trying to sound indulgent.

He never ejaculated inside her, he preferred to finish on her face, and later, when Yasna's body took shape, on her breasts, on her ass. It wasn't clear that he liked these changes; over the five years that he raped her, he lost interest, or desire, several times. Yasna was grateful for these reprieves, but her feelings were ambiguous, muddled, maybe because in some way she thought she belonged to the assistant, who by that point didn't even bother to make her promise not to tell anyone. The father would come home from work, fix himself some tea, greet his daughter and the assistant, then ask them if they needed anything. He'd hand a thousand pesos to him and five hundred to her, and then he'd shut himself in for hours to watch the TV dramas, the news, the variety show, the news again, and the sitcom *Cheers*, which he loved, at the end of the lineup. Sometimes he heard noises, and when the noises became too loud he got some headphones and connected them to the TV.

It was precisely the assistant who urged Yasna to organize her fifteenth birthday party ("You deserve it, you're a good girl, a normal girl," he told her). At that point he'd been disinterested for several months; he would only touch her every once in a while. That night, however, after the beating, when it was already almost dawn, drunk and with a pang of jealousy, the assistant informed Yasna, in the unequivocal tone of an order, that from then on they would sleep in the same room, that now they would be like man and wife, and only then did the father, who was also completely drunk, tell him that this was not possible, that he couldn't go on fucking his sister—the assistant defended himself by saying she was only his half sister—and that was how she found out they were related. Completely out of control, his eyes full of hate, the assistant started to hit Yasna's father, who as she knew from then on was also his father, and even gave Yasna a punch on the side of her head before he left.

He said he was leaving for good and in the end he kept his word. But

during the months that followed she was afraid he would return, and sometimes she also wanted him to come back. One night she went to sleep with
her clothes on, next to her father. Two nights. The third night they slept
in an embrace, and also on the fourth, the fifth. On night number six, at
dawn, she felt her father's thumb palpating her ass. Maybe she shed a tear
before she felt her father's fat penis inside her, but she didn't cry any more
than that, because by then she didn't cry anymore, just as she no longer
smiled when she wanted to smile: the equivalent of a smile, what she did
when she felt the desire to smile, she carried out in a different way, with a
different part of her body, or only in her head, in her imagination. Sex was
for her still the only thing it had ever been: something arduous, rough, but
above all mechanical.

The writer eats some cream of asparagus soup with half a glass of wine for
lunch. Then he sprawls in an armchair next to the stove with a blanket over
himself. He sleeps only ten minutes, which is still more than enough time
for an eventful dream, one with many possibilities and impossibilities that
he forgets as soon as he wakes up, but he retains this scene: he's driving
down the same highway as always, toward San Antonio, in a car that has
the driver's seat on the right, and everything seems under control, but as he
approaches the tollbooth he's invaded by anxiety about explaining his situation to the toll collector. He's afraid the woman will die of fright when she
sees the empty seat where the driver should be. The volume of that thought
rises until it becomes deafening: when she sees that nobody is driving the
car, the toll collector—in the dream it's one woman in particular, one he
always remembers for the way she has of tying back her hair, and for her
strange nose, long and crooked, but not necessarily ugly—will die of fright.
"I'm going to get out quickly," he thinks in the dream. "I'll explain."

He decides to stop the car a few meters before he reaches the booth and
get out with his hands up, imitating the gesture of someone who wants to
show he isn't armed, but the moment never takes place, because although

the booth is close, the car is taking an infinite amount of time to reach it.

He writes the dream down, but he falsifies it, fleshes it out—he always does that, he can't help but embellish his dreams when he transcribes them, decorating them with false scenes, with words that are more lifelike or completely fantastic and that insinuate departures, conclusions, surprising twists. As he writes it, the toll collector is Yasna, and it's true that in an indirect, subterranean way, they are similar. Suddenly he understands the discovery here, the shift: instead of working at a bank, Joana will be a collector in a tollbooth, which is one of the worst possible jobs. He pictures her reaching out her hand, managing to grab all the coins, loving and hating the drivers or maybe completely indifferent. He imagines the smell of the coins on her hands. He imagines her with her shoes off and her legs spread apart—the only license she can take in that cell—and later on an inter-city bus, on her way home, dozing off and planning the murder, now really convinced that it is, as they say in Mass, truly right and just. After she's done it she heads south, sleeps in a hostel in Puerto Montt, and reaches Dalcahue or Quemchi, where she hopes to find a job and forget everything, but she makes some absurd, desperate mistakes.

The last time he saw Yasna, they almost had sex. Up until then they'd seen each other only during those lunches in the city center; whenever he'd asked her to go to the movies or out dancing she'd pile on the excuses and talk vaguely about her perfect, made-up boyfriend. But one day she called him, and then she showed up at the writer's house. They watched a movie and then they planned to go to the plaza, but halfway there she changed her mind, and they ended up at Danilo's, smoking weed and drinking burgundy. The three of them were there, in the living room, high as kites, stretched out on the rug, uncaring and happy, when Danilo tried to kiss her and she affectionately pushed him away. Later, half an hour, maybe an hour later, she told them that in another world, in a perfect world, she would sleep with both of them, and with whoever else, but that in this shitty world she couldn't sleep with anyone. There was weight in her words, an eloquence that should have fascinated them, and maybe it did, maybe they were fascinated, but really they just seemed lost.

After a while Danilo let out a laugh, or a sneeze. "If you want a perfect world, smoke another one," he told her, and he went to his room to watch TV. Yasna and the writer stayed in the living room, and even though there was no music, Yasna started to dance, and without much preamble she took off her dress and her bra. Astonished as he was, he kissed her awkwardly, he touched her breasts, caressed her between her legs, he took off her underwear and slowly licked the down on her pubis, which wasn't black like her hair, but brown. But she got dressed again suddenly and apologized, she told him she couldn't, she said she was sorry, but it wasn't possible. "Why not?" he asked, and in his question there was confusion but there was also love—he doesn't remember it, he would be incapable of remembering it, but there was love.

"Because we're friends," she said.

"We're not such great friends," he answered, completely serious, and he repeated it many times. Yasna let out a peal of beautiful, stoned laughter, a real and delicious guffaw that only very gradually wore itself out, that lasted ten minutes, fifteen minutes, until finally she managed to find, with difficulty, the way back to a serious and resonant tone with which it would be appropriate to tell him that this was a good-bye, that they could never see each other again. He didn't understand, but he knew it didn't make sense to ask any questions. They sat with their arms around each other in a corner. He took Yasna's right hand and calmly began to bite and eat her fingernails. He doesn't remember this, but while he looked at her and bit her fingernails he was thinking that he didn't know her, that he would never know her.

Before they left they sat for a while with Danilo, in front of the TV, to watch an eternal game of tennis. She drank four cups of tea at an impressive speed, and she ate two *marraqueta* rolls. "Where's your mom?" she asked Danilo suddenly.

"Over at an aunt's house," he answered.

"And where's your dad?"

"I don't have a dad," he answered. And then she said:

"You're lucky. I do have one. In my house there's a rifle and I'm going to kill my father. And I'm going to go to jail and I'm going to be happy."

By now it's three in the afternoon, he doesn't have much time left. He urgently turns on the computer, annoyed by the seconds the system takes to start up. He writes the first five pages in a matter of minutes, from the moment the detective arrives at the scene of the crime and realizes he has been there before, that it's Joana's house, until he climbs up to the attic and finds the old boxes with clothes from the time when they were a couple, because in the story they were a couple, but not for very long, and in secret. He also finds the globe he'd given her—but without the stand that held it—and a backpack he thinks he recognizes in among the fishing rods and reels, the buckets and shovels for the beach, the sleeping bags and rusted dumbbells. He keeps looking around, impelled more by nostalgia than a desire to find evidence, and then, just like in books, in movies, and also sometimes in reality, he finds something that would not be conclusive to anyone else, but that is, immediately, to him: a box full of drawings, hundreds of drawings, all portraits of her father, ordered by date or series, but each more realistic than the one before, at first sketched in pencil, and then, the majority, in the green ink of a Bic pen, fine point. When he sees the accentuated contours, gone over so many times that the paper is often torn, and when he notices the exaggeration of the features—though never to the point of caricature, they never lose the aura of realism—the detective understands what he should have understood a long time before, what he hadn't known how to read, what he hadn't known how to say, hadn't known how to do.

The writer works at a cruising speed through the intermediate scenes, and takes great pains over the final two pages, when the detective finds Joana in a boarding house in Dalcahue and promises he will protect her.

She tells him in great detail about the crime, put off so many times over the course of her life, and while she cries she seems to grow calmer. Maybe they stay together, in the end, but it's not certain. The ending is delicate, elegantly ambiguous, though it's not clear what it is the writer thinks is ambiguous, or delicate, or elegant about it.

It's not a great story, but he sends it off with a clear conscience, and he even has time to drink a pisco sour and eat some yucca *a la huacaína* before his friends get to the Peruvian restaurant.

It's not a great story, no. But Yasna would like it.

Yasna would like the story, though she doesn't read, she doesn't like to read. But if it were made into a movie, she would watch it to the end. And if she caught a repeat of it and she didn't remember it, or even if she remembered it well, she would watch it again. She doesn't often watch movies, in truth, nor does she often recall the writer. She doesn't even know he is a writer. She did remember him a few months ago, though, when she was walking in the neighborhood where he used to live.

They had declared her father terminally ill, and recommended she give him marijuana to help with the pain. She'd thought of Danilo's plants, hence that walk through the old neighborhood, which seemed erratic but was not: she enjoyed the luxury of walking around aimlessly, peripherally, even reaching the end of a street and then retracing her steps, as if she were searching for an address. But she knew perfectly well where Danilo lived, still in his family home; she merely wanted to enjoy that luxury, modest as it was. Her father was sleeping more calmly by then, with less pain than on previous days, so she could go out for a walk and take her time.

"I hope you haven't killed your father," he said to her when he finally recognized her, and since she didn't remember her words from that night almost twenty years before, she looked at him with alarm. Then she remembered her plan, the air rifle, and that crazy afternoon. She felt an uncomfortable happiness when she remembered those lost details, as Danilo talked and cracked jokes. She liked that house, the atmosphere, the camaraderie. She stayed for tea with Danilo, his wife, and their son, a dark-skinned, long-haired boy who spoke like an adult. The woman, after looking at Yasna intensely, asked her what she did to stay so thin.

"I've always been thin," she answered.

"Me too," said the boy. She bought a lot of marijuana, and Danilo also threw in some seeds.

It'll be a while before the plant flowers. She is watering it now while she listens to the news on the radio. Her father doesn't rape her anymore, he wouldn't be able to. She hasn't forgiven him, she's reached a point where she doesn't believe in forgiveness, or in love, or in happiness, but maybe she believes in death, or at least she waits for it. While she moves the furniture around in the living room, she thinks about what her life will be when he dies: it's an abstract feeling of freedom, maybe too abstract, and for that reason uncomfortable. She thinks of an ambiguous pain, of a disaster, calm and silent.

She hears her father's complaints coming from the kitchen, his degraded, corrupted voice. Sometimes he shouts at her, berates her, but she pays him no mind. Other times, especially when he is high, he laughs his labored laughter, utters disjointed phrases. She thinks about the will to live, about her father clinging to life, who knows what for. She brings him another marijuana cookie, turns on the TV for him, puts his headphones on for him. She stays awhile beside him, looking at a magazine. "I didn't believe in God, but only with his help could I overcome the pain," says a famous actor about his wife's death. "It's simple: lots of water," says a model on another page. "Don't let public tantrums get to you." "It's her second TV series so far this year." "There are many ways to live." "I didn't know what I was getting mixed up in."

She hears the trash collector going by, the men's shouts, the dog barking, the whisper of canned laughter coming from the headphones, she hears her father's breathing and her own breathing, and all those sounds don't alter her feeling of silence—not of peace: of silence. Then she goes to the living room, rolls herself a joint, and smokes it in the darkness.

BLIND SUN

by **JOCA REINERS TERRON**

Translated by Stefan Tobler

I

Stefan Czarniecki was never going to get used to the sun in the tropics. It had a white, direct, broad, deep, dense luminosity that was almost solid, and that pulsed in the optic nerve behind his left eyeball as he went round the shacks with the military policemen. What was he, a Polish insurance broker, doing in a São Paulo *favela*? Even closing his eyes didn't help; his eyelids were too transparent, his eyelashes like a lab rat's. This attack on his senses was just the sun's rude way of saying *Good afternoon.* They left the alley lined with damp fencing, the smell of burnt food and the dark heads peeking out of slits in windows. His sandals raised reddish dust with every step; it was gathering in the corners of his toenails. Just ahead, the heel of the policeman's boot was splashing through a puddle. They stepped onto a soccer pitch. Tufts of dry grass. Clods of mud from last night's rain, now hardened by the heat. Drops of sweat ran down his forehead, blurring his vision. The silhouettes of vultures in the sky indicated that they had arrived. One of the goal posts had fallen over; the goal had never looked more undefended. But no chance of scoring here, nor of winning. On the white stain of the sun-bleached ground an even whiter patch stood out. And then, at the epicenter of the painting, there was a red smudge. The stink of coagulated blood. Under their soles the dirt had the consistency of soaked sand. It was as if the painter of the scene had decided with broad brushstrokes to add a bloody cube to the pure expanse, in order to challenge the monopoly of white. Stefan squinted to see better. The policeman said, *Christ, I've never seen anything like this*.

The red cross on the back window indicated that the cube was an ambulance. A pile of raw meat filled the back. There must have been fifteen bodies where the stretchers normally went. Who knows, maybe twenty. No one checked to see if that count was right. Stefan looked without wanting to.

"And the wheels of the ambulanz?" he said.

"Pfff!" said the policeman. He was cleaning his teeth with the same toothpick he had just used to scratch his ear.

"Pfff?" said Stefan. "I don't underrrstand."

"Pfff," said the policeman, flapping his hands like wings. "They flew off."

On the floor by the front passenger seat Stefan found a handkerchief. He thought quickly of another handkerchief like it, one that had belonged to his late grandfather. But this one was a child's. It was pink, with a name embroidered on it: *Carolayne*.

With one handkerchief in his hand and another in his head, Stefan closed his eyes and saw a group of black spots. He saw them for just a second or less; when he opened his eyes again he couldn't say how many vultures there were. Was it a definite or an indefinite number? The problem was tied to the problem of God's existence. If God existed, the number was defined, because God knew how many vultures he had seen. If God did not exist, the number was indefinite, because there was no one who could count it. In this case, Stefan was sure he had seen fewer than ten vultures perched on the ambulance and more than one, but that he had not seen nine, eight, seven, six, five, four, three, or two vultures. He had seen a number between ten and one, which was not nine, eight, seven, six, five, etc. The whole number was inconceivable. *Ergo*, God did not exist.

"We couldn't put the bodies in the bags," said the policeman, scaring off a vulture with his baton, "because you can't see where one body ends and another begins."

Stefan excused himself with a quick gesture, stumbled back up toward the beam of white light that spanned the alleyway, and retched up his lunch.

2

Stefan Czarniecki, Stefan Czarniecki. There was no way out for him but to obey his boss's orders (that is, my orders) at WTF's Munich office and fly to São Paulo to negotiate the renewal of the policy covering that city's fleet of ambulances. Luck had never been on his side, I know, but I still sent him. To be honest, had you watched him drag his 290 pounds out of the hired car parked in front of Lapa district's town hall on the morning after his visit to the soccer pitch, sporting a flower-patterned shirt and Bermuda shorts, it would have been difficult to know what the man's qualities were. He did have one special quality for sure, but it was well hidden. One of the car-watchers came up and asked for money to watch his car. Stefan did not understand, he could barely see the kid because of the glare. The kid said *Dólar, dólar*, rubbing his thumb and index finger together in front of Stefan's rather red face. In the end he understood, but not before turning a deeper, beetroot red. The car-watcher was black and really thin; Stefan was a fat redhead. If it had not been for the kid's rudeness, it might have seemed like a meeting between two interplanetary travelers.

Stefan was Polish. When it came down to it, he wasn't unaware of things: he knew it was ironic to be a Pole working for a German insurance company. Germans had never been known for giving Poles a sense of security. In the two weeks leading up to his trip to Brazil, he had studied Portuguese by Skype with an Angolan teacher who lived in Berlin. He had thought it might be a good idea to throw in all his chips and not take the flight back. After all, Europe was not in a good way. And he had learned that South American marijuana was good stuff, and that the Brazilian president, a kindhearted, mustachioed socialist who went around in a Panama hat and lived on a farm, was legalizing drug use. Staying there had seemed like an attractive option. There was the sun, too, of course. He was looking forward to getting a tan on a beach, although he had his doubts as to whether that would happen. His freckles burnt so easily.

When he landed at Cumbica airport and saw the sniffer dogs lifting their snouts toward his Hawaiian shirt, which reeked of hash (he had not washed it in six months), he thought he had gotten on the wrong connecting flight. He had made a mistake, in fact, but not with the flight, as he later discovered on the Internet: the country that planned to legalize marijuana was called Uruguay and the Brazilian president had a beard, not a Panama hat. Stefan had never heard of Uruguay and, when he looked it up on the map, he saw why.

The phone woke him in the middle of his first night in Brazil. It was his boss. One of the city ambulances had been damaged. He didn't have the details yet. The boss just let him know that, because he was there on the ground, Stefan would have to do the inspection. The hand of chance always drives the cars we insure, his boss liked to say, and he said it again at that moment, while Stefan imagined the hand of chance hesitating, causing an aerial disaster above a marijuana plantation. This was Stefan's main weakness: his concentration rapidly went up in smoke.

Two days later, after getting away from the car-watcher, Stefan went into the town hall, where he had an appointment with the local Secretary of Health. On the wall of the waiting room, where council employees dealt with the public, there was a photo of the Secretary in a military uniform. Since his arrival, Stefan had seen soldiers everywhere, and now he had found one here, in the local government. Wasn't the country a democracy? Or was Uruguay the democracy? There was an enormous line. It looked like the Secretary had a lot of problems to deal with. People with black clouds instead of faces. Stefan tried to count: there were more than fifty, fewer than one hundred. The military policeman who had accompanied him to the scene of the accident recognized him and led him to the back of the line. The doors lining the corridor each sported the same poster: DISRE-SPECT SHOWN TO PUBLIC OFFICIALS AS THEY CARRY OUT THEIR DUTIES IS A CRIME PUNISHABLE BY SIX MONTHS' TO TWO YEARS' INCARCERATION OR FINE, they said.

In a long row of occupied chairs, there was one woman who was crying. Her body was doubled up, her head lay on her thighs, and a little child was holding her hand. Her crying was low and brief, sobs without any intervals. Stefan remained silent like everyone else, and stroked the pink handkerchief in his flower-patterned pocket. It was the best way to attract Zofia's spiritual attention. He thought: A vehicle used to save lives, stuffed full of murdered people. But how did the handkerchief end up in the ambulance?

3

One week before the massacre, Brayan was in a cold sweat on the bus going to work. The sun was beating down that day, but even so his hands felt as cold as a frog's forelimb. He had not had a steady job in ages, ever since he had been fired from his position as the janitor's assistant in a condo-minium out in the Eastern Zone. Now he worked as an electrician, a joiner, and a builder, but he was not properly any of those. Coming back from church one day he had met old Dumpster, a master builder whose specialty was constructing churches for evangelicals. He'd had some work he could offer, in a mansion in Morumbi, and he offered it. The money was bad, but Brayan's daughter was really ill and so he accepted. Now he got off at the nearest bus stop and walked over a mile to the mansion. At the gate, other unemployed people from his neighborhood were waiting. One uncle, three cousins, and two nephews. They said it was the pastor's house. The place seemed to be completely covered with vegetation, from the stone walls protecting the house from the street to the roof to the walls overlooking the inner courtyard, which was where the work was to take place. Reflective glass in the windows blocked the view inside. A huge bald black guy in a flashy suit and tie showed everyone in. The only words he said were that they should work in silence. The way he said it left no room for ambiguity: they would have to work without talking, just like they would have to keep quiet about the details of the job. Old Dumpster showed the stonemasons the architect's plan, which was a drawing of an enormous swimming pool in the shape of a woman's ass. The angle was striking: from the front (or the back, to be more precise), it was covered in tiles of varying shades of skin tone that gave a gluteal elevation to the bottom of the pool, soon to be filled with sky-blue water. At the center of the ass, in the spot corresponding to the anus, a lit fountain would be installed. In the same bind as Brayan, the other stonemasons—all members of the same evangelical church and all unemployed—did not raise any objections about the shamelessness of the design. They started the excavation so silently that it seemed like they were building a tomb and not a pool.

4

While he waited to be seen, Stefan did some sums. The sun was so strong that it burst through the louvered windows along the corridor, illuminating the people waiting. A ray of sunlight fell on the prostrate mother and her child, turning them transparent and unreal. In order to be able to see them, Stefan had to squint, which caused his eyes to tear. The tears clouded his vision even more. In his briefcase he had a spreadsheet that detailed all the costs and figures of the WTF's multimillion-dollar policy, as well as all the discounts and advantages that were necessary to convince the Secretary to renew it. The city had 171 vehicles, of which 140 were in operation and 31 kept in reserve. It was not a bad number. By his calculation, there was an ambulance for every 82,000 inhabitants, which was within the bounds of the World Health Organization's recommendation of one ambulance for every 150,000 inhabitants. Before joining the line to see the Secretary,

Stefan had taken a look at the ambulances parked in front of the Barra Funda emergency room. They were in good condition, new vehicles. Everything seemed fine. However, there was an inconsistency in the figures. Although the number of ambulances was more than sufficient to serve the population, the number of emergency departments was not. That was why there were seemingly endless lines outside the hospitals and almost all public offices. Unable to receive treatment in hospitals, people gathered in front of desks at the Centers for Disease Prevention and Control, at Vaccination Posts, at the Transport Department, and at any other government office that dealt with the public—always with the hope of being seen by a doctor. Except there were no doctors there, or in any of the other offices. The sunlight penetrated the steamed-up window and drew more tears from Stefan's half-closed eyes. Without thinking about what he was doing, confused by the bright light, he pulled the pink handkerchief from his pocket and wiped his face. As he did so, he saw that, at the other end of the corridor, the crying mother lifted her head for a moment to look at him. Or rather, she stared at the handkerchief in his hands. She recognized something.

5

Coming home in the early hours after his first day of work at the mansion, Brayan found his wife sitting on the doorstep. Their youngest girl was braiding her mother's long hair. Brayan did not say anything, but clambered over them slowly and went straight through the kitchen to their only bedroom, which they shared with their two daughters. Carolayne was lying in bed, looking at the holey zinc roof, her eyes white. In the past, in better times, she used to say that the holes looked like stars. Beside the bed a plastic bucket was almost full of vomit and traces of blood. His wife joined them in the room.

"Did you manage to get a place for the little one in the nursery?" asked Brayan.

"No," she said. "I wasn't at—" her voice crumbled, and she was unable to finish her phrase.

Brayan put his hand, sweaty as a frog's skin, on his girl's forehead. She was burning up with fever.

"She's much worse."

Afterward, he sat silently on the doorstep, lit a cigarette, and enjoyed the real stars, not the holes in the zinc roof. He wished he could find some way of helping his daughter, but the only sums he could do had unfathomable answers. He was not good at math. The work would be done in two weeks' time, so he was sure to receive his money three weeks from now, maximum; it would be enough to pay the last two months' overdue rent and the bill at the market, or at least part of it, but it would not arrive in time to take Carolayne to a private clinic. Tuberculosis. A neighbor had said he didn't believe that people still died of it. So what was happening to his daughter, if she wasn't about to die? The numbers got mixed up in Brayan's head, and he stopped doing the math without having reached any conclusion.

And what if he asked Dumpster to be paid early? But the foreman had acted strangely that day. He no longer seemed to be the devoted brother that Brayan knew from the evangelical church services. He kept his distance from the stonemasons as they worked, standing in silence next to the black guy in the suit. You could see the bump of the gun holster under the man's jacket; he always had his earpieces in, never saying a word. When Brayan went to get a drink of water, he passed close to him. He could hear that the guy was only listening to static in his earpieces—static at such a high volume that it could be heard by anyone near the drinking fountain, where the man stood all day, as solid as a statue. What kind of person listens to static all day? Most people listen to music, however bad their taste in music. It just wasn't normal.

Dumpster seemed to be scared.

From deep in the corridors of the mansion a blast of cold air escaped and sent shivers down the spines of the stonemasons.

6

On his second night in Brazil, back in his hotel room after his inspection of that gory ambulance, Stefan ran his fingers over the child's handkerchief and remembered the handkerchief belonging to his grandfather, who had been killed in the massacre in the Katyn Forest in Poland in 1940. A family relic. When the tragedy occurred Stefan had not been born yet, but he knew of it from his grandmother's telling and retelling of the story.

Stefan put the pink handkerchief on the bedside table and took a deep toke on his joint. It was pretty good. The boy who had sold it to him at the gas station opposite the hotel hadn't been lying. Brazilian dope was really good. What a shame the Brazilian president wasn't the Uruguayan president and Brazil wasn't Uruguay. South America could have been really good, but it wasn't quite all that. It just seemed like a pretty chaotic place.

The phone rang once, twice. Stefan answered it, thinking it might be his boss. It wasn't.

"Hi, Granny. How are you?"

It was his grandmother, who had died a few years ago. At first the calls had scared Stefan. Then he'd gotten used to them and even started to like them. The strangest thing about them was that his granny always had a story to tell about an object resembling whatever happened to be in his pocket at the time; if he had a handkerchief he had found at a crime scene, for example, she would tell him something about a handkerchief. If he had a lighter, then she'd talk about that. Right now she wanted to tell him, once again, the story of his grandfather's death. It always happened when Stefan had a joint. On occasion it even happened when he didn't. This was Stefan's greatest quality: he talked to his grandmother.

She started her story. Stefan's grandmother had traveled to Smolensk to meet her parents just one day before her husband had been taken prisoner in Kozelsk, many years ago. Hitler had just invaded Poland. Stefan's grandfather was an officer in the Polish army. The Soviet army executed twenty-two thousand Polish soldiers in the forests around Katyn.

Your grandfather was one of those soldiers, Stefan.

"I know, Granny."

Well, the story of your grandfather's handkerchief is even more interesting: how it was recovered and reached our house. I didn't tell you that yet, did I? Obviously, the people living around there who managed to survive knew about the massacre, although the Soviets didn't admit to it. When the Germans discovered the mass grave in 1943, they wanted to prove the Stalinists' guilt. They brought those butcher-doctors who do autopsies to Katyn from all over Europe, and they rounded up the remaining local Poles, who were hunting rats to survive. Like your uncle Witold, who was captured as he answered the call of nature in a thicket. The Germans needed all kinds of witnesses, even a liar like your uncle Witold. It was the worst night of his life, and let me tell you, he had his fair share of terrible nights, especially when he used to drink in Piotr's pub in Gnezdovo. The Nazis tied your uncle to the trunk of an oak tree and started to drag bodies out of that enormous hole. Although no one would say Witold had a delicate constitution, he was not strong enough for that. After seeing hundreds of bodies exhumed, he fainted, and didn't wake up until hours later. I expect he'd been drinking before heading into the woods, Stefan. That would have been just like your uncle, God rest his soul (far from alcohol). He and I were just talking about the harm drink can do, but I remembered that he doesn't drink anymore. The dead are teetotalers. Against their will perhaps, but they are. In any case, the truth is the Gestapo took good care of him that night, because they needed his statement to support their propaganda against the Communists.

"Best get to the point, Granny Zofia."

Relax, boy. The Nazis left Witold in a shed to recover with some other poor devils. In the middle of the night your uncle managed to sneak out and make off in his underpants. It was winter. The temperature was below zero. Luckily it didn't snow, Stefan, otherwise he wouldn't have made it. As he ran on, he found himself deeper in the woods, and the temperature kept dropping. That was when Witold stumbled headfirst into a thornbush. When he got up, he realized he had stumbled over a corpse. The dead man's face was completely disfigured, but not his Polish officer's uniform. Witold didn't hesitate for an instant. He tore the coat off that man. By the end of the next morning he'd arrived in Gnezdovo, where old Piotr hid him in a place he must have loved, especially after almost having almost frozen to death: the pub's cellar.

That was where, by the light of a candle, your uncle Witold found the handkerchief in one of the coat's pockets. It was as good as new. There was not a single stain of blood or mold on it. It still bore your grandfather Henryk's name, which I had embroidered on it with these hands that the ground hasn't swallowed up and never will.

"Every time I hear this story it gives me the creeps," said Stefan. "Granny Zofia? Granny?"

The line went dead. Her calls tended to stop in that abrupt way. Stefan leaned back on his pillow and looked at the pink handkerchief folded on the bedside table. It too was intact. *Carolayne.* Who would have embroidered that name? The dope wasn't quite the shit he'd thought it was. The high had passed, leaving a raging migraine in its place. In the ceiling mirror Stefan saw that he was sunburned. His body was red and his underpants white: he looked like the Polish flag. His freckles were red-hot, burning hot, like they were about to go up in flames.

7

When he got to the Morumbi mansion for the second day of the job, Brayan noticed an ambulance parked at the building site. Old Dumpster had not turned up for work, and the black guy was still stroking the butt of his automatic under his jacket and listening to his static. The other stonemasons continued to work in silence, broken only by their grunts as they shifted stones.

Shortly before leaving home, Brayan had helped his wife to apply Vicks VapoRub to his daughter's hot chest, then held the girl as she'd coughed over the pan of hot water from which she was inhaling the steam. He wondered whether those treatments had any effect, or if they just made Carolayne vomit even more. This time the amount of blood she threw up was frightening. He needed to do something.

Brayan looked at the patio where they were building the pool. Why have an ambulance at a construction site?

The man in the suit looked at Brayan, put his index finger to his lips, and smiled. The color of his teeth was the same as the whites of his eyes, while his face got blacker and blacker, disappearing like a shadow in the dark corner of a corridor. Brayan could hear the deafening sound of the static from the man's earpieces. A chill wind whistled from out of the house, raising a whirlwind of cement dust and scattered sand. Hugging themselves against the cold draft, the other stonemasons witnessed Brayan take the nearest shovel, turn around violently, and hit the guy in the suit on the temple. Seeing him laid out on the ground, Brayan heard the noise of the earpieces' static oscillate and then disappear. He got into the ambulance. The key was in the ignition.

"Lift home, anyone?" he winked at the others. "I'm only asking once."

8

"Stefan Czarniecki," came a woman's voice from among the cubicles behind a half-open door. The pronunciation of his surname was wrong. But, because there were not likely to be any other Stefans there, Stefan Czarniecki stood up and followed the thin secretary whose hips swayed gently ahead of him. She turned another doorknob and motioned for him to enter. As immobile as if they were doorposts, two large black men in suits stood inside with their arms crossed. They reminded him of eunuchs, but without the fans. Times had changed; there was a fan on the ceiling, instead. But the static Stefan heard was coming not from the fan, but from the security men's earpieces.

The uniformed man Stefan had seen in the photo outside was now lounging in an armchair before him. He was wearing an expensive suit, although the jacket was hanging on a nearby chair. It was impossible to see his face. It was almost completely hidden in a carton from which fat noodles slid, splattering the table with tomato sauce. Lifting his chopsticks high in the air and rattling his gold watch, the man signaled for Stefan to sit down. There was a Bible on the desktop. The former military man was now an evangelical pastor, as well as Secretary of Health here. In short, he was responsible for the well-being of his citizens' bodies as well as their spirits.

"Buon diea," said Stefan, in what he hoped passed for Portuguese.

The Secretary picked his teeth with a toothpick, stuck out his belly, unhooked the bib from his shirt collar, and lit a cigar. Right behind his Brylcreemed hair was a sign saying that smoking was forbidden.

"Oh! *Bom dia*," replied the Secretary. "You're from WTF Insurance, right? Let me see your new calculations. This is why you came, right? Come on, come on!"

Stefan handed over his spreadsheets, staining them a little with tomato sauce, and continued in broken Portuguese:

"One hundred seventy ambiulaanz, minus one, that police took for crrrime," said Stefan. "You know, the massaaker."

"Huh? I don't know anything," said the Secretary. "Congratulations, you speak Portuguese really well. Do you understand figures too? Here, let me spell this out for you with noodles."

With the skill of a Chinese calligrapher, the Secretary drew 30% with cold, floppy noodles on the desk. Stefan admired his talent. He should have pursued an artistic career, and not become a Mafioso in the guise of a religious politician.

"That's lot."

"It's that or no deal. There's a bucketload of insurance brokers hot for the ambulances. You talk to your German man."

"It's lot. No can't do deal. Need talk to Munichi."

"Mieow-Nicci—is that some drag queen's name? Go and talk, then," said the Secretary. "I'll give the German a day to sort it out. God bless. Now scram."

Stefan was led to the exit by the Secretary's secretary. When the door opened, the woman who had been holding hands with her little girl was standing in the middle of the corridor, waiting for Stefan. She stretched out her hand, palm up, and asked to see the pink handkerchief he had put in his pocket just moments earlier.

9

When Brayan stopped the ambulance in the road below the slope where he lived, his wife had already received the text message telling her to take Carolayne down to the corner. The stonemasons, perhaps fifteen or twenty men, got out of the back and gently took the girl from the arms of her mother, who only had time to give Brayan the pink handkerchief through the driver's window. Although they didn't know it, the passing of that handkerchief from her hand to his was their good-bye. Then the ambulance shot off down the gravel road, turned the corner, and skidded toward the boiling asphalt of Avenida Giovanni Gronchi, which its driver intended to take all the way to the Children's Hospital on Rua Seraphico Prado. Perched in the back, those unpolished men, whose skin had turned into old leather after years of work under the hot sun, were jammed together shoulder to shoulder, vainly trying to reduce themselves to the size of children. In the middle, Carolayne put on the airs of a princess as she lay on the stretcher holding her pink rucksack. The stonemasons laughed their toothless laughs and hollered out their stories, guffawing at the sudden turns Brayan took. It was like a holiday trip in a school bus, maybe a trip to the beach or a theme park. They turned on the lights of display panels and medical equipment. They played with the oxygen mask and gave each other little shocks with the defibrillator, which only tickled their strong builders' chests. Brayan put the siren on, clearing the road of other drivers; the paupers in the back laughed harder and made signs at them through the windows. Carolayne felt so happy that her nose stopped running and her cough stopped, which is why Brayan forgot to pass her the handkerchief that ended up falling on the seat and from there was pushed by the breeze to the floor, where it was found the next day by Stefan. My daughter is going to be treated immediately, thought Brayan as he put his foot on the gas, the lights flashing and the siren blasting out at top volume, not knowing what awaited them around the next corner.

IO

Stefan Czarniecki's big problem was always his complete lack of focus. He had been sent to sort out a particular problem, which he had not managed to sort out. Instead, he'd ended up sorting out something else entirely.

As soon as he had told his boss the terms demanded by the Secretary to renew the policy, he hung up. Then he turned to look at the woman in front of him with the pink handkerchief in her hands. Opening it, she revealed the embroidered name: *Carolayne.*

"You see, her name is written here," the woman said. "My daughter, my little girl. Her father disappeared, and she did too. They didn't come home."

"I found it in the ambiulaanz at the crrrime. It was on the frront seat."

The woman hugged her only daughter and started to cry.

I I

The next morning Homicide received more information about the ambulance massacre. The faces had been mutilated beyond recognition; the fingerprints had been burnt off; the teeth had been torn out. There was no way to identify the victims. They had found the girl's body among those of the men. They knew it was a child because of its small size and the absence of pubic hair. They had also found a small school rucksack, inside of which they found a milk-white tooth. A DNA test showed that it was Carolayne's. The evangelical Secretary wrote a polemical article in the papers about the cost of such tests: they were too expensive to be wasted on everyday criminality and banditry. A Brazilian's life was not part of an American TV series, he said. As the stonemasons did not have papers or medical records, they were buried in paupers' graves. Their church made no effort to reclaim even their souls.

WTF did not renew the policy. The afternoon after Stefan's meeting, the town hall's cleaner got rid of the numbers the Secretary had laid out beautifully with noodles on his desktop. Thirty percent went into the bin.

In the coach on the way to the airport, Stefan saw an ambulance, its siren blaring, speed through a traffic jam. In São Paulo it was the only way to avoid the congestion. Only police cars and ambulances managed to get around the city's immense network of roads with any efficiency; the city was the biggest car park Stefan had ever seen. Not a single car was moving. Suddenly the ambulance turned off its siren and slowed down. The light on its roof slowly stopped flashing. For the patient it carried, the rush was over. Ambulances are vehicles that sometimes talk without wanting to, he thought.

His cell phone played the *Simpsons* opening theme. The display said BLOCKED, so he thought it was his boss calling. But it wasn't.

"Hi, Granny."

She didn't normally call his cell, so it must have been urgent. She asked where Stefan kept his dead grandfather's handkerchief.

"In the same drawer where I keep my weed, uh—my tobacco."

The old woman started a long sermon about the dangers of smoking.

If the Nazis hadn't arrived first, smoking would have finished off your grand- father. That no-good Witold still smokes. I can't understand how they let him, here of all places, she said, and started to cough.

"Why was that ambulance at a construction site, Granny Zofia?"

After a few more coughs mixed with static, the old woman told him that the ambulance had been used to transport building materials for the pool. The pool's owner had been in a hurry, a big hurry, and that was how he'd gotten around São Paulo traffic. He was a very scary man, she said, and in that very instant the Secretary leaned back in his chair and imagined diving into his ass-shaped pool for the first time.

The coach went into a tunnel and the line went dead. Stefan closed his eyes and felt the blind sun heating the freckles on his arm. He realized that if he opened his mouth and said what he thought, he would end up setting fire to the coach's curtains.

Arriving at the airport, he found out his flight was two hours late. Joining the line to board, he closed his eyes for a moment. It was already night, but the light of the sun still blared behind his eyelids. He did not want to stay in that place another minute.

AMÉRICA

by JUAN PABLO VILLALOBOS

Translated by Rosalind Harvey

The perpetrator had killed his neighbor because of an argument about soccer. The motive did not merit a murder, but most of the blame lay on the fact that there had been a loaded weapon close at hand. A machine gun, nothing more and nothing less. A Mendoza C-1934 machine gun, to be precise. The perpetrator had inherited it from his father, an incorrigible chatterbox, who had appropriated it while doing his military service decades before, in the previous century. The weapon had hung on the wall in the living room of the man's house until he and his wife both died, when the Hotel Regis was destroyed in the earthquake of 1985. Anyone who came to the house before that would end up being told the father's favorite story: the tale of the adventure in which he and two fellow soldiers, just for a laugh, had sneaked the machine gun out of the barracks in some loaves of stale bread. The Mendoza C-1934 was the regimental weapon of the Mexican army, the father would tell them; the Mendoza factory had been founded during the Mexican Revolution to supply General Villa. The father said *General Villa*, not *Pancho Villa*. What he didn't tell his listeners was that the gun was loaded. The perpetrator, who had heard the story a thousand times, did not know this either.

When he inherited the machine gun, together with the house, the perpetrator put it in the closet, under a pile of old sheets, where it remained until the night of the murder, when it emerged, according to the perpetrator, "to give my neighbor a fright, but not to kill him." The neighbor was an América supporter. The perpetrator supported Cruz Azul. Do we need mention that América had just won the final match of the championship on penalties, with ten men, after having scored two goals in the last minute to force extra time? And with a goal from the keeper! Like in a bad movie, like on a TV show. It can't be a coincidence that the man who owns América also owns a TV station.

The perpetrator told all this to the police officer in the early hours of the morning, after giving himself up voluntarily. The worst thing about such an absurd, unlikely testimony was that it was true.

The inspector takes his first sip of the boiling-hot coffee his secretary has just served him. The coffee tastes burned, but the inspector doesn't know this: he thinks that this is the taste of authentic coffee. Every morning, his secretary puts the coffeemaker on at eight fifty a.m., so that the coffee is ready by nine. The inspector shows up, at the earliest, at ten. Gingerly, he takes another sip; he doesn't want to scald his tongue. He is sitting in his office. Today's newspaper lies open on his desk, and he scans the headlines mechanically.

That shitty journalist again.

A fortnight ago, in a nightclub in the south of the city, two young women were killed by machine-gun fire. An assault rifle, this time, nothing more and nothing less. An AK-47, to be precise. The official weapon of the Soviet armed forces. The police have managed to catch the perpetrators, but some commentators are still stirring up public opinion. It's a serious matter, because the dead girls are middle-class.

The inspector calls for the sub-inspector, who appears three minutes later, sipping and blowing on an identical cup of coffee.

"Have you seen the paper?"

"Uh-huh."

"That shitty journalist. And the worst thing is today everybody's gonna read the paper, because of the game."

"Actually the worst thing is what the chief said."

"What did the chief say?"

"Didn't you see? He said that today there was going to be important news about the case."

"He said that?"

"Yep."

"And? Do we have anything?"

"Nothing."

"Nothing?"

"Nothing."

"Is the chief in yet?"

"At this time? What do you think?"

What are the chances of a goalkeeper scoring a header in the last minute of a championship final?

The chief puts his head under the covers and says, "Not so fast, not so fast." The chief's girlfriend takes note and sucks more slowly. They are in the apartment the chief uses to meet up with his girlfriends. The place can be rented by the day or by the week. Furnished. Cable TV. Internet. Electrical appliances. Cleaning service. A concierge who doesn't ask questions. The girlfriend keeps trying, but it's no good: the chief just won't get hard. He must be tired from being up all night, from the alcohol and the coke. Or maybe it's that the chief, at his age, is starting to suffer from a different kind of problem.

The girlfriend sits up, making the covers slide off the bed. She is naked and skinny. Nineteen years old, although she looks sixteen; a childlike face with huge eyes and big lips.

"Get your gun," says the girlfriend.

"What?"

"Would you like to stick your gun up my ass?"

Blood rushes to the chief's groin; his member twitches as if from an electric shock. The girlfriend smiles with a mouthful of perfectly aligned little teeth.

"You're so bad! You think I'd let you do that? But you know what you can do? You can point it at my head while I suck you off."

The chief retrieves the pistol from under the heap of clothes discarded by the side of the bed. It's a Beretta 92, nothing more and nothing less, the same pistol used by American soldiers in the Gulf War. The pistol used by the Spanish Civil Guard, by the Argentine National Gendarmerie, by the armies of Albania, Brazil, France, Peru, Colombia, the Philippines, Turkey, and Slovenia. Oh, and, of course, by the Mexican police.

The girlfriend returns to her task. The chief leans over slightly to the right so he can push the barrel of the Beretta in among her blonde curls. With his left hand he fondles her diminutive breasts. He has a monumental erection and can't decide whether to carry on like this until the end or to enter her. The girlfriend is in no doubt. She hasn't slept a wink, one client after another at the lap-dancing club, her body is crying out for rest. She wants to finish this off once and for all, as soon as possible, but the chief wants exactly the opposite and won't finish, is never going to finish, not ever. It's time to perform the maneuver that never fails: she spits onto the fingers of her right hand and slowly slides them between the chief's legs.

"Mmmmmm."

"You like that, baby?"

The girlfriend massages in a circular motion under the chief's scrotum, slips her middle finger between the folds of his anus, and when the semen erupts in a savage spurt, the Beretta 92 goes off.

What are the chances of a gun staying loaded for over fifty years without anyone realizing?

"Do they not have enough business in the north?" the candidate asks.

The conversation is taking place in the party offices, right after the weekly meeting. The candidate and his companion sit at a long oval table alongside ten empty leather chairs. On the table are twelve cups of coffee with the party logo printed on them, eleven of them empty. The candidate picks up the only full cup and takes a careful sip of the boiling-hot coffee, burned after sitting on the hot plate all through the two-hour board meeting. He thinks about asking his secretary to make another pot, but he has no intention of prolonging this encounter, and so resigns himself to the heartburn. He turns back to the campaign's canvassing coordinator, who has requested a private meeting to discuss "a very interesting proposal."

"They just want to be on good terms with you, sir."

"Those days are over, my friend. That style of doing business worked when we had seventy years of the same old story. Now no one offers support in exchange for vague favors."

The door of the meeting room opens and the upper half of the campaign manager's body appears. He looks at the candidate without speaking, allowing his eyebrows to express yet again the perplexity of those who know they have been excluded.

"It's a private meeting, I'll be done in five minutes," the candidate says.

What can the canvassing coordinator have to discuss with the candidate without the knowledge and the participation of the campaign manager? Somehow the candidate has already forgotten what he's just said, about them not being in the age of the same seventy-year-old story anymore, about the candidate no longer being an omnipotent figure whom everyone respects with unconditional reverence. Although in truth that all stopped even before the seventy years were up. It stopped after sixty-four, the day Colosio was murdered.

The door closes. The canvassing coordinator continues.

"You're totally right, sir; times have changed. Don't misinterpret this, but we can't afford to turn down the support they're offering us. And anyway, these people are talking to all the candidates."

"All of them?"

"The ones who have a chance of winning."

The candidate looks at him. "The problem, my friend, is that we have a deal with some other people, you see?"

"I know, and these people know it too. That's why they came to speak to me and not with you, or with my colleague in charge of the campaign funds."

"This could cause a lot of problems."

The canvassing coordinator picks up a pen from the table, the candidate's pen. It's a Montblanc Meisterstück 149, nothing more and nothing less, in black and gold resin. The same pen used by John F. Kennedy. He writes a telephone number on a piece of paper and holds it out to the candidate.

"I hope you won't take this the wrong way, but we must accept this offer. They're not giving us any other alternative."

The newspaper offices look strange in the morning, with all that light coming in through the windows. The so-called shitty journalist doesn't usually show up before six p.m., and everything is different now: not just the brightness of things, but the people (who are few, and different) and, above all, the calm rhythm with which the atmosphere seems to vibrate, which contrasts with the frenzy at the end of the day. He walks past the mostly empty desks toward the offices of the editor in chief, who is waiting for him, his door open. Before going in, the shitty journalist pours himself a cup of coffee from the pot on the editor's secretary's desk. Carefully he takes a couple of sips, trying to clear his head, if only a little.

The editor is looking at something on his desk. The shitty journalist knocks four times on the door frame with the knuckles of the hand not holding the cup of coffee and goes into the office. Into the office, too, comes the stench of damp and tobacco his clothes give off.

"Congratulations. You look like one of Onetti's characters."

"I've come straight from a brothel. That's the risk you run if you call me here at this ungodly hour. The coffee's burned, by the way."

"Since when are you such a gourmet?"

"It'll give me heartburn."

"Sure, it's the coffee. Not all that junk you eat on the street."

"Increase my expenses and you'll soon see me eating in the finest restaurants every day."

Contrary to what one might expect, there are no stacks of newspapers in the office. On a corner of the desk, neatly folded, lies today's edition. Hanging on the back wall in a little gold frame is a national prize for journalism, next to an Ibero-American one. There are no family photos. The editor picks up an iPad from his desk and hands it to the shitty journalist.

"We have the photos."

"How modern. Already you've shattered my illusion of being a character from Onetti."

The shitty journalist looks without surprise at the photos, as if they were merely the graphic representation of an obvious truth. And this is what they are.

"Are we going to use them?"

"Depends. Request a meeting with the chief of police."

"The chief? That poor jerk doesn't know a thing. We'll have to squeeze the candidate."

"Not so fast. Let's go for the low-hanging fruit first."

"The chief can't stand the sight of me. What do I say to get him to see me?"

The editor picks up a fine-nibbed Stabilo pen, nothing more and nothing less. Gray ink, manufactured by the inventors of the highlighter, a German factory in existence since the middle of the nineteenth century. He notes down the name of an illegal high-class brothel, as well as the names of two women and of the owner, who is known to control all sorts of trafficking in the western part of the city.

"Tell him I've talked to these people."

The shitty journalist looks at the names the editor has written down. "And where the hell did you get these from?"

"I have my sources. Don't forget I'm a journalist too."

"Seriously. What's your source, Google?"

The piece of paper ends up between the pages of a notebook with black covers that the shitty journalist stows in the back pocket of his pants. He shakes the editor's hand good-bye and starts for the exit, but the editor stops him.

"Hey, don't leave your cup here."

The shitty journalist goes back to the desk, picks up the coffee cup, and begins his retreat again. This time he stops of his own accord.

"So where did the pictures come from?"

The editor pretends to be concentrating on his iPad.

"It was the campaign-team people, right?"

"It's best if you don't know."

What are the chances that an ejaculation caused by massage of the prostate results in a reflex action of the index finger of the right hand?

Two officers are putting the girlfriend's corpse into a body bag. The chief passes the Beretta 92 to the inspector, who in turn passes it to the sub-inspector. Another three officers remove the sheets, the mattress, a rug, and a bedside table. Anything that might have been spattered with the girlfriend's blood. The sub-inspector searches the apartment from top to bottom; no one is calling it the "crime scene," because no crime has happened there.

The chief's cell phone rings. The ring tone is a children's song currently in fashion. The chief looks at the inspector and says, "My daughter put that on there." When he looks at the screen and sees who's calling him, the chief goes to the other room in the apartment and shuts the door.

"How can I help, Mr. Candidate?"

"The people from the north have been approaching my team. Do you know anything about this?"

"There's a rumor they want to fight for this territory."

"Now? In the middle of the campaign? Talk to your boss and tell him I don't want things to get any more out of hand until September. We've got enough on our plate with all the other shit going on at the moment."

"All right, sir."

The candidate is talking to the chief, but the chief in turn has a boss. The structure is limitless, police hierarchy is like the Himalayas. The candidate communicates with the chief, and not with the chief's boss, because the chief is the only person in the police force in whom he has complete confidence. The chief and the candidate were at primary school together. Of course, if the candidate wins the election, the chief will become the chief of chiefs.

"One other thing. Did you read the papers today?"

"Yes. We're taking care of that too, sir."

"Did they close the investigation? They're ruining our campaign."

"We're on it."

"But didn't you tell the journalists there'd be a development today?"

"It was to calm them down."

"Well, it didn't work. Sort it out, for Christ's sake."

The chief presses the little red button to disconnect the call and goes back into the main room, where they've just put a new mattress on the bed. The inspector and the sub-inspector are whispering about something over by the window, their backs to the non-crime scene. The chief approaches surreptitiously to try and catch what they're saying; are the sons of bitches talking behind his back? He tiptoes over until he's almost breathing down their necks. No, they're talking about soccer, about the goal scored by América's keeper.

The chief's cell phone rings again. The inspector and the sub-inspector jump from the shock. It's the shitty journalist.

At the end of the day, how long has it been since there was a serial killer in Mexico? (Not counting the presidents of the Republic, of course.)

The shitty journalist takes a seat at a table by the window overlooking the street. On it he places the black notebook and a blue Bic ballpoint pen, the pen created by Marcel Bich in 1950 in Clichy, a pen exactly the same as a hundred thousand other ballpoint pens sold all over the world. The café is half empty: only three tables occupied out of a total of twelve. He has gotten there twenty minutes earlier than the time he'd agreed on with the chief of police, as a precaution, because he didn't want to be late. The place was a long way from the newspaper offices, a long way from the apartment where he lives, a long way from the cantinas he frequents, a long way from all the ambits in which he usually moves. But today the traffic in the city has been relatively quiet. The waitress comes over to take his order. She is small and dark, her hair in a short straight bob that falls just to the nape of her neck. Slim. Large breasts. Just as he likes them.

"An espresso."

"We don't do espressos. You can get an Americano if you like."

Where has this national obsession with using the verb "to get" in inappropriate contexts come from? It's "Can I have an Americano," "Can you make me an Americano," or "Can you serve me an Americano"; even, capitalistically and prosaically, "Can I buy an Americano." "Can I get an Americano" sounds like a badly translated phrase from another language.

"Will you make it now, or is it already made?"

"We make it all the time."

The shitty journalist squints over at the bar and has to stand up to make out, at the back, two coffeemakers, their lights on and their glass jugs full.

"It's impossible to get a decent cup of coffee in this city, it really is."

"Would you prefer a tea?"

"I want a coffee, but I want you to make it for me now."

"We make it whenever it's finished."

"How long since those machines were switched on?"

"Just a minute ago."

He looks into the waitress's eyes to gauge her sincerity and the only thing he can detect with any certainty is the weariness accumulated from days spent on her feet, tracing over and over again the Sisyphean route between the kitchen, the bar, and the tables.

"If you don't like it, you can send it back," she says.

"You got it."

As he watches her walk off to fetch his coffee he recalls, or is again reminded, that there is nothing more futile than attempting to seduce a waitress. Even if one succeeds, they can't leave their jobs, and when they finish work they're always too tired to do anything. But the shitty journalist has a tendency to be fascinated by projects doomed to failure. This is why he loves Onetti. There is a reason he has ended up looking like a character from one of the Uruguayan writer's novels.

What was the first book of the man's that he read? *Bodysnatcher.* It was when he was a teenager, that sixties edition published by Seix Barral that he found in a secondhand bookshop, with the tiny type. They don't make books like that anymore, thank goodness.

The waitress places the cup of coffee on the table and scurries off, not giving the shitty journalist time to do or say anything. He blows on the liquid, which is giving off a steam that is far too white (a terrible sign). He takes a sip. It's burned. At least he'll have a pretext to talk to the waitress again. He looks up to see where she is at the same moment a whistling sound opens a hole in the window. The bullet from the Beretta 92 enters through the shitty journalist's left temple.

In the inspector's office, today's newspaper is still lying on the desk. Even though it's five in the afternoon, it's as if yesterday's news has aged twenty years.

"The perpetrator has no wife, no kids, no family, nothing. We can say anything we like. We could say it was a crime of passion," says the sub-inspector.

"The dead man has a wife and kids," replies the inspector.

"And that means he can't have been a fag?"

"Are you trying to say he killed his boyfriend and then went out looking for hookers at a lap-dance club?"

"He didn't go out looking for hookers. We'll just put the girl's body somewhere else. The closer to the journalist, the better."

The inspector leans back; his chair creaks. He looks up at the ceiling and squeezes a little anti-stress ball. He imagines that, at that very moment, somewhere in the world, a writer is looking at the ceiling, trying to think of a plot for a detective novel. The sub-inspector's chair also creaks, but because of the impatience consuming the body of the man occupying it.

"Why didn't the chief just get rid of the body? That would have been the simplest option."

"He wants the family to bury her."

Three knocks are heard on the door to the office. The inspector shouts, "Come in!" An officer enters, apologizes for interrupting, and hands the sub-inspector a piece of paper, then asks for permission to leave. The sub-inspector reads the report carefully.

"The Beretta's clean."

"Are you sure?"

"As if it never existed. As if it were fresh from the factory."

"If we have the clean weapon and the signed confession, then it's all sorted. The suspect kills his neighbor in the night—if you want to call it an argument between fags, I don't care. The next day he goes mad or paranoid or whatever, kills the girl and the journalist. And we let slip that we suspect the guy of being involved with that double murder at the night-club, that we're investigating the connection. Something really vague, just to gain time."

"It sounds terrible put like that. We've got to get a good story together, piece together the suspect's movements, clarify the motive, get hold of the psychiatric report if necessary. No one's going to believe us, otherwise. We'll end up looking ridiculous."

"Where do you think you live? Did you read the suspect's original statement? He killed his neighbor with a Mendoza from the fifties, for Christ's sake! This is a country that believed that a mythical eagle warrior killed a candidate for the presidency. We had an attorney general who hired a clairvoyant to find a corpse, remember? They ended up digging up the bones they'd planted themselves! What more do you want? This country's never liked well-told stories. Isn't this enough?"

"The country's changed."

"Sure it has. It's changed so much that everything's the same."

The laptop on the desk emits a high-pitched bleep. A similar alert sounds a moment later on the inspector's cell phone.

"Hold on."

The inspector double clicks on the mouse pad, and an internal memo flashes up on the screen. He takes a long gulp of cold, burned coffee as he reads it.

"Bingo."

"What is it?"

"They've just announced the disappearance of twelve people from an after-hours club in the center."

"Fuck off."

"Get the suspect right away, prepare the press release, quick as you can. In two hours no one will remember this. And hurry. I'm going to see the chief tonight at the party."

"What party?"

"The one for América."

"But the chief doesn't—"

"The candidate supports them. That's what matters."

What are the chances of a journalist being murdered in Mexico?

The party for the championship is being held in a five-star hotel. All the players are there with their families, along with the club's trustees, a select group of sports journalists and society columnists, actors, actresses, singers, TV presenters, and all sorts of other people from the wonderful world of showbiz, all of whom are also employees of the club's owner. And politicians, of course, of diverse affiliations, not just fans of América: politicians who support the Chivas, the Pumas, Atlante and Necaxa, even Cruz Azul. No one wants to miss the party.

The chief of police and the inspector surf the wave of the crowd, slowly approaching the candidate. People whirl around him, shaking his hand, embracing him, patting him on the back, praising and congratulating him on his magnificent campaign. The chief gives a final push and plants himself in front of the man. He embraces him theatrically, so that everyone there can see the great friendship between them.

"Good news, sir," says the chief of police, with a smile of genuine relief, genuine happiness.

"Not now, not now," the candidate says. "I've got to get a photo with the goalkeeper."

WHITE FLAMINGO

by ANDRÉS FELIPE SOLANO
Translated by Nick Caistor

The watch was a little star that seemed to light up the hotel lobby just to attract Mariela. The man was wearing it on his left wrist. It was as chunky as the tins of menthol balm they used to sell in the shops of the vile neighborhood where she'd been born.

For a dozen nights after she'd gotten out of the clinic, she had thought about going back to that hole. She'd pictured herself smiling, showing off her new body, which had been worked on to perfection in the gym of her apartment at the Commodore. She was living there at the time with Caliche. In her fantasy they stood in line in a pharmacy in the old neighborhood, where they'd gone to buy aspirin, and Caliche ran a hand through her locks. Yes, "locks," not "hair." Hair was what the beggars had, the ones who collected cardboard boxes from the sweatshops around the corner from her house. Their hair was a dry, genital mop, as if a dead animal had been placed on their head. What Mariela had were locks. At different times she had dyed them red, or jet-black with highlights, and even sprayed them purple. The first time she'd dyed them, in a tiny hairdresser's in Hialeah, she had made them blonde, of course. Blonde hair had been a childhood dream, ever since she'd gazed at Ursula Andress on posters outside the movie houses in the center. At twelve she'd tried to bleach her locks in the yard, but her mother arrived just when she had the bottle of peroxide in her hand. She'd snatched it away and given Mariela a slap that left her top lip swollen. Perhaps that was why she kept them blonde for so long, when she finally had the chance.

Mariela had established a network of contacts in the city's grandest hotels. A few banknotes here, others there, to a receptionist at the Conrad, the Loews, or the Victor, were enough to get the details she wanted—makes, colors, distinctive marks. If she doubled the tip, she could discover the exact reference number of any timepiece in the hotel. Caliche, her first husband, had taught her that certain watches—Rolex Daytonas, say, or Breitling Navitimers—suggested an addiction as powerful as sleeping pills. According to him, nobody could show their Ferrari at a restaurant table, or the paintings hanging in their Key Biscayne mansion; a special-edition Cartier Santos, on the other hand, could be discreetly displayed while its owner was studying a document or signing a check in a work meeting. For powerful, truly rich men, comparing watches was like adolescents comparing pricks in a toilet.

Mariela had fallen into the watch business after trying all the typical jobs for immigrants. She had washed yards, handed out leaflets, changed diapers on toothless old men. She had been in this line of work for more than a decade now, and sensed that a golden age was about to dawn. Her hotel contacts knew her well; each month she brought them *Men's Watch Collector* magazine so that they could recognize the key makes. When they tipped her off to the arrival of a multinational executive, or the son of a brewery owner, or the manager of an airline, she would be there within the hour. Then, armed with the information she needed, Mariela would go up to the man in question and, with great discretion and charm, offer her services as a dealer. In order not to scare them, she made contact in public places, as she now intended to do with this man in the lobby of the Ritz Carlton in Coconut Grove. If he was friendly and wanted to chat, Mariela would offer him a small hook as she pointed to the watch she was interested in. "What a coincidence," she would say. "My husband has the very same one."

She knew how to lie. Otherwise she would not have been able to make her way in Miami, leaping like a frog in a puddle from the poverty of Hialeah to the mediocrity of Kendall and then to the dazzling triumph of Miami Beach. Of her two husbands, only Leandro, the second one, an Argentine she had met at an auction, was still alive; whereas her interest in watches had come from Caliche, it was Leandro who had refined her taste. Thanks to him she knew about wines, daggers, and even postage stamps. Leandro had taught her to repeat the names Pollock, Warhol, Basquiat at cocktail parties. He'd tried for years to get her to share his passion for cigars, without success. He used to say she was the perfect woman for a Rosa Cuba Media Noche. Over time, the smell on his breath became unbearable. That was why she'd separated from him, and since then she had not been out seriously with anyone.

She didn't miss Leandro, though. Not the way she missed Caliche. He had been so good to her: he was the one who had offered to pay for all the surgery. Caliche had been living in Miami since the end of the seventies. He was a pilot. They'd met at the 1235 Club, where Mariela had been working behind the bar. A week after she told him her secret they began sharing a bed. It was as if, when he met her, a powerful mechanism had started up inside this man with rough hands, a mechanism that only stopped when he died.

Waiting in the lobby for her possible client to finish his phone call, Mariela remembered Caliche's death in the chicken restaurant. That was the only thing he had not been able to forget from the time he had been poor in Colombia: roast chicken with salty potatoes and homemade chili sauce. Because of that stupid weakness he'd been killed. As soon as the burial was over, Mariela decided to go into hiding. That hail of bullets was the alarm bell. She had not risked everything and started a new life just to be found one night in some alleyway with her guts spilling out. She took two of Caliche's Omega watches with her.

One of her tricks consisted of giving a client her business card and then lazily stretching out her arm, so that he saw her gold Rolex Submariner. A man's watch on a woman's wrist aroused a lot of them, especially if it was eighteen carats set against copper-colored skin like Mariela's. She never slept with her buyers, though—it was a rule. She had learned a long time ago that she had to have at least one rule, if she wasn't going to lose her sense of direction. She had broken it only once, with Leandro, after she was sure that neither of them was going to be taken by surprise. She hated surprises. She had armor-plated herself on all sides to keep them out of her life. That was why, when she saw the man across the lobby hang up, she felt sick when she recognized the bracelet, with its two initials, on his wrist.

Without waiting for him to turn around, Mariela walked over to the hotel bar and asked for a crème de menthe. After half an hour on her own and a second drink, she went over to reception. She handed Xiomara a couple of banknotes. She always carried a thick bundle of new currency that a friend at the bank reserved for her. It was important for her to give her contacts freshly minted notes, as crisp as crackers, so that they wouldn't think they were doing anything underhanded. All those years on the streets had taught her that old, greasy banknotes created a sense of guilt that took a long time to fade.

The man was going to be in the hotel for four nights, the receptionist told her. His name was Alfonso Duque.

Duque sat staring at his feet for a long while. The damp patch on the instep of his right foot was bigger than the one on his left. Fair enough, it had been a long day: pine trees, airport, taxi, airport, palm trees, but even so Duque couldn't understand why one of his feet sweated more than the other. He hated tea, hot mornings, weeping old folk, and many other things, but above all he hated having to come back to this city and see his feet sweat.

144

After what had happened, he had avoided Miami time and again, despite the huge amount of work that had appeared there since the eighties. Instead he had done jobs in Colón, in Lima, on a couple of Caribbean islands; he had even agreed to go to Budapest to take care of a loose cannon, someone who had wanted to strike out on his own. But now Ramiro had insisted he go back to Miami. Duque thought that in his old age Ramiro must be giving in to his whims, to bad smells, to the start of madness.

The boss had been put in jail at age fifty. He had gone in with one of those huge, square bodies that made even the most everyday things difficult, from sharing an elevator to sitting on a toilet. Now, ten years later, Ramiro looked as if he were made of green pap. He had spent his last month inside prison filling three pages with unfinished business. He'd shown the list to Duque the first night they'd met up at the mountain retreat, one of the few properties that hadn't been taken from him. "To start afresh we have to clear the path," he'd said, holding a cigarette and a glass of cold milk in his hand. The first name on the list was Jairo's.

Duque could understand the old man's hygienic impulse, but he didn't comprehend why they had to go after Jairo after all these years. When he'd come back alone from Miami, he had often had the same conversation with his boss. "He vanished. I didn't find him in his room, and he never reached the airport. That's all I can tell you." Ramiro had believed every word, but he'd also made it clear that it had been Duque's responsibility to keep track of his partner, and that therefore it would be up to him to close the circle someday. Ramiro liked circles. He liked the full moon, liked the shapes traced by the blades of a fan. Duque liked parallel lines, married couples who slept in separate beds, freeways.

He searched for a pair of clean socks in his case, put them on, and lay down again on the bed cluttered with pillows. The room cost three hundred dollars a night. Duque had administered Ramiro's money carefully, so that there was enough left for them both to enjoy a comfortable retirement. He couldn't get it into his head why on earth the old man was so determined to explore a new line of business at this stage in their lives, to say nothing of the crazy scheme he was proposing. Duque would have understood if they were talking about gold, or silver, or emeralds, but no—old man Ramiro had gotten hold of several hectares of jungle land that contained these metallic-gray rocks. Coltan. He'd put a sample in Duque's hand when they were in the Jacuzzi and explained that the mine was close to the border with Venezuela. They would have to go there, excavate, and then transport the stuff by boat down the Orinoco, then by truck to Bogotá, and from there get it to a port.

Ramiro was methodical when it came to business: he already had a contact in Germany and another in China. Duque would be in charge of the open-cast mining operation. He wanted to hate Ramiro for this, to hate him as much as he hated plastic tablecloths and baby prams (though not necessarily babies), but the fact was that it was Ramiro who had kept him alive. He had gifted Duque with a life. So his loyalty to the man with those extraordinarily long, now gray hairs sprouting from his nipples would send him to the jungle, and that same loyalty had brought him back to Miami. Because of Ramiro, Duque was lying on a double bed in the Ritz Carlton, his stomach upset after eating pork chops with potato purée when he wasn't really hungry.

He closed his eyes and tried to recall the hotel he and Jairo had booked on that distant night. He was sure it had been in the city center—what was its name? Yes, the White Flamingo. Duque had an excellent memory, he made decisions rapidly and could foresee the consequences of his actions, like a fencer or a professional climber. In his line of work, it wasn't just the hands and eyes you had to look after; you had to protect your head. Other, much younger people had gone to rack and ruin from too much whoring, cocaine, and rum. Perhaps that was why he was still so annoyed at the mistake he'd made back then. How often had he been told he should always take a double room, rather than two separate ones? But Jairo had insisted, he'd said they had more than enough money and he didn't want to spend a sleepless night listening to Duque's snoring. People often think that only fat men snore, but that isn't true at all—Duque had snored all his life, though he was as thin as a stick of incense. He was sure it had to do with his prominent Adam's apple. He had never gotten used to it; every time he saw it out of the corner of his eye it looked as though it was a second nose stuck to his throat. Duque hated his Adam's apple as well, just like he hated the sound of buses in the early morning, oval faces, tinned meat.

Finally he couldn't stand the sight of the sweaty socks anymore. He got up and threw them in the metal trash can. He remained standing for a moment, feeling the letterhead on one of the sheets of paper on top of the heavy desk. He ran his finger over the golden lion's head, trying to touch its tiny tongue. His resentment, Miami, the metal pin in his knee that hurt every now and then, all disappeared for a moment with the realization that he was in a hotel that still cared about such details. He had noticed the shoehorn earlier, in the bathroom, while urinating a bright yellow stream— almost orange, thanks to the vitamins he had started taking. In some hotels, even among the best, shoehorns and headed paper were things of the past. Now they offered unlimited access to the Internet instead.

He congratulated himself on having resolved the question of the instrument so promptly. He had gotten it this afternoon, within an hour of his arrival, and now it lay ready in his man-bag—which he had bought some-time in the mid-eighties—well wrapped in a handkerchief so that the edges wouldn't mark the leather. Tomorrow he would have to start asking around about Jairo. Ramiro still had eyes and ears everywhere. Before Duque caught the plane the old man had given him several contacts, retired people who had been given short sentences in return for their possessions, and who had stayed on to live in Florida as honest citizens who had made a mistake in their youth. The business had been taken over by a number of small clans, and nobody knew anymore who was at the head. It was like a nest of cock-roaches: as soon as anyone switched the light on, they went scuttling off in all directions. Perhaps old man Ramiro was right, and the best thing was to take a risk on something completely new, on those rocks, on coltan. "We have to put our money on technology, my boy," he had told Duque when they climbed out of the Jacuzzi, past the sleeping terrier, Oscar, the old man's lifelong companion, who was now crippled by arthritis.

Duque switched on the TV. He had learned a smattering of English years ago, when he'd had to hide in a cousin's house in Jersey City. He liked the voices in gringo advertisements. One of those smiling, luminous voices was going to receive him at the gates of hell, he was sure. After an ad for yachts, the big metal sphere he had seen with Jairo that December in 1982 appeared on the screen. He recognized it at once. They had driven from Miami to Orlando in a rented car to celebrate a job well done. Other people celebrated in whorehouses; they preferred to celebrate like this, in an amusement park, as happy as a loving couple. The park had been commemorating thirty years in existence. Duque tried to pronounce the name of it in his head, but got it jumbled up. He felt like going to Orlando again. He did some calculations. He could give himself a day before he began searching for Jairo. Satisfied with this conclusion, and with his stomach finally settled, Duque gradually fell asleep without undressing or switching off the light. This time his own snoring didn't wake him up as it usually did, when he was very tired.

He paid the entrance fee to the park. With his ticket he was given a leaflet in several languages. It took him a few moments to walk through a garden, and then he found himself confronted by the giant sphere. Next to him, a young couple was taking photos of it as if it were a cathedral or a pyramid. He decided to find a bench where he could sit and contemplate it in peace.

He had to go to the side of a lake. He remembered the lake. You could get on a boat and go around the world in half an hour. There were buildings representing Mexico, France, Japan, China, Italy, Canada. He asked himself if Canada was that important, if there existed such a thing as a Canadian civilization. At last an old woman and her husband freed up a space on their bench for him. The man smiled; one of his eyes was covered with white gauze. He was behaving like a little boy alongside his wife. As he sat down, Duque realized that his feet had begun to sweat again. In his car he had a spare pair of socks that he had bought in a supermarket when he'd stopped to make a phone call. He didn't have a cell phone and never had. Coltan was used to make cell phones and computers less heavy, Ramiro had explained. Duque didn't understand why people wanted everything to weigh less. He liked his watches and his instruments the way they were. He had five guns at home, of different calibers, although he hadn't used them recently. Now that Ramiro was free, he'd had to get them out of the garage to oil them. "One thing is forced leisure in jail, another is leisure you choose. That kind of leisure is harmful," Ramiro had said, showing him a map with the exact location of the mine. He'd pointed to it with his index finger. His fingers were short, stubby, like a dwarf's. "We have to employ Indians. Some settlers, not many. Indians are better. If they don't want to work, we have to give it to them straight. Leisure kills."

Duque imagined the camps, the brown water, a crowd of bare-chested Indians extracting the rocks. He wasn't sure he could start all over again. He would have to find the strength to hold conversations in cafés in desolate villages in the middle of the jungle, surrounded by sullen, hungry people. He would have to rediscover the confidence to place a weapon on the table without hesitating, alongside a bottle of beer or an empanada. He would have to give orders. He felt tired. His shoulders hurt, as if he were carrying a sack of sand on his back.

He still had the leaflet in his hands. He glanced at it. It told the story of the park, and of the sphere, which represented a spaceship. The tour inside it covered the history of communications. On one page he found the opening words of the tour's original script: *Where have we come from, where are we going? The answers begin in our past.* One of the things Jairo had liked best was the image of a secretary with her hair done up, sitting in front of a screen in an office. Duque could picture Jairo now, smiling, studious, dark-haired, with a woman's skin. He'd never shaved, never had a single bristle on his cheeks. They'd met at school. Their parents had the best houses in the neighborhood. Old but spacious, with lots of rooms and a terrace. They'd liked riding motorbikes and American pop music: Chicago, Foreigner, Toto. Jairo had been a good singer.

Ramiro had found them leaning on their bike, mango with salt and half a bottle of aguardiente in their hands. They were riding around the hills on the outskirts of the city. They'd gone up there to look at the columns of smoke that always rose up into the sky in the evening. That day Ramiro was with a police sergeant by the name of Galindo, who later was drowned in a swimming pool by his enemies. The deal Ramiro offered them was simple. If they accepted, he'd give them a new bike. "That one's very old," he'd told them, not getting out of his car. "You deserve something better. A Kawasaki, or something similar." They thought it over that night on their terrace, and the next day called the number Ramiro had given them. They had no problem with their first job, transporting a heavy bag that felt as if it were full of hammers. That was all. Ramiro suggested another couple of tasks after that, which they completed scrupulously. After a year of working for him, Ramiro invited them to a farm full of banana trees, where Galindo taught them to shoot beside a huge water tank. They learned quickly, Duque especially. Jairo simply followed his lead. They completed their jobs on time and without leaving anything behind, like good plumbers or expert builders. They became known in the city. They were respected. Nobody bothered them for leaving parties early. Then Ramiro suggested they go to Miami.

They were sent there to take out a Colombian-Lebanese who was getting rich from Ramiro's business. They dealt with him in a shopping mall in broad daylight, and their hands didn't tremble. The next day they bought shoes and rented the car. Jairo had a disposable camera. This was precisely what Ramiro liked about the two of them; they forgot the work quickly, and were able to get on with their lives as if nothing had happened.

The leaflet also mentioned the person who had written the first story-line for the sphere. Apparently he was a famous writer, by the name of Ray Bradbury. Duque remembered the scene almost at the end of the tour—a boy sitting alone at a personal computer. He was alone but at the same time accompanied. That was how Duque had felt throughout his life. While he was thinking all this, somebody sat down beside him.

It was an elegant woman, a bit younger than him, and possibly with too much makeup on. She seemed to be asking the sphere for something with the same intensity with which people ask a favor of a bleeding Christ in a church. She couldn't take her eyes off it. She smelled nice, Duque thought. A moment later she stood up, and Duque tried to get a look at her legs, but she was quickly lost amid the crowd. A group of red-faced tourists arrived then, and their presence made him give up on the idea of queuing to go inside the sphere. He no longer wanted to see the future. He had seen it already, anyway. It was death and destruction.

He looked one last time at the structure's strange surface. It appeared to him as if it were made of coltan. Before leaving the park he bought a key ring in the souvenir shop.

Instead of switching on the air-conditioning, he drove back to the city with the window down. He stopped at a gas station to relieve himself and make a call; he produced the same cloudy, orange-colored stream. Crossing a bridge, he thought intently of that woman, her way of sitting with her back ramrod straight, her long neck, and gradually the circle began to close in front of his eyes.

He was back at the hotel before nightfall. He had a shower, changed his clothes. Then he went down to the lobby carrying his man-bag. He didn't care that his trousers were crumpled. For dinner he had tomato soup: he couldn't eat anything more. In reception he asked an employee for the address of the White Flamingo. It took her a while to reply, she didn't seem much good at the computer, but finally she told him it was twenty minutes away by car.

Mariela took a phone call just as she was about to plunge her feet into the warm water. She had put in a pinch of magnesium sulfate, another of bicarbonate of soda, and a squirt of glycerin. It was Xiomara. She said that Señor Alfonso had just asked her for an address in the city center, and then had left the hotel. What an ugly name he had chosen to register with. Alfonso. When the girl told her Duque's destination, Mariela's breath caught. My God, she thought; first the theme park, now this. She had wanted to talk to him on the bench, but hadn't dared. How do you strike up a conversation after thirty years?

She wasn't going to try to postpone what couldn't be postponed. He knew she was watching him, clearly; now she wanted to hear the voice of her adolescence. She would ask him why he still wore that ghastly copper bracelet Ramiro had given him, like a shackle.

She found a parking space with no difficulty. Before getting out of her pickup she checked her makeup. Rouge, lipstick, mascara. Then she walked to the hotel where she had buried her previous life. A man behind a window, pale from watching too much television in the dark, told her the room number. She didn't have to give him a crisp banknote. At the last moment, outside the door, Mariela looked down at her fingernails and shuddered, exactly as she had done when she had left this very same spot years ago, carrying only a small case. She knocked loudly.

She heard footsteps, and the door opened. She hadn't noticed the bags under his eyes when they had been on the bench together. She would have to recommend calendula. Duque turned his back on her and returned to the brown chair he'd been sitting in. His cologne mingled with the smell of cigarettes and stale semen in the room. Everything seemed exactly the same, there in that rundown hotel. Mariela sat down on a corner of the bed, her bag across her knees. She was wearing a pair of sheer black stockings, reinforced at the heel. Her first instinct was to straighten the bedspread, but she restrained herself. From outside came the sound of car horns, the alarm at a jeweler's. The neon sign of the White Flamingo flooded the room intermittently. Duque was the first to speak.

"I thought it was just neighborhood gossip, but it's true."

"As you see."

"What's your name these days?"

"Mariela."

"Such an ugly name."

"How about Alfonso?"

"It was my grandfather's name."

"I didn't know. It's still horrible."

His voice was as impressive as before, melodious but deep, almost as beautiful as the priest's who'd led Mass at their school. Mariela had often confessed to him simply to hear that voice.

"Have you seen Ramiro? I imagine that's why you're here."

"He reckons he wants to do business with minerals now. A rock they call coltan."

"I've never heard of it. It's a precious stone, or what?"

"No. It's to make microchips with. Cell phones, computers, that kind of thing."

"He never stops working."

"I know. That's what I told him. He's still got lots of money."

"What about you? Do you have money? Did you get married?"

Duque didn't reply. He stared down at his shoes. He jiggled them as though there were ants inside. Mariela grew impatient. She wanted to move the conversation on.

"How did you recognize me, at the park? My mouth, my neck? You always wanted to give me a kiss, but you never had the guts. I thought you were going to, that evening before we met Ramiro."

"I'm no queer."

"Nor am I. I'm a woman, Duque. Look at me. Can you see any difference? I always was one, even if I had to wait a few years."

Duque shifted in his chair. He was uncomfortable. He leaned his elbows on his knees, ran a hand through his hair. He looked at Mariela.

"Shit, you had it all planned. That's why you were so pleased when he told us we had a job to do here."

"No. You're wrong. The idea of escaping came to me that night, right here. It happened, that's all. Accept it. I didn't mean to cause you any problems with Ramiro. I'm sorry."

Mariela knew it was too late for apologies. But she didn't want to run away again, and she had missed him all these years. That was why she had followed him. Perhaps Duque would have even believed her, if she told him this.

"In the neighborhood they said you'd had the operations to escape. So that he'd never find you. You could have gone to any other city. This is a big country. You didn't have to do all… this, to yourself."

Duque waved vaguely toward her face, her breasts, and then between her legs.

"Did you have an operation there, too?"

"You haven't understood a thing. I didn't have the operations to run away from Ramiro. Do you remember Roberta Close?"

"Obviously."

"Beautiful, admit it, really beautiful. I think I look a lot like her. Look how long my legs are." Mariela stretched them out to the side, taking the chance to look at the black heels of her shoes. "My voice was always a bit high."

"If you'd been born with an Adam's apple like mine, nothing you did would have been any use."

"I suppose you still hate it. You always hated so many things. I got out so as not to carry on hating." She looked up again. "Except that theme park, I suppose. You still love it there, don't you?"

"And you? Why did you follow me? Weren't you afraid? Why did you come?"

Duque had almost called the woman Jairo, but stopped himself. They were both weary. Their momentary wish to play games had vanished.

"Because I still remember the rule we promised to keep," Mariela said.

"Which one?" Duque asked.

"You know which one. You made it. We never killed a woman. I thought it was stupid, but you always insisted. You said we at least had to have one rule, just one."

Mariela stood up. She had become nervous when she saw Duque's dilated pupils.

"What are you going to do? You could stay here, with me. Ramiro doesn't have as much influence as you think. Except over you. D'you want to break rocks again? You've got nothing there. We could go to Los Angeles. Actors love watches. You could help me find a Patek Philippe. Number 3449. There are only three of them in the world. If we found it, we wouldn't have to work another day ever."

Duque said nothing. The neon sign flashed in through the window and lit his profile. Mariela looked at his man-bag and repeated her question.

"What are you going to do, Duque?"

For a moment, he hesitated. But the metal sphere came to his aid, spoke to him. He saw the future at his feet once more. It was death and destruction. He took out the weapon. The copper bracelet gleamed. He aimed at the center of her chest, between the two prostheses, below the artery throbbing in her neck. He couldn't shoot her in the face, as Ramiro had ordered.

The jungle awaited him. Now more than ever he would need to carry on taking vitamins. He wouldn't wear socks, he thought. He'd go around barefoot.

1986

by **RODRIGO REY ROSA**

Translated by Jeffrey Gray

I

When he woke up, the ants were still marching through the hut, but they weren't climbing over his body the way they'd been before, in the dark, when he'd woken briefly to find himself shaking as if in *delirium tremens*. He was cold and badly needed to urinate. He was lying in a ramshackle room, its roof thatched with fronds torn from guano palms, surrounded by trees whose branches were shaking in the wind. Where had he been earlier that night? The weak light that entered like needles through the cracks in the walls had a faintly pink tone. Was it the moon? He'd fallen asleep a little before dusk, when the gray sky had already lost its last flush. The ants signaled rain, he remembered.

He had the urge to cry out. But he'd done so already, once, on an earlier night—he'd let out a series of howls—in the end uselessly, he remembered with sleepy surprise. He came to the conclusion, once again, that he was a prisoner. But whose?

During the past few days, his food—black beans and country tortillas of a bluish-green hue, or cold corn *atol* with powdered milk and a strange mineral taste (which could account for his gas and the horrible stomachaches, the hedonist prisoner thought) had been served on a pewter plate, introduced into the cabin by means of a little hatch in the wall at ground level. He never knew who brought him his food, which always came very early in the morning and then again at sundown; he was just able to see, through the hatch, a pair of feet, shod in rubber boots, and the hand that pushed the plate toward him. *Fuckers*, he said to himself. The croaking of the frogs outside stopped suddenly. As if they were obeying a command, he thought.

The water hitting the guano leaves reminded him at first of a snare drum with a mute. Then the sound changed to a vast roar, which comforted him in a way—the rain was familiar by now. But his desire to urinate had become overwhelming. The reeking bucket he was supposed to use as a toilet was full. He stood up to aim the stream through a chink in the wall. The droplets that sprinkled his legs and feet felt hot on his cold skin.

He had started to get used to the dim seven-by-ten-foot hut. He had spent a lot of time there. He knew that a ray of sun, filtered through the palings, would reach the food hatch before long. He knew that a flock of parrots would fly over the hut a little later. But how much time would pass between one flight and another? A lizard, sooner or later, would appear among the leaves of the roof. He would hear the sound of a rat scurrying. He'd become used to all this. But even these familiar sensations seemed unreal, and he knew that his inner clock was off: the hours—or days, weeks, months?—had passed by behind the curtains of a hallucinogenic mist. He didn't know what drugs they'd given him (or even who *they* were), but he guessed that the state in which he found himself, between somnolence and thought, was the result of some substance combined with opium.

He could remember walking, with great difficulty, along a narrow path through the trees, while other young men, fitter than himself, climbed past him. Was it a punishment? Some kind of contest? He'd had a big plastic jug of water tied to his shoulders, he remembered; the idea was to see who moved the jug fastest from the pond of cold water at the bottom of the ravine to the bare mound, kilometers higher, where the guards stacked the containers in metal frames that looked like honeycombs, handing back empty jugs to the students.

"Fuckers," he said again. He was going to kill them.

With an almost pleasant weariness he closed his eyes again. He slept deeply until dawn.

He woke to a church bell tolling. It didn't startle him; in fact, the sound had something happy about it. But at that moment he couldn't remember whether the bell had rung yesterday or the day before. He imagined that today could be Sunday. Or was it that he hadn't slept, that night, in the same hut as on the previous nights—but in one almost identical, from which one couldn't hear the bell? The day before felt far away, as if time were a tunnel, a pipe that branched out, got tangled up, petered out, and finally disappeared just when he wanted to examine it. The bell kept on ringing.

On hearing steps draw near, and then knocks on the thorny wood door, he sat up. The walls of the little hut on whose bare earth floor he was stretched out did not seem the same as the ones he remembered.

"He's calmed down now," a voice said.

It was not an assertion; it was an order. This man, whose voice he'd heard before, he remembered—but from where?—communicated exclusively in the imperative, and with a marked English accent. Even his questions were put as commands, the hedonist would think later. He lay down on his back again, saying nothing.

The man, whose silhouette he could almost make out through the crannies, pounded—with a stick?—harder on the door.

"When he calms down, I'll come back," he said.

"I'm calm," said the hedonist.

"Fine." He heard the noise of chains, then the sound of a key turning in the padlock. "I'm coming in."

The light was very soft. The man was tall. He wore a cowboy hat and a light yellow guayabera, and, at his waist, a police baton. And wasn't that a pistol that bulged under his guayabera, to the right?

"Who are you?" the hedonist asked, sitting up on the ground, careful not to touch the wall of the hut with his shoulder.

"I'm part of a medical team. You're not well. We want to cure you."

"I'm not sick. I feel fine."

The visitor kept himself from laughing.

"Get up. The doctor is going to see you."

The hedonist stood up very slowly.

"That's good, Dario."

"Darío," he corrected. "You're not the doctor?"

The visitor made a face to suggest the stupidity of the question.

"Sir," the hedonist went on—and he was surprised to hear himself make the protest—"the ants have been coming into the hut, and at night they crawl across me."

The other man snorted.

"They like your blood!" he said with maniacal force. "It's the garbage you have in your system. When that's been purged, they won't bother you anymore."

"They're carrier ants," the hedonist answered calmly, his tone rational. "I've lived in the country and I know about them. I was in their way, so they climbed over me. They don't bite or sting, but they're *uncomfortable*."

The visitor (or better, the hedonist thought, the Cowboy) shook his head.

"Come on," he ordered. "Today you can have breakfast with the others, if you like." He looked outside over his shoulder. "Diogenes is going to bring your shoes and your clothes. Then we're going to hear some music in the meeting room. Diogenes will take you there."

He turned on one heel and left another man, Diogenes, in his place, silhouetted against the door frame.

Diogenes was a small man with dark skin and gray eyes. His angular face seemed to have been carved with a knife. He smiled incomprehensibly. On one arm he carried a bundle of clothes, neatly folded, and a pair of rubber boots. In the other hand he clutched a long machete, unsheathed, which the hedonist supposed he was never without.

While he dressed he asked Diogenes, who remained standing, with his back to the hut's interior:

"What is this place? A prison? What have I done that they've got me in here?"

Diogenes turned to look at him.

"A sanatorium. And I don't know," he answered. "I'm just trying to make a living."

"Fuck," said the hedonist. He put his boots on. They were surprisingly comfortable.

"If you're ready now, we'll go," said Diogenes respectfully. At least this one knows his place, thought the hedonist, his vanity satisfied.

As they walked from his new hut—Diogenes confirmed that he had been moved to what the man called "Sector A"—toward the meeting hall, he thought that there was no way this could be a sanatorium. Diogenes was a simple peasant; he had nothing of the nurse about him. And the Cowboy was no doctor. They followed a path among enormous trees, where the light was faint. At a fork, they passed a soldier (a Kaibil, a commando?) in camouflage, and suddenly the hedonist had a bad feeling: he was in a detention camp. The path led to a clearing, where in addition to the meeting room there was a dining room in the form of a little open-walled *rancho*, from whose grimy palm roof the smoke of an earthen stove rose up lazily. And another hut, a bit bigger than his own, which must have been the storehouse.

Alongside a muddy road stood the bell, hanging from a length of timber between two wooden props, within arm's reach, unprotected. It wasn't ringing anymore, and now one could hear only the birds' cries, while the mist dissolved above the grass of the clearing in the first rays of the sun. The air was cold and humid and smelled of damp earth and rotten leaves.

In front of the meeting room, which was itself a circular *rancho*, blind and dark as an African hut, several guards had gathered, dressed like

Diogenes. Other, younger men and women—their clothes not as clean, the hedonist noticed—were entering the semidarkness. Inside stood a little set of bleachers, crescent shaped, each section built from three planks of rough wood. Hanging from the palm roof by cords of maguey were two large speakers; all of a sudden, a big organ began to play. Bach? the hedonist wondered. Or Palestrina? Diogenes led him inside, and as his eyes got used to the darkness, he could make out the source of the music—a cassette player on a rattan table by the door.

The effect of it—music that ordinarily he liked—was strange: startling, even oppressive, high up there among the clouds and the tall trees. The other young people, sitting now on the bleachers, about twenty of them, their heads shaved close (those of the women too, about six of them altogether), watched him with curiosity. From time to time one could hear them slapping their arms and swatting themselves on the neck to crush the mosquitoes that were thick around them. The hedonist sat on the edge of one of the benches.

A man dressed completely in white, with a star-shaped medallion around his neck, came through the door with an air of solemnity. His eyes were intensely blue, and his expression, undermined perhaps by his faint smile, appeared benevolent; this was a man capable of the greatest forbearance, his face suggested. There was something womanish about him, the hedonist thought. And he was limping very subtly. He carried a cane that converted into a tripod seat. The young people bowed to him slightly. Surreptitiously, one of them made the gesture of vigorously jacking off, syncing the motion with the music.

The music stopped. The man in white sat down at the table and closed his eyes, self-satisfied—as if the music had been his own, the hedonist thought. The Cowboy came in, then, and stood in the center of the room, facing the bleachers. He addressed himself first to the room in general, with a serene, well-modulated voice and a paternal attitude. Then he looked directly at the hedonist.

"Welcome, Darío Alaluf, of San Pedro Sula, Honduras." A pause. Some giggles among the youngsters, some coughs. "Here we are all sick in spirit, or in mind, but we are going to heal ourselves. *His* sickness, his hedonism"— he looked at Darío again for a moment—"comes from profound ignorance. You are all here to learn." He paused again, for quite a long moment, as if to invite objections. "Allow me to explain. There are rules that should be very clear; violation of them means punishment. The punishments you have received and that you will receive in the future are part of a plan. They were ordered out of a disinterested love, a universal and superior love, which you must never forget. Let us now review some of these rules."

As the Cowboy spoke, the man in white listened, his face turned upward, his eyes still closed.

"In the first place," the Cowboy explained, "under the roof of the meeting room, students are forbidden to speak unless invited to. If you break this rule, you will be forbidden to speak *anywhere* for an entire day. The punishment for not complying with the punishment is the doubling of the punishment. Furthermore, you are forbidden to speak about anyone's past, or to sing, or to refer to the person of the doctor director"—the man in white—"under any circumstances."

Once the Cowboy had finished his speech, the man in white rose from his chair and walked to the center of the circular room. The Cowboy sat down on the bleachers with the students, who kept an almost perfect silence—no laughs, no coughs. The wood of the bleachers creaked once under the weight of the Cowboy.

"Any questions?" asked the man in white, but no one dared say anything. He spoke then about the ants, about superior intelligence, and the collective soul. He looked at no one as he talked, his gaze lost at some point above and beyond the congregation. He had no opinions, he said toward the end; then he asked for questions again, and a young woman (American) asked him what he thought about injustice.

"What is it to be a woman, after all?" he said, and closed and opened his eyes. "To me it is the same as to be man. We need not think of these things; they are not part of our higher nature."

The music began to play again. The students, like automata, marched toward the door, passing by the man in white, who had placed himself next to it. He gave each student a pat on the back as a kind of benediction as they passed by. One of the girls—a chubby blonde, with the face of someone without many friends—refused the pat and began to scream and to rain blows on the man in white. Two of the guards threw her down on her back and sat on her on the mud floor.

"Mysolene!" shouted one student, not too loud, once out in the fresh air.

"Dilantin!" another replied.

"Silence!" came the Cowboy's voice.

Neither the young woman nor the man who had made the jacking-off motion was seen again for many days.

He would never know how long it took him to accustom himself to the routine of the supposed sanatorium. Time, apart from the present moment, continued to be a mystery. But before long he discovered that almost all the rules could be broken, as long as neither the man in white nor the Cowboy nor their collaborators were nearby. Among the students, communication usually took the form of written messages—in the mud, on the trunk of a tree, on a palm leaf. And with some of the guards it was possible to talk during the long walks they led the students on.

The man in white didn't come to the camp often. Sometimes he arrived by mule, sometimes by military helicopter, landing in the clearing between the meeting room and the forbidden zone, as they called the housing area beyond the fence line. On each visit he would inspect the premises and then give a sermon—on karma, say, or on the fact that for the enlightened man the sky was not blue, or on some theme so abstruse that no one understood him at all. The hedonist had noticed that he was never without his cane, and that he always carried a pistol, though it was usually concealed. His deputy, the Cowboy, lived in a big house in the forbidden zone and was not as strict as the man in white, though he too carried a gun.

There were two distinct groups of students: North Americans, and Central Americans from Guatemala and El Salvador. Apart from meals and the musical sessions, which took place every morning before breakfast, they mixed on very rare occasions—usually only to have hand-to-hand fights or battles with sticks, which the guards had to stop. The North Americans, about a dozen in all, weren't as young as the others. The hedonist had heard that three of them had fought in Vietnam; one of them was clearly insane. Sometimes you'd see him wandering around, sniffing the contents of a plastic bag, his guard keeping a certain distance: it was his own shit in the bag, the guard said. The hedonist was the only Honduran. The music in the mornings was almost always Teutonic, and almost always played on an organ.

The hedonist had heard that beyond Sector A, and Sector B—in which he had passed an indeterminate amount of time—a Sector C existed, where there was just one single hut for one student, or prisoner. But nobody seemed to know anything about this man. Maybe there was no one there anymore, he thought to himself at times. Maybe that lone student had died. Or been released. Or escaped.

II

It was one of those rare moments in which he was able to talk to someone. Early that morning, the sound of the helicopter had announced the departure of the man in white, and when they came out of the circular hut after the music session, the Cowboy was nowhere in sight. One of the women smiled at the hedonist, who had lagged behind as they moved toward the dining room. Her name was Juliana. She was tall, stocky, and attractive, he thought. She said to him in a low voice, "You like the music, don't you?"

It was true. The doctor's deputy didn't have bad taste in classical music. That morning he'd played Mozart's Requiem in D minor.

"I do," the hedonist said. "How about you?"

She shook her head.

"I like rock."

"But…" he started to say. "I mean, me too. It wouldn't be bad to have some rock as well, for variety's sake. And you—why are you here?"

"My father stuck me here, because of drugs."

Juliana's dad was a military man. He couldn't afford to have a strung-out daughter in public view—this was the explanation. She had to get herself together, one way or the other. They'd told her they would send her to a rehab center in Belize, by the sea. It would be a vacation. On the eve of her internment, her mom had gone with her to shop for beach clothes. But it had been a ruse. The next morning, two undercover cops came for her, forcing her into a car with smoked windows. On the way toward the Atlantic, they drugged her. She barely remembered the climb, on the back of a mule, to the top of Mount San Gil, where—she told the hedonist—they were now.

"In Izabal—you know?"

It was the first time he could remember hearing this.

Suddenly, in the midst of speaking softly with Juliana, he had a sharp memory of a family portrait: his adoptive father and his sister (his mother had died a few years back), arms around each other, looking into the camera, in the garden of his mother's house.

"Who's the man in white?" he asked Juliana.

"The big boss. He's an English gringo. A *huge* asshole. He thinks he's God Almighty."

They had come to the dining room. A goose let out a trumpet blast from somewhere beyond the kitchen. They entered in silence and sat down at the big table with the others, facing their mugs of powdered milk and cold *atol*. It was difficult to swallow the powder, but everybody did.

A few days later, as the Cowboy and his wife were cutting the hair of two or three students who sat in cane chairs in the clearing next to the bell, the hedonist and Juliana strolled toward the heliport. The Kaibiles who usually guarded the area were absent that afternoon. The noise of the cicadas was deafening. She began:

"We're gonna get out of here, me and Martín." Martín was a very young student who'd just finished a stint in Sector B.

"You're going to escape?"

"Uh-huh. Tomorrow."

"Diogenes says…"

"You believe that son of a bitch?"

He had tried to rape her, she had told him.

They stopped walking. There was nobody in sight. A firefly passed by, dragging its useless little bundle of light. They watched it for a moment, till it was lost among the trees and became a tiny glow in the shadows.

"Can I come with you? What's the plan?"

Juliana assumed a pained expression. He couldn't come with them; she and Martín had made a deal.

"You can make a break for it a little later. I'll tell you the way to do it."

"All right," he said.

It was best to try it on a weekend, she said, when the guards were less vigilant and when the students themselves weren't worn out from hauling water. And it had to be in the daytime, when the light would help him get some distance from the camp. Anyway, as he knew, at night their shoes were taken away, and you'd be crazy to try to run without shoes. Martín, who had tried to escape five times over the three years he'd been there, had covered a lot of ground on two attempts, but on both occasions he'd been captured by the police or the military after he hit the highway. So this time they were going to try to head in the opposite direction, uphill at first, following one of the streams that descended from the summit.

On the other side of the mountain, Juliana said, was the wide Rio Dulce, between Lake Izabal and Amatique Bay. They hoped that the Indians there, traditionally enemies of the ranchers, the gringos, and the military, would help them get away. Martín already knew how to recognize all kinds of edible plants and vines with water, so that would be no problem, she said. They could eat fish, too, and *jutes*, the little black snails that the streams were full of.

The hedonist knew about edible plants and berries; in Honduras, his father had had a farm in the lowlands. He'd spent a good part of his child-hood there.

"We'll take four machetes between the two of us," Juliana went on. Martín, in his last attempt, had taken only one. It broke as he was cutting a palmito.

"He was fucked after that, brother," Juliana said.

Everything was going to depend on how they were treated in the first village they planned to contact. It was called Río Bonito, and the people there were all Kekchí.

III

Diogenes had taken on the role of teacher. During their walks toward the Cold Pond, or when he accompanied the hedonist back to Sector A, where he took off the hedonist's boots and locked him into his *separo*—as the staff members called those huts wrapped with barbed wire—the man gave his little lessons. In addition to the palm hearts and the peach-flavored wild berries of the ujuxte, a large tree the hedonist hadn't known in Honduras, Diogenes taught him to recognize, by the shape of the leaf, a particular plant whose fruits were poisonous.

"Your stomach will swell up if you eat from these pods," the man said. "It'll take you days to die, with horrible pain the whole time. Nobody survives this."

He had been counting the days that passed—marking them on cane stalks—since Juliana had made her escape one Sunday at noon. He had made twenty-one marks now, and still no one seemed to know anything about where they had gone. That Sunday Juliana had avoided talking to him. Martín had also stayed apart from the group. At breakfast, the hedonist had watched them surreptitiously; he had seen Martín hide some tortillas under his shirt, and listened as Juliana drew near the stove, where the cooks were gathered, to speak to Doña Aura, who guffawed loudly as they talked. Doña Aura was Diogenes's wife, a good-looking mestiza, one-eyed and cheerful.

Juliana asked her something about the moon and the rain. It was going to rain that night, Doña Aura told her; she'd seen the ants and the crescent moon. The tips were pointing downward, she said, and laughed.

The rain was a good thing, the hedonist had thought. It would wash away their footprints.

Near the storeroom, which the North Americans called the "inventory," he'd seen on several occasions a little girl about twelve years old, who, it was said, was the daughter of the enigmatic man in white. She was pale, with thick tresses of hair that fell almost to her waist. One day, after the hauling of the water, the hedonist saw her at the door of the building. At her belt she wore a short machete. He stayed behind the column of students and approached her. She looked at him without expression.

"Hello," he said. "How are you? My name is Darío."

Finally the girl smiled.

"My name's Laurel," she said.

"How old are you, Laurel?" he asked.

"Eleven."

"And you're already using a machete?"

The girl nodded her head.

"It's necessary," she said. "For the snakes. And the rats."

"Rats?"

"Sometimes they come here by the hundreds. The other day, here," she said, and looked inside the warehouse, "I killed more than twenty."

"Really? With that little machete? Horrible!" He made a face of disgust.

The little girl giggled.

"Yes, horrible," she said, wrinkling her little freckled nose.

"You speak Spanish really well," he told her. "Where did you learn it?"

"From the guards."

The Cowboy let out a shout from the dining room.

"We'll talk again, all right, Laurel?" he said to the girl.

"I'm not supposed to, but okay," she said, and her little nose wrinkled again. It was a kind of smile, the hedonist decided.

"Laurel! Watch out!" the Cowboy shouted behind her.

Laurel went into the storeroom without saying anything more.

There came a day when, thanks to the daily chore of the water jugs, he began to feel in pretty fair shape.

In setting out, he would have to avoid the well-traveled roads, where the Kaibiles patrolled. There were two of these roads, he now knew; one ran down the southern slope of the mountain till it came to a village called Los Ángeles, and the other, toward the east, cut through a cattle ranch owned by an army officer. Juliana had explained this to him. It would be better to follow her route upward, which wouldn't be easy; cutting down a palm or a liana could give him away, Juliana had told him. She had suggested following the stream, where his footprints would be erased quickly.

He saw Laurel again, in front of the temple, one morning after the music.

"Hi, Laurel," he said. "I like your machete."

The girl touched the handle of her machete, which was sheathed in leather engraved with designs: a pyramid, a quetzal. He noticed she was missing half of her left index finger.

"I can't give it to you."

"Of course not."

The little girl looked at him.

"Are you going to escape?"

"Shhh," he said, taken aback. He looked around him.

"Me too, someday," she said. "I'm going to escape."

He looked at her. "Can you help me get two machetes?" he said.

"I don't know." She looked down, tracing a half circle with the tip of her boot. "I guess I can try."

"Really?"

The girl nodded her head.

"You're a little angel," the hedonist said.

The girl wrinkled her nose and lowered her eyes to the ground again.

"What happened to you?" he asked. He pointed to her finger.

"A horse. It's karma. For making a bad sign, Father says."

"No way," he said. "The horse bit you?"

The girl nodded her head up and down rapidly.

It was on a Friday at noon that he talked to her again. He was following the group, crossing the clearing on the way to the dining room, when he saw her half hidden behind the bell. Diogenes had gone ahead to talk to Doña Aura, who, as always, let out peals of laughter at the slightest provocation.

"I got them," said the girl. "They're by the last curve of the Río Frío road. Behind a round boulder. Under some leaves."

He thanked her. You're truly an angel, he told her.

"Good luck," she said, with an intensity that surprised him.

IV

Like his predecessors, he left the hospital at noon, while the guards were having lunch. Doña Aura's laughter, those happy and wild gales that reminded him of the cries of a mad bird, was the last human sound he heard before entering the woods.

As he put the camp behind him, he imagined the reaction of the guards and the other members of the staff. Would they come after him? How many? Which direction would they take?

He headed quickly toward the Cold Pond, where the previous afternoon the guards had dunked the crazy North American—the one with the shit bag—until he shit himself and fainted. According to Diogenes, it was a kind of exorcism, or maybe some kind of punishment. He slipped on the wet ground, running when the terrain allowed it, fell among the shrubs, and found himself in the mud more than once. The machetes were there where he'd hoped they would be, hidden under some leaves, and with them he kept on going, with caution. Beyond the pond, during the first hours, his course was uphill. He was getting winded fast; he started to wonder whether he was really in the kind of shape he had to be to undertake this venture. And what would be his punishment if they caught up with him? He had the machetes, at least. For a while he walked by the riverbed, where he gathered some snails, but he had no luck catching fish. Then he moved away from the water to look for berries, palm hearts, ujuxte fruit.

The first night he slept up in a tree with a massive trunk. A woodpecker just above his head woke him up. It would peck at the trunk, then turn around quickly to see if some insect hidden under the bark had come out on hearing it; then it would seize the bug in its beak and swallow it. The next night he spent at the foot of a huge boulder still warm from the heat of the day. He woke up surrounded by mist, which the sun quickly dispelled. By mid-morning he'd reached the summit; he could see the coast in the distance, and, parly covered with a vast mantle of fog, the widening river.

V

The descent was harder than the ascent. After he passed the crest of the mountain, he came to the edge of a precipice that he had to find a way around. He'd left the stream behind him, and he began to run out of water. Now he was in the hot country. He cut down a few lianas and drank from them. But wouldn't these cuttings, ever more frequent, give him away? Wasn't he being followed? At sundown the mosquitoes started to plague him. He slept very badly that night, worried he might be coming down with a fever.

The morning of the fifth day he could make out, close to the bank of the river, behind a hill of Indian cornfields, the palm-thatched roofs of a small village. On the sixth day, hiding one of his machetes in the roots of a ceiba on the outskirts of the settlement, not without apprehension, he approached the houses. A little black pig was nosing around, sniffing the ground. Then a woman (she must have been Kekchí, since she wore the native blue skirt and white *huipil* that exposed her navel) suddenly appeared in his path, and looked at him with surprise. Frightened, perhaps.

"Good morning," he said. "I'm here in peace. I need help."

The woman spoke very little Spanish. She called out, and a moment later an adolescent with very large eyes appeared behind her. The boy spoke Spanish.

"What do you want?" he asked.

The fugitive student repeated:

"I need help."

The boy spoke with the woman in Kekchí; then turned to the hedonist and said:

"The others told us that someone like you would come."

Relieved, he followed the Kekchís to one of the houses, where they invited him in. They offered him a seat in a worn hammock and gave him a glass of *atol* and some tortillas with salt, which he devoured.

As Juliana had said, these people didn't much care for their North American neighbors on the other side of the mountain. Nor did they care for the *ladino* laborers or the soldiers who followed their orders, and who kept the Kekchís from going up the mountain to hunt. They were ready to help him in his flight.

They showed him a pool of greenish, lukewarm water, then gave him a ball of soap and a worn-out towel, and even a disposable razor that looked new. The fugitive student thanked them effusively. His clothes were in shreds, but they gave him some clean ones; except for the pants, which barely came to his ankles, they didn't fit too badly. After shaving, he looked at himself in a small splintered mirror. How long had it been since he'd seen himself? His head was almost shaved; he'd never seen himself that way, and he didn't much like what he saw. They gave him a big lunch of black beans and rice, and in the evening he dined with them on wild turkey cooked in achiote sauce.

He must have spent thirty-six hours in the village. He talked a great deal with the boy with the deer eyes, whose name was Calín. He learned the Kekchí greeting, addressed to the heart. ("How is your heart?" one said. Or sang. *Ma saa laa ch'o'ool?*) Early on the morning of his third day there, he presented to the boy's family the two machetes that Laurel had given him. Then two men rowed him upriver in a cayuco—and they rowed fast, leaving behind the green and blue slopes of the San Gil, which looked like a wave on the point of breaking. They passed some fishermen of varying ages, who cast their nets with amazing equilibrium as they stood upright in their little boats, and then began to encounter little coves where pleasure boats and white yachts were anchored in the still green water. The men took him up to the town called Rio Dulce, under the west side of the big bridge on the highway that linked the Petén with Izabal, and there they said good-bye.

VI

Now he was alone, a man without papers. He walked slowly up a muddy little street, down the middle of which meandered a dirty, stinking stream of water, which he took care to avoid with his knockoff sneakers, a gift from the Kekchí. He could never have imagined the generosity of the Indians; they had lifted his heart, he thought. It was another phrase they had taught him.

There were crowds of people out on the highway, which also functioned as the main street of the town until it turned into the huge concrete bridge over the river, a bridge that seemed to belong more to the future than to the present. On both sides of the street little stores were crammed together—groceries, food stalls, two or three hardware stores, a little bank agency. Trailers with cattle or cane, buses with passengers buying junk food from shouting vendors, and dilapidated jeeps and pickups rolled very slowly through the crowd. With their overheated engines and tires, they made the already excessive heat even worse. The fugitive noticed two backpackers, one with a camera, who seemed to be searching for the picturesque in that ugly place.

He toyed with the idea of dirtying his face with mud, making himself look like a beggar. He asked a woman selling fruit and milkshakes how much the bus fare was to Bananera, the town on the bank of the Motagua river where Honduras began. Thirty quetzales, she said. She added that the bus would pass by at three p.m., coming from the Petén, and she pointed in the direction opposite the bridge.

The two backpackers with the camera were coming back, having gone down the street into the little bank, in front of which a Kaibil was posted. When they passed him, he heard them speaking French, and decided to follow them. He spoke a little French—that was a good thing, he thought.

He followed them for a good distance, losing sight of them just at the point where the road curved up to become the bridge. To one side of the embankment was a narrow little street that went down toward the river; near the river's edge were several little food stands. In one of them, a shed painted orange, a couple of foreign women could be seen drinking beer. The two backpackers reappeared from behind another stand and went to join them.

The fugitive headed down the little street, where the shade made the air cooler, though it smelled of rotten fruit. One of the women was a real beauty, he thought, her legs and arms shining with some sort of cream. Seeing her, he felt his blood pound. He waited till the men had sat down, and then came up to the table. He said:

"*Bonjour.*"

It was difficult not to look at the shining legs of that Aphrodite, but he didn't want to make a bad impression. He managed to keep his gaze level.

"I don't want to bother you. Something incredible has happened to me."

The four foreigners looked at each other, a little alarmed.

"No, thanks," said Aphrodite, whose eyes, in his weakened state, he looked at inadvertently. She averted her gaze.

"Please, I'm in danger," he said in his rudimentary French. "I can explain."

"Leave us alone, *señor*, if you don't mind," she said, without looking at him.

The photographer leaned toward him, as if to listen. He stood up.

"Come," he said, and began to walk away from the stand toward the river. Then he slowed down and said, "*Bien. Je vous écoute.*"

They took a few steps toward the water. On the muddy riverbank, a boy with Dravidian features was sitting on a rock, repairing a net. The sun was high in the sky now, and it stung the skin. The fugitive began to give the photographer a brief version of his situation.

About a year ago, possibly more, he'd been kidnapped after a night of drunkenness. He had alienated his father, a despotic bourgeois and a judge, with his drug use and his unwillingness to work; he had already dropped out of a rehab facility in Honduras. The only other things that interested him, besides drugs, were reading and writing poetry. Eventually his father had gotten fed up, and decided to send him to a harsher place.

He pointed to the mountain, which could be seen—the blue summit with its shifting hood of gray mist—beyond the bridge, and explained that he had woken up, half naked, on the floor of a hut, the door locked with chains. He had managed to escape, he said, but he was afraid that his captors were coming after him. He was afraid to speak to the authorities—as the Frenchman advised him to do—because he was sure they'd take him back to the sanatorium, which was guarded by Kaibiles. He had friends in San Pedro Sula, Honduras, and all he wanted to do was to return there. Could they help him get to the border? He knew it was possible to cross the Motagua without being noticed, and from there he would have no problem getting to San Pedro…

"*Et qu'est-ce que vous voulez que je fasse?*" asked the photographer.

"I need money for the bus."

"Where to, exactly? And how much is it?"

The beggar explained that it was to Bananera, a plantation on the border; he could make it with fifty quetzales.

The photographer looked at the water; the sun was turning into little gold coins that glittered nervously on the surface. He reached into his pants pocket and extracted a rubber coin purse. He opened it and took out a roll of bills, which he unwrapped in order to pull off an orange-colored bill.

"Here," he said, and handed it to the fugitive, who thanked him and put the bill into his pocket.

"Come on," said the photographer. "We'll have a beer—if you want."

They walked up toward the shack.

"Can I take a photo?" the man wanted to know, while they were still in the sunlight.

"No, please."

"Okay, let's go."

The three or four seconds he waited before following the photographer were enough to make him decide against the beer. The other three foreigners had their backs to him. He walked alongside the shack, and with a sideways look, raised his hand waist-high by way of saying good-bye. He didn't turn to look back over his shoulder.

He got to the main street. He saw a military patrol, bound for the Petén, and instead of following them over the bridge, he headed down the highway, his hands in his pockets, head down, pensive. He remembered the camp, the punishments for violating the rules. He'd seen a student chained to a tree; through a whole day he'd heard his screams in Sector B.

Another group of tourists was coming down the street. North Americans. Their baseball caps and shorts told him as much. He thought of asking them for more money, but restrained himself. A man with a country face passed by; he asked:

"Excuse me, sir. What day is it today?"

"Saturday, the tenth."

It wasn't noon yet. With a little luck, he would cross the border before nightfall, and he could be in San Pedro by Sunday, the eleventh, sometime in the morning. Eleven was his lucky number, and Sunday was a good day to enter the house, he thought. As for the year, he had just learned it as he passed by a newspaper vendor: 1986.

VII

Sitting just behind the driver of a run-down bus, he fell asleep. As if through a thick fog, he saw a column of young people, carrying big jugs full of water on their shoulders, clambering up a path among the trees. And then he remembered those ants that carried bits of leaves, which, once decomposed, would form the soil for mushrooms, their food, inside their little anthills. The hot wind came in gusts through the bus window; the smell of rotten cane, of cowshit, of grass—it all acted on him like a balm that kept him from remembering his rage for minutes at a time.

They got to Bananera in the red-hot sun of the afternoon. The bus stopped in an open plaza, and the passengers got off and dispersed in all directions. It was a dirty, noisy village—evangelical loudspeakers, rumba, hawkers— and grass grew in the streets, with shreds of plastic garbage caught in it. The beggar headed toward a soft-drink stand on a little raised area. On the other side was the Motagua, a brown-colored strip running through hills of various shades of green.

He drank a soda, very hurriedly.

"Can I get change in lempiras?"

"With pleasure."

He looked toward the other side of the river, where Honduras began.

"Listen."

"Go ahead."

"Where can I cross over?"

The vendor pointed toward the general area behind him.

"From here to there, it's free, as long as immigration doesn't see you. Coming the other way is harder."

There was still plenty of light when he got to the little beach with its coarse gray sand that crunched under his feet. Before he saw the corpse, the breeze hit him with the smell. A dead cow, leather puffed up like a balloon, right near the water. Two buzzards were pulling its entrails out of its back-side, giving little hops as they worked. Animal witches, he thought, or arthritic nuns. Maybe he could compose a poem with that image.

VIII

He waded across the river with difficulty, the water running smooth a little above his waist. A group—two women and three men—watched him from a grass-colored hill, on the Honduran side. They didn't say or do anything. Maybe, he thought, they were waiting for the right moment to cross over themselves, in the other direction, when there was less light. He made it to the shore and kept walking.

A horse trail led alongside the grassy hill. He followed it upward, then down, and kept on going, beyond, walking through a plain that lay between fields of new rubber and African palm, where the only sound was the song of the cicadas. Two hours later, in the last light of the day, he found himself on the outskirts of a little town. Little wood or cinder-block houses, painted bloodred or bright blue, turquoise or pink, stood under the banana trees or in the shade of a cedar or a ceiba. On a football field, in the center of town, multicolored garbage shook in the breeze. A little boy was playing with a cloth ball beside the trail.

"What's this place called?" he asked the boy.

"Las Margaritas."

"Do you know how far we are from San Pedro?"

"By bus? Three hours, more or less."

"Is there anywhere to sleep around here?"

The boy nodded. Next to Don Lencho's shop, which was on the other side of the field, they let rooms.

IX

The next day, at Don Lencho's shop, he breakfasted on a pineapple juice. He took the first bus to San Pedro, getting there at nine o'clock sharp.

As she did every Sunday, his sister would be taking their father for an outing, which included lunch at the coffee farm they had outside of town on the road toward La Ceiba. Except for Bobby, an old German shepherd, the house would be empty till well into the afternoon.

He'd thought of going to the market to spend his last lempiras on a corn coffee and some tortillas, but he decided it would be better not to go anywhere near the neighborhood yet. Someone—a local employee, a maid, a street person—could recognize him, and he didn't want to run the risk. It would be better to stroll around downtown, even though he'd have to endure his hunger a little longer. There would be plenty of time to have a good meal in the kitchen at home. Then he'd have a long bath in his own bathroom, put on clean clothes, and arrange things as they suited him.

The house—which as a kid and even as an adolescent he had used to impress his friends, since it was a grand building, surrounded by an ample garden that, now that he thought of it, seemed like a patch of jungle—was hidden from public view, at the end of a cul-de-sac. Nobody saw him arrive there, nor saw him leap—with the practice of years—over the white stake fence. The dog was nowhere to be found; maybe he had died, he thought. The cries of the grackles sounded from the lychee tree planted by his maternal grandfather, the agronomist, almost a century ago. He stood a moment in the white gravel driveway, looking up at the facade of the wooden house, which seemed to lean back against the solid promontory behind it, like a Maya mound. The place was built in a New Orleans style, crowned with gables and green tiles. The landings of a semicircular staircase rose among the trees—pitanga cherry, lychee, jaboticaba, avocado. The judge, for the time being, was master here, and had been since the hedonist's mother's death. But that, he said to himself, was about to change.

X

Inside the garden, he was someone else. He inhaled as deeply as he could, until the air hurt his lungs. He leapt up the balcony steps and, after confirming that the French windows were locked, climbed to one of the upper windows (with catlike movements, he fancied, feeling proud of his physical condition), forced open one of the panes, and knocked out the screen with one blow. He put one leg through, then his torso, then the other leg, letting himself fall to the floor inside. There, as he had expected, between a white rose and a candlestick, on a kind of altar above the fireplace, stood a photo of his mother. His mother as she had been, young, beautiful, smiling, before she'd met the judge.

He walked up and kissed her forehead through the cold glass. Then he sank one finger into the melted wax around the little flame and smeared a bit of it on his forehead. A simple ritual, secret and strangely comforting.

From the living room, he passed down a hallway with parquet flooring— white acacia and caoba wood—to his bedroom, happy to be alone in the large empty house that had been his since childhood and that the judge and his daughter had made unlivable for him.

He continued on to the judge's studio, a well-furnished little library lined with statute books and volumes of history, where he fell back into the black leather chair behind the big black wooden desk. One of the drawers was locked, but it wasn't difficult to force open. Inside, as he'd hoped, he found a pile of papers, a small strongbox, which he didn't even try to open, an account ledger, and a revolver.

There were three letters from a Dr. Burden, dated between 1984 and 1986, which he read with mounting interest. AREYP—the Association for the Reorientation of Young People—was, he realized, the name of the place he had escaped from. An advertising brochure included with one of the letters displayed attractive bungalows, saddle horses, happy-looking girls and boys. The director of the hospital, it was said, used naturopathic methods combined with spiritual exercises, musical therapy, and other innovative techniques. Total discretion was guaranteed.

It seemed that the judge had paid the doctor handsomely to keep the hedonist in that oppressive sanatorium. Elsewhere among the papers he found a clinical chart (from another hospital) with his own name at the top.

The patient demonstrates the typical symptoms of affective paranoid disorder, including hallucinations, delirium, and delusions of grandeur. Although of a hedonistic nature, he is insecure, dishonest, and vindictive. His inferiority complex, which is clinically pathological, can be attributed to certain genetic features: notably, his Indian, Semitic, and Negroid ancestry. We recommend immediate sedation and antipsychotic medication (thorazine, among others). The treatment is complicated, the duration indefinite, and the prognosis doubtful.

It had been almost two years since the judge had paid Doctor Burden—who was not really a doctor, as the hedonist would learn later—for the time of his captivity.

The account ledger offered better news. He was going to be a very rich man.

XI

His pangs of hunger having returned, he headed for the kitchen. He opened the refrigerator, saw it was full, and closed it again. He went into the storeroom and came out armed with a cured pork leg and a bottle of red wine, which he set on the pantry table. At last, he thought, he was going to have a feast.

After his meal, his next stop was the bathroom. As he let the water run in the tub, he began to whistle; the water was steaming as he got undressed. He leaned over the toilet and vomited up some of his excessive meal, then washed out his mouth and got into the tub, where he fell asleep instantly and remained so till the water turned cold.

Brimming with well-being—the feeling was almost magical, in a way—he went to his bedroom, which was just as he had left it. He took clean clothes from the closet and got dressed.

Then he went through his dresser drawers, taking out a wad of bills and several documents: his passport, his driver's license. He left behind his savings book, check pad, and calendar. Now the memories were crowding his head. With a slight seasickness he fell onto the bed, his fingers linked behind his head.

*   *   *

The rest would appear in the newspapers and is all verifiable. The judge and his daughter died in the flames that night.

Darío Alaluf, who once again crossed the border clandestinely the night of the fire, lived for the next three years apart from the world in San Andrés Itzá, in the Petén. Then, declared sole heir to the judge's estate, he returned to settle down in Honduras.

Today, after more than twenty-five years (Burden now dead of old age and the phony sanatorium abandoned and forgotten), he can tell his story—though he does not wish to reveal his actual name. The law cannot really touch him, at this point, nor would it want to—as those same statute books that fed the flames in the judge's studio would say, patricide is a crime subject to the statute of limitations in Honduras. And Darío has become a man of honor and respect, as they say around here.

EMUNCTORIES

by **RODRIGO BLANCO CALDERÓN**

Translated by Daniel Gumbiner

For Hermán Sifontes

This story takes place in July 2012. It had been ten years since I'd been back to Venezuela, and it was the fiftieth anniversary of the first printing of *The Time of the Hero*. It sounds crazy, but it's the second date that's important.

When I awoke to the sight of Sofía's back, I told myself that of course I had to return from very far away—had to be, in some way, other—for the bitch to finally get in bed with me. But that's a lie. Really I'm only thinking that now, now that I can't get Superintendent Cursio's "Bitches, bitches," out of my head. In the moment, I couldn't think of anything but my stomach cramps, and I barely made it to the bathroom.

The snacks at the embassy hadn't sat well with me. Or it could have been the beer we drank afterward. Who knows. The whole country didn't sit well with me, and I didn't sit well with it. It was because of this that I was thrown in jail a few hours later, and at this point I don't think I'll ever go back.

I flushed the toilet and forced myself to look at its contents, as if to remind myself that I had, at one time, been *that*. I stuck my head into the bedroom for a moment to see if Sofía had heard (or smelled) anything, but another contraction forced me back to the toilet. This is when I remembered the warning Sofía had given me when we arrived:

—There's no water.

I clenched my butt cheeks as best as I could and left on a reconnaissance mission around the apartment. If, in the drunkenness and stumbling of the morning, Sofía had been able to warn me like that, she must have taken certain precautions—there had to be, in the laundry room or kitchen, some bucket of water. But no. Or maybe my haste kept me from looking carefully. What happened is that I had to run to the bathroom once again, still trying not to wake Sofía, her body a corkscrew of flesh beneath the wrinkled sheets.

I grabbed the wastebasket, lifted up the cover, and defecated. I wiped myself as best I could and closed the wastebasket. I left the bathroom, went into the closet, and grabbed a Nina Ricci bag. The thickness and the color of it gave me confidence. The wastebasket fit inside easily. And so, shit in hand, I found the keys and went out into the street.

I didn't notice anyone in the hallway, or the elevator, or by the front door. Upon leaving the building and seeing the color of the sky, the ridges of Avila in the distance, and the main intersection of Los Palos Grandes completely empty, it occurred to me that it was still very early on Sunday morning.

Then, just before I reached the trash bin on the sidewalk, a motorcyclist flew by at full speed and snatched the bag. I watched him disappear toward Fourth Avenue.

One of the things that had surprised me upon my return to the homeland was the fact that the motorcyclists had become the scourge of the city. For a moment I was happy that, without trying, I had exacted some small measure of vengeance against them.

I had shit on them, one could say.

"Life is an affront; the organism is a network of emunctories," I recited.

I was too ashamed to tell Sofía what had happened. And it was in that instant, when I realized that I didn't have anyone to whom I could relate this anecdote, that I accepted that I had lost my country. Or, in reality, that I had never had it. Julián was my only friend left in Caracas, but he was in jail.

It was on his behalf that I had accepted the invitation to the gringo embassy. It was the perfect excuse to visit him. An acquaintance had informed me of his situation: how the minister of the economy had sacrificed him to appease the president, the three months he had endured without seeing the light of day, the comments he had made to various writers about my absence and my silence.

My stay was to be brief. Three days would be sufficient to present my new edition of Ramos Sucre's poems, visit Julián, and sign the necessary papers so that a lawyer could put my parents' house on the market. Columbia University had talked to the cultural attaché about my translations. They had spoken so highly of them that the invitation had transformed into something of a tribute.

Sofía hadn't left my side the previous night. During the interview, which she conducted, I felt her gaze move beyond the standard journalistic interest she owed to her interviewee—beyond, even, the interest owed to an old friend she hadn't seen for many years. It was during our conversation that I found out that Sofía had not graduated with a Literature degree, as I'd thought. She had graduated in Communications and now wrote for the society pages of an evening newspaper.

After the interview she accompanied me to a bookstore, where I bought the Real Academia anniversary edition of *The Time of the Hero*. Prison had made Julián more reflective, more disciplined. He was learning Italian and reading the classics, and I thought he would enjoy the novel.

—Classic Vargas Llosa, Julián?

—Of course, Gilberto.

They let Julián use his cell phone. I learned that night that Sofía and Julián were friends. It was she who gave me the number for the phone he used in prison.

—It's tapped, was the first thing Julián said upon hearing my voice. Some secret SEBIN civil servant had been picked to listen to a debate about classicism and realism in contemporary Latin American literature.

—You're coming tomorrow, then?

—Of course. What time?

—Come at ten. SEBIN headquarters.

—Okay.

SN, DIGEPOL, DISIP, SEBIN—these were the acronyms that the political police had used in Venezuela for the past fifty years to disseminate their spiritual cacophony. It could have been this that confused me; I never asked Julián about the location of the SEBIN headquarters. Instead I chaotically reconstructed some memories from my university days and, at nine twenty in the morning, found myself in front of the Helicoide, that monstrous shopping-mall-turned-detention-center built during Pérez Jimenez's dictatorship. It resembled, I thought, the great piece of shit that has been our nation's history. I didn't pass by my house. I barely had time to kiss Sofía's sleeping shoulder, grab the book, and leave.

At the first checkpoint they didn't know who I was talking about. One of the policemen looked me up and down while the other made a phone call.

—You have to wait until eleven, he said after hanging up.

—My friend told me I could visit at ten.

—Eleven is the second shift.

I left and went to the bakery on Avenida Victoria. There I devoured a *cachito de jamón* and drank a half liter of Riko-Malt, savoring it as though it were an exquisite wine. I thought: this cachito and this Riko-Malt are the only things that justify the existence of a country as miserable as Venezuela.

The prospect of seeing Julián in this situation disheartened me. He had built a fortune, and he was dedicated to investing it in the country. Worse still, he had invested it in that absurd venture they call "culture." And for what?

I began to leaf through the Vargas Llosa. *Cuatro, dijo El Jaguar.* Cavas. Boa. El Poeta. Arana, El Esclavo. The story was intact, not only in the book but in my memory. Before I knew it, it was after eleven. The chemistry exam had been stolen by the peasant, the Circle had officially formed, and soon the revenge would unfold.

Back at the Helicoide, the policemen asked me more questions—the same ones, actually.

—Julián Rangel, I said again.

The same policeman made another call, and this time they let me pass.

I walked quickly up the enormous curve of the Tarpeian Rock, which led to the main building. Looking down, the whole ghetto of San Agustín seemed like a squashed crowd waiting for some kind of divine act. The miracle would never come to pass, of course; the multitude knew this, but they also knew that the only thing keeping them alive was the hope that it might.

I came to another checkpoint. It was manned by a national guardsman who, like the others, asked me who I was there to visit. The guard, a fat guy with the air of a bus driver, made his own phone call. Then he hung up. He asked me for my ID and my cell phone. He made a note, placed my cell phone and my ID in some sort of slatted wooden box, and gave me a numbered chip.

After that there was a concrete terrace that led to an empty parking lot and a door guarded by another policeman—this time a big, strong guy carrying a large machine gun. In the parking lot two Hummers and a string of five or six motorcycles—all black—gleamed in the sun. It cast a strange and brilliant light upon them.

The gorilla at the door asked me yet again who I was looking for. I repeated Julián's name and entered what seemed like a visitor's waiting room. Inside, another policeman, who was making a family sign in on a registry, told me to sit on a brown leather couch. The wall in front of me was covered with a grid of cubbies. The only thing I was carrying was the Vargas Llosa novel, so I didn't have anything to store.

The policeman finished with the family and motioned for me to come over.

—Who are you coming to visit?

It all seemed like a nightmare. I gave him the name.

—What relation do you have with the aforementioned?

—Friend from childhood.

—Location of residence?

It was at that moment, for the third time that day, that I took a shit.

—Los Palos Grandes.

I don't know why I lied.

The policeman's gaze drilled into me.

—The third avenue, I added, burying myself deeper into the plaster I had set. An enormous, helicoidal plaster.

The policeman's glare softened. He even gave me a half smile.

—What are you carrying there?

—A book.

—Can I take a look?

—Of course.

Instead of leafing through the pages, he reviewed the front and back cover, as though he weren't a policeman but rather a literary critic.

—Come with me, he said, still carrying the book.

I would not leave until the following morning.

By now the reader will have realized two fundamental things. The first is that this was not the headquarters of SEBIN. Or that, in any case, Julián was not imprisoned in the Helicoide. And the second thing, more important still, is that this policeman was the motorist who, just that morning, had grabbed my bag.

It would take me some time to realize all this. At first, I was too busy trying to decide which of my cellmates was going to rape and kill me. Or would they all rape me, one at a time, and kill me after? After a while I was able to calm down. There were three petroleum engineers in there with me, who had been accused of starting a refinery fire; the fourth man was the director of a government food program, the one directly responsible (according to official sources) for those containers of spoiled food that had appeared in different ports around the country.

—And you, asked one of the engineers. —What death are they trying to pin on you?

I said I didn't have the slightest idea what I had been accused of.

Right then a new man entered, introduced himself as Centeno, a civil servant, and told me I was to follow him to the detective's office. Reclining in an armchair in that office, with his feet on a desk, was Detective Pulido. That's how he introduced himself, and I introduced myself in return.

—Gilberto Porras, he said, reading my ID.

I remembered that I still had the numbered chip that the guard outside had given me. Without knowing why, I gave it to the detective. Pulido took the chip, looked at it closely.

—I'm going to bet with this. This is definitely my number, he said as he returned my ID.

I didn't like where this was going, and I began to talk compulsively. I started to explain, in great detail, who I was, where I worked, how long I had lived in the United States, what my relation to Julián was, and my planned departure the following night.

Pulido observed me with pleasure, barely containing his smile.

That smile frightened me even more, and I began to speak faster when Pulido took his feet off the desk, ducked down to look for something on the floor, and placed the Nina Ricci bag in between us.

I wondered, first, whether or not my method had worked. No smells overwhelmed the room. When Pulido pushed the bag toward me with his index finger, I realized that it was empty.

I felt myself turning pale. Pulido had stopped smiling.

I could hear someone screaming in the hallway. The Dutchman, another prisoner, had freed himself from his handcuffs. Pulido left the office; our encounter, apparently, was over. A few seconds later he reappeared with Centeno, who brought me back to the cell.

My companions assured me that there wasn't anything serious to be afraid of. Unlike Dorancel Vargas, they explained, the famous "Humaneater" who ate male flesh, the Dutchman only ate female flesh. He was wanted in various countries in Europe and nobody had any idea how and why he had come to Venezuela.

—He likes to eat ovaries, one of the engineers said.

Every few minutes you could hear the distant yells of guards mixed with incomprehensible remarks. They were almost done soothing the Dutchman. I must have had an expression of horror on my face, because Henry, another of the engineers, stepped forward and told me:

—The drubbing they gave Diomedes was worse.

Diomedes was a Colombian drug smuggler who had been beaten into submission when he'd arrived a few nights earlier. Since then he had not left his cell except to go to the bathroom.

—But apart from that, said Rafael, the one who had spoken of ovary eating, —this is calm for around here.

I passed the afternoon in my two-meter-by-two-meter cell, lying on my cot, which was a thin mat that had been placed over a shelf of cement. I spent the whole time crying and cursing Julián, my parents, Sofía, and Ramos Sucre. The stories I had heard about Venezuelan prisons were so plentiful and so terrible that I feared for the worst.

It was about five or six in the evening when I heard a *cuatro* play a few songs. I stuck my head out of my cell and saw Henry, Rafael, and Daniel, the three ex-*pedevesas*, and Sebastián, the food-program man, starting what seemed to be some kind of a parade. Upon seeing me, they stopped and invited me to join them.

—Today is my birthday, said Henry. —We gave a little something to Cursio, and he let us bring out the cuatro and the little bottle of whiskey.

They gave me a drink of whiskey.

—Who is Cursio? I asked.

—The chief of this shell of a place, said Sebastián.

Then they told me all about Cursio, Centeno, and Pulido. When the bottle was halfway gone, things seemed to turn around; we entered into that phase of exalted friendship. We took pity on our friend the Dutchman, and Henry sang him a song:

—Yo soy un niño caníbal nadie me quiere a mí / No me quedan amiguitos porque ya me los comí.

I recognized the Virulo tune, and I accompanied Henry with a choral bass and hand claps.

—Is there a party?

The silence was consuming, as if someone had disconnected a previously deafening sound system.

—Yes or no?

We opened up a space for Diomedes. His eye was practically closed because of the swelling, but the rest of his face, particularly his expression, seemed to suggest that nothing had happened.

—And the old ladies? A party without old ladies is the saddest thing in the world.

Diomedes got up, leaned his head through the bars of the common room, and yelled:

—Hey, Centeno! Yes, you, bitch. Who else? Get me Superintendent Cursio.

Instead of bringing Superintendent Cursio, the civil servant dragged Diomedes from the room. We all feared the worst. After a bit Centeno returned, opened the cell door, and threw Diomedes back in. Centeno walked back down the hall. To my great surprise, he had left the gate open.

—What's happening? asked Henry.

—We're going to celebrate your birthday as God would have wished, bitch. That's what's happening, said Diomedes.

Centeno returned carrying a sound system. Diomedes left the cell, as though he were at his own house, and returned with a bottle of champagne. Shortly thereafter a dispatch of ten bottles of twelve-year-old whiskey arrived.

During the first few drinks, none of us knew exactly where things were heading. Cursio appeared. He looked like Marlon Brando from *Apocalypse Now*, only dark-skinned. He sat in between us like a host and greeted us one by one. He had the strong, good-natured accent of a rancher.

It was then, in the few silent seconds between one *vallenato* song and another, that we heard some sounds on the roof.

Dogs, I thought. Dogs from the anti-drug squadron. It sounded as though a regiment of fingernails were marching methodically.

Diomedes turned down the sound system's volume and pointed toward the roof with an air of fake intrigue, like he'd just spotted Santa Claus. A few seconds later, accompanied by the *tic tac* of their heels, the prostitutes entered.

Cursio and Diomedes were the commanders of the party. They let us drink as much whiskey as we wanted and dance two or three dances with the women. Seeing as there were four girls, I figured they had calculated one for each of them: Diomedes, Cursio, Centeno, and Pulido.

—Where is Pulido? I asked Centeno.

—He's got guard duty today, he said. —You know, keeping an eye on the Dutchman.

I imagined other parties, and other monsters.

Centeno was talking to me as if we were old buddies. Or worse, as if I were a policeman too. The pistols rested on the table.

From there on in, everything was very confusing. I remember that, in the middle of my drunkenness, I began to talk about Ramos Sucre with one of the prostitutes. I remember that the woman nodded at my words as if she knew who Ramos Sucre was, or what existed in the depths of poetry. I remember Cursio rubbing his bald spot while one of the girls, the brunette, danced for him. I remember Daniel using a pistol to lift a napkin off the table, and then setting the weapon back down. I remember one of the women convincing Centeno to pull out a few grams of cocaine.

The bathroom was located at the end of the hall, down a snail-shaped staircase. When I got up to go, I saw Pulido in some sort of utility room between two cells, his back to the door. He was stretched out in a chair, his feet resting on a plastic stool. It seemed like he was sleeping. I continued toward the bathroom. On my way back, I stopped in front of the door.

I could take advantage of the inconceivable camaraderie of the party and speak to him, beg his forgiveness for whatever it was that I had done, and beg him to let me go. I was about to do it when I heard the unmistakable scratch of a page turning. Pulido wasn't sleeping. He was reading the Vargas Llosa.

I backed away in silence and slipped back into the party. Despite what happened later, I don't regret it. Tormentors have a right to read in peace as well.

When I got back to the room, the coke was up and running. Out of all of us, only the ex-director of food agreed to take a few hits. Cursio began to scream "Bitches, bitches" and didn't stop until finally, much later, one of the women took him up to the rooms on the floor above us.

Centeno and Diomedes partied with us until very late. Afterward, each one left with his corresponding woman without saying good-bye to anyone. Immediately after that, the engineers went to bed. The fourth woman, the one with bleached blonde hair, got up from the sofa and went to the bathroom. I was the only one still awake, besides Sebastián, and for a while I listened, between yawns, to the frenetic ramblings of the food-program man.

At some point I fell asleep. I must not have slept very long. Less than two hours, I imagine. I didn't have a single dream or premonition.

When I woke up I was alone on the sofa. There wasn't anyone in the rest of the room either. Someone had taken the care to turn off the lights. The gate that separated the common room from the hall of cells had been left open.

I went to the bathroom.

I saw Pulido sticking his head out of one of the cells, grabbing the thick bars like a prisoner. He heard my steps and pulled out his weapon. The light from the reading room was on and allowed him to identify my face. I saw his, also. Then I saw what was on the floor of the cell.

The blood nearly reached the hallway. The metal base of the gate formed a dike that prevented the current from flowing through. The bleached blonde had a murky wound in her stomach, as though she had fallen on a grenade, or suffered a bite from a hidden land mine.

I imagined the Dutchman watching me sleep and shutting off the lights, his orange beard soaked in blood.

I peed myself.

Pulido watched the puddle form at my feet and began to laugh.

—It's okay now, he said, opening the door. He led me to the office, gave me back my cell phone, and took me back up to the surface.

—I can go? I asked him.

The Hummers and the motorcycles were still parked there. Without the intense light of day, they looked like a coven of ravens and vultures.

—I'll tell Cursio I was asleep. That's what I'll tell him.

—But what are they going to do?

—The Dutchman will turn up. Or maybe he won't.

—And the woman?

—The prostitute? Her? She's just a prostitute.

In my mind I saw again the torn stomach of the blonde, her chewed ovaries, and I had to turn away to vomit.

—If you open your mouth, I'll kill you, Pulido said as he gave me a hard slap on the back.

I stood there a few moments staring at my vomit on the asphalt, identifying the remains of the cachito and the Riko-Malt, as if it were a Rorschach test.

I began to walk down the slope. It was cold out. Looking out at the shantytowns, I could see the first lights of the day switching on, mixing with the bulbs that had not been turned off all night. The shelter they offered was uncertain, but it was shelter nonetheless.

I turned on my cell phone. I saw a message from Sofía.

Will I see you again?

All of the sudden I felt someone grab my shoulder. I had almost walked down the entire path. I was paralyzed for a few seconds.

The Dutchman, I thought.

It was Pulido. He had run to catch up with me.

—It was El Jaguar who killed El Esclavo, wasn't it? he asked, still panting from the effort.

    I said the same thing to him that I said to Sofía.

    —I don't know.

IN THE DARK CORE
OF THE NIGHT

by ANDRÉS RESSIA COLINO

Translated by Katherine Silver

I 'm standing in front of the house, a glass of whiskey, no ice, in one hand and a cigarette in the other, listening to Dardo's string of fairly capricious and anyway inconsequential appraisals of someone or other in the back and watching how the wind blowing in from the ocean keeps livening up the ember of my cigarette and how the paper burns in a crackling helix, releasing the nicotine that should be entering my lungs instead of being lost forever in the fields behind us. I'm thinking about how to get rid of Dardo, even though it was me who wanted to come out front with him. It's summer, and I feel like we're trapped, not precisely here in this house, but in this part of the world that might as well be called New Ciudad Juárez, but is more commonly known as Punta del Este.

"They're all a bunch of sonsabitches," Dardo insists.

Who isn't? And aren't we in bed with them, in a way?

"You know what Juanma's problem is, don't you?" I ask.

He doesn't know, but the question fills the emptiness.

"I'm going to do something," Dardo says.

It would be much better if Dardo would stop saying the things he says, and stop thinking them. He carries his pathetic life around with him everywhere he goes, and the only things he ever talks about are products of his impoverished imagination. If he killed himself this very instant, it wouldn't make much difference. The only thing out of the ordinary would be the number 4 stamped on his coffin, and this just to bring our generation up to speed on how many others in his family had done it before him.

"Ever thought of suicide?" I ask.

His face shows sorrow disguised as surprise.

"His, I mean," I add with emphasis. "Wouldn't it have been a whole lot better if he'd just killed himself?"

"What the hell are you talking about?" he says, turning around to look behind him. "These people don't even understand what that is... It's too elaborate. Requires too much introspection."

A valuable construct given the context, Dardo, but sad and false, nonetheless. Anyway, you're forgiven. I know you'll never again be able to talk about suicide without feeling ashamed. I don't much like picturing Bet, your sister, in the wake of her attempt, injected with that mixture of fertilizers and herbicides for soybeans or whatever it is, the syncopation of her vital organs, one of her kidneys expelling lithium and the other downers, her liver swollen with antipsychotics, all her limbs making signs her mouth doesn't notice, a smile sponsored by a pharmacological ice pick spread across her face. To tell you the truth, I, too, fear their possible effects on her, while she lies in the sun in the morning trying for the perfect tan. And though everybody blames Juanma for her crisis, we would all pat you on the back and tell you that madness is essentially a feminine problem.

Dardo lights a cigarette, and we smoke in silence.

"You're not saying anything," I say.

Dardo rarely doesn't say anything. And so he adds:

"Juanma's a motherfucking bastard. He didn't leave that girl by the side of the road like he said he did."

I hate white Mercedes-Benzes, but I still can't help watching them closely when they're prowling around. One with tinted windows passes slowly by the house while Dardo is carrying on a debate with himself, then stops a little farther on, where I can still see it. Dardo flicks away his cigarette butt and turns to go back inside. I have to stay and watch. I finish my whiskey, toss the glass with almost complete indifference under the bushes that mark the property boundary, and light another cigarette.

The car pulls off to the side and stops, sinking into the starboard side of the ditch the dirt road drains into. A woman I can just barely see gets out and, not bothering to close the door, starts strolling down the road, making the loose gravel crunch with each step she takes. A little later and through the same door, a fat man I figure to be about forty or fifty appears. He coughs and clears his throat and, straightening his back with an exaggerated movement, chuckles loudly a couple of times into the night. The woman turns around and says something to him. I figure he's a bad guy, or at least a very unpleasant one. She walks back up to him, slams the door shut, and, lifting her arm, seems to be giving him orders. Next to him, she looks very young and slim; then they both turn and start walking toward me.

When they're about ten feet away, the man fulfills my sordid prediction to a T. He looks sweaty and bloated, with greenish bags for eyelids, his large bald spot stripped with thin and tangled clumps of hair. A few moles stand out sharply on his forehead against his bright red skin, burnt by the January sun. The same color spreads over his broad, fleshy nose and flaccid cheeks. He swings back and forth as he walks, more hastily than forcefully, and that enormous belly jutting out in front of him seems uncomfortable to carry around. But she's the surprising one. Noticeably younger than he, maybe even under thirty, she looks and walks like no other woman I've ever seen in the thirty-odd miles from José Ignacio to Punta Ballena. With slightly bowed legs in opaque black jeans and no high heels or platforms under her feet, she takes long strides while moving her slightly curved trunk; she carries her right shoulder slightly lower than her left, and her head leans in a little toward her companion, as if she were clinging to an expression of disinterest from some past conversation but with the tension of a tic frozen in place. Her full lips seem to be whispering, and her lively eyes pleasantly remind me of a lab rat's.

I'd thought they were walking toward me, but now it's clear that her object of interest lies behind the front door. I even know where they're headed. They pass so close to me that I could jump them without any warning, but they don't even look over. It bothers me, but I know that in a few minutes they'll be retracing their steps, their task accomplished, their palms sweaty and their heart rates reset.

Suddenly, she seems to think of something, stops right before entering the front door, and whispers to the man, who doesn't pay much attention to her and continues into the house. Then she turns and starts walking toward me; as she approaches, she looks me right in the eye and outfits her nervous face with a shy smile.

"Hi," she says, as she shoves her hands inside the pockets of her jeans.

"Hi."

"Excuse me... have you got a smoke?"

I pause before answering, and I hear her swallowing her saliva, her tongue pressed against her teeth.

"Sure," I say, as I pull my pack out of my pants pocket.

I don't want some stupid, forced dialogue. She takes the cigarette I offer and waits for me to light it. I can see her better under the flame of the lighter. Her skin is a little dry and her lips are chapped and cracked, her dark hair just barely wavy. Her shoulders are bony and her summer dress shows her freckles. She gazes off into space as she takes a long drag, which she holds for an added moment. She twitches her nose, like a rat, before she blows the smoke out to one side. She doesn't speak, nor does she return the lighter. She looks at the Mercedes as if it were evoking a clear memory of something or other.

"Is there somewhere around here to buy a pack?"

"If you don't want to waste twenty dollars on Marlboros, there's the gas station at La Barra."

"Is that far away?"

"A little."

"Do you mind coming with me? Truth is, I always get lost around here."

There's no insinuation in her voice or her body, only a sudden and straightforward lilt of helplessness at the end.

I don't answer. I'm taking my time, only because I have the opportunity to do so.

"Okay. Let's go."

She walks to the Mercedes without looking behind her. I watch as she rescues it from the ditch and waits patiently for me. The second I shut the door, she steps on the gas and asks me my name. Hers is Lili. I limit myself to giving her short instructions as she drives through the dark, narrow streets of the seaside resort, without traffic but lined with poorly parked cars and ridiculously wide SUVs that constantly force her to swerve. She seems nervous. Not much changes when we reach the wide and well-lit highway that hugs the coastline except that she presses hard on the gas pedal, the car accelerating to seventy-five miles an hour in what feels like a split second. In spite of my deep-seated disdain for Mercedes-Benzes, the interior makes me appreciate its solidity. The leather seat supports my body comfortably, and there is enough space to stretch out my legs. I ask her if it's her car, and she laughs in a way that seems to be saying six or seven things at once.

I suddenly find myself in the position of Dardo's sister, or one of those other teenagers Juanma has managed to get into his car, whose legs he loosens up by accelerating as fast as he can. I have put myself in the hands of this woman's expertise and criteria. Lili, whom I don't know from Adam.

Now would be a sensible moment to put on my seat belt, but it would also be a terrible way to make friends. I'm sure those teenage girls wouldn't do it, tempted as they'd be by the imminent contact, watchful of Juanma's hand moving from the gear shift to the steering wheel until, according to his accounts, he takes a curve to the left at full speed and places his left hand on the top of the steering wheel, then quickly moves his right hand to the girl's thigh, where he buries it between her legs, always bare, and where it gets scorched by the heat he invariably finds under her bikini panties. If there's any resistance, he says, he just shakes the wheel a little and, like an automatic reflex, the pressure between her legs changes and shivers run up and down her spine. I doubt very much that Lili would dare do anything of the sort, but a fantasy starts to take shape in my head.

I pull my eyes away from the coastline outside the car, which I know by heart, and look at her.

"Careful as you approach," I say.

"Why?"

The traffic in La Barra forces her to drive at a crawl. It's backed up for about half a mile, luxury convertibles and enormous SUVs vibrating with the bass of their audio equipment. Alongside, a two-way parade flows by, the men impeccably dressed and groomed and the women unequivocally thin, perched on five-hundred-dollar shoes. A gathering less variable than it might appear, adorned with a backdrop of lighted bar signs and the bright lights of the high-end car showrooms, with their offers of champagne and their white leather armchairs. A different kind of gathering, made up of a score of promotional models wrapped in patent leather, doesn't manage to attract anybody's attention.

"And the gas station?" she asks angrily.

"At the other end."

*   *   *

Lili parks the car along the side of the road, far away from the pumps, and walks to the dimly lit, glass-walled store. I get out of the car and move a few feet away to have a smoke. This was where she was last seen, Juanma's latest girl. I look at the roof over the pumps with the same close attention that only the employees probably give it during the most monotonous moments of their shift. I see the cameras, almost a dozen, their focuses crossing, reverse and panoramic angles, twenty feet from the ground.

It's a little early for the recurrent scene that Juanma and the young lady with the initials M.N. starred in eleven days ago, and that new actors repeat every day at dawn with a better outcome. The groups of young people milling around the edges of the station's cone of light are still relatively quiet, the motorcycles aren't revving their engines with despair, there are only a few cars, and I even see a policeman or two come to buy a Coke at the shop, but it would be easy for anyone to guess exactly how it happened. Juanma and his friend were in his BMW, the girls laughing and guzzling booze in the dark across the street, in between the motorcycles and one or another car they used as an improvised bar, showing their best profile to the cars that were driving by, scorning them with delicate indifference, and waiting. Then Juanma stops not too far away and his friend calls the girl over and gets out of the car as she approaches; they greet each other with a kiss on the cheek, and she smiles, but her attention is really focused on the one inside. She leans over the open car door to continue the conversation that has already gone into several chapters, and finally accepts *going for a spin* with him, taking the place of the friend who has crossed the street to the station.

In the picture one of her friends took with her phone, thinking how much they'd laugh at it later when they looked at it together, you can see the sky bursting with a color one could reasonably assume to be the first light of a summer day. The car, black or dark blue with yellow headlights, can be seen a little ways away up the street, about twenty linear yards from the eyes of the cameras that would have best been able to capture it.

*   *   *

Lili returns from the store with a couple of packs of cigarettes and two small bottles of beer. When our eyes meet, she smiles, and the set expression on her face, which I thought by now was part of her features, starts to dissolve.

"Full of kids," she says, getting into the Mercedes. Surrounded by fumes of gasoline and diesel, she immediately lights a cigarette and pulls out onto the road.

I feel like she's trying to tell me something. Maybe it's just that she's looking at me for the first time, uneasy and wanting to get a quick idea of who I am, as if only now realizing the implicit risks of getting into a car with a man at dawn. She scrutinizes me so summarily that she seems rash, and the very next instant she surprises me by abruptly turning down a much darker lateral road, where she continues driving for a few feet, then stops. With a boldness that clearly seeks complicity, she grabs the beer out of my hand, takes a gulp, and returns it to me. Twitching her nose, her lips pressed together, she digs into the tight pocket of her pants. It's obvious what's coming.

As I watch her reliably handle the tiny paper package and metal tube, and make sure to inhale just the right dose, I get a visceral sense of her sex. All my attention is focused on her sharp, slender fingers, her short nails painted with dull dark-red polish that's slightly chipped, the white crystals obeying the skillful procedure. I'm attracted to her hands; I would like them to brush against my skin accidentally at some point in the next ten minutes. I watch her inhale another line. I wonder if it's better or just about the same as what there's so much of at home. I still can't decide if the fat man who was with her came to buy or to make a delivery, but I'm not going to get an answer to that question right away. I accept what she offers, taking the weapon and its ammunition with feigned apathy. Accidentally, my index finger brushes against the pad of her thumb.

The car bounces along a road that Lili's never driven on. It's a winding road through low hills and forested parkland, a dark road that leads away from the coast, adding an unnecessary detour of about twelve miles to our return in order to avoid *all that shit in La Barra*, as Lili expressly requested. Anyway, I am not in the least eager to get back. We converse with the stereotypical frankness that usually ensues, and I try to tell her that not a single square foot of the terrain we are now driving through is free of the shit she just reviled and thinks we have avoided. If you ever had the chance to be invited to one of these properties, I try to tell her, you would end up first sympathizing with and then missing the sincerity of most of the people hanging out down there on the main road, who are so thoroughly disgusting on their own. On the left, you can see the now traditional-seeming smaller properties that border the lake, with their private golf courses and their framed photographs that testify to the visits, in the nineties, of Israel's tenth prime minister, of the Pimpinela duo, of Diego Armando Maradona, of Don Augusto Pinochet with a friendly smile on his face, and, just a little later, of Bush senior with his arm around Julio María Sanguinetti and Luis Alberto Lacalle, an unforgettable trio to finish off the century. A little farther on, the walls of the shining new development await you, its circular footbridge docks stretching over the mirrorlike water, its berths and heli-ports contained in a single structure. If you want to see something even more awe-inspiring, just turn a little to your left for the sumptuous chalets perched on the mountainside, with panoramic views of the lake and fifteen miles of coastline from a luxurious living room where you can converse face-to-face with the living corpse of Adolfo Yabrán, officially declared dead eleven years ago, after which all charges of murder and arms trafficking against him were dropped, by Divine Providence. Then you'd really be up to your ears in shit, and in its purest, most physiological form, so to speak. Shit that still hasn't seen the light of day and flows through the intricate circumvolutions of material intestines with fluidity and comfort, still in communication with the rest of the system, sustaining for years the richest known enterobacterial colony and loads of restless intestinal parasites. Shit that delights in the vision of a papal toilet where it can finally rest, and pays for it. I would like to confess all of this to you, Lili, but I manage to articulate only a minimum part of this speech that boils and bangs around in my brain, pointed like the Mercedes toward the cliff we're about to drive over. A girl shouldn't drive like this, nor should I let myself be driven like this. I see her smiling at my stumbling verbal diarrhea and a new urge to take possession of her shakes my own numb body. I move my hand to her leg and grab her thigh just above her knee. I move my palm along her jeans till I reach the creases in her pants at her hips and I find her zippered belly and sink my fingertips into it to measure the density of her flesh rather than the cloth. I move my hand up and down, then return over the same route. Lili breathes in through her mouth and moves her jaw while her eyes remain glued on the road, her hands clinging to the wheel. She accelerates, and there isn't much more I can do.

For a moment I want to be Juanma, grab a handful of Lili's hair, twist it around my fingers and pull until I feel the strength of its roots, bite into the spot where the neck muscles are inserted behind her ears, twist her head around and invade her mouth, press hard up against her chest, dig my fingers into her vagina with only the tiniest bit of prudence, spreading open her legs while they struggle against me without conviction. But I am sitting in the seat of the one who submits, and any attempt to control the car from my position would be suicidal. I suddenly imagine the world of the girl in my position who has taken this wrong step. All she can do is beg in silence for an unlikely rescue.

Blue and red blinking lights and white lights flashing without any discernible pattern appear ahead. They disappear around every curve we take, and reappear again with greater intensity. Lili lifts her foot off the accelerator, and I remove my hand from between her legs. It takes us a while to understand that it's an ambulance ahead of us, driving in the same direction, and that it won't be long before we catch up to it. Relative to the speed we've been traveling, the present pace now seems tedious; considering our state and my confused arousal, each revolution of the car's tires and of those in front of us eats into my composure a little bit. We drive around curves and up steep inclines, but there are no straight stretches where we can overtake the ambulance. The brightness of its lights looks ridiculous at the speed it's going, and their stochastic flashing perturbs the continuity of my thoughts. I should either stop looking or jump out of the car. Lili seems relaxed, but I have no idea what her silence means. I lower my window, light a cigarette, and distract myself for a while trying to make out shapes in the dark and hilly landscape.

Some time has passed before Lili finally shows some reaction. She leans back in her seat and asks for a light, then agilely takes a cigarette out of the pack and places it between her lips. The ambulance seems to have begun a process of infinitesimal deceleration that increases the silence between us. The landscape is now flat, and the road is straight and open through the lifeless fields. I think I hear the croaking of frogs over the sound of the tires on the rough road, a sound that becomes more and more distinct and atomized as our speed diminishes. Lili takes a drag on the cigarette and blows the smoke out slowly. She could easily overtake the ambulance now, but the flashing lights remain in front of us. Maybe she's being patient. Or maybe it supports a conspiracy theory—a plan to keep me at her mercy, or at the mercy of whoever is in charge. An express kidnapping: empty my bank account at an ATM or charge up my credit cards, or extortion based on a ridiculously optimistic evaluation of the affection my affluent father has for his thirty-year-old failure of a son.

The ambulance finally stops. We pull over, too. I'd like to ask Lili why we don't continue on our way, what she's waiting for, but I am terribly confused, feeling the uncomfortable symptoms of anticipated abstinence and drowning in embarrassment from awareness of my own voice. The ambulance turns left, onto a path not visible in the darkness. I see it bouncing around, enveloped in a cloud of dust that softens the unbearable flashing of the lights. Its distance from us increases. Lili smokes her cigarette until the filter is burning, and then there is nothing left to do. We kiss.

When I am once again able to watch us from a distance, I see myself cupping my right hand over one of her breasts, which I find a bit small but firm and with a well-proportioned and upturned nipple, enormously attractive. I am eager to free my effortlessly established erection from its confines, but before that I caress her breasts and reach up to her neck, which stretches out for me to kiss. Under my fingertips I feel her muscles, hard as tendons, and the rough surface of her windpipe. For a moment I have it under my thumb and horrific images rush through my mind—I imagine myself tightening my grip, as if feasibility were the only criterion for choosing a path. I briefly pull away from Lili and see her half-open mouth, her chin, and her neck. *It might be madness, but today I would do it*, said the poet. But true madness is never named. Her nipples are still erect, and her chest swells and retreats noticeably. Suddenly I am sure I will kill Juanma when we get back. How the hell could he have gone through with it?

We kiss again and I place my hand between her legs. Lili moves and bends over a little as she drops her arm from around my neck. I manage to unbutton her jeans and burrow under her panties. Her movements fill me with impatience, her hands are touching something but not my body, and my erection, which has become uncomfortable, wants to be held. I am thinking about guiding her there when her touch startles me. I look down without thinking, and everything contracts. In her hand is a gun, resting on the bulge of my cock inside my jeans. She smiles at me with damp, swollen lips, and her ratlike eyes switch back and forth, looking into one of my pupils, then the other, as if she needed to reassure herself again and again that she has garnered my full attention.

"That's as far as we go," she says delicately.

My right hand is inside her jeans, my arm immobilized by hers, which is crossed over it and holding the gun between my legs. I want to pull away immediately, but I'm terrified the gun will go off. Lili smiles and kisses me, pressing the metal against me and looking for my tongue with hers.

"Put your seat belt on," she suggests, and pulls the gun away.

*   *   *

Lili stashes the weapon somewhere on her left and starts up the Mercedes, accelerating impatiently. She shifts it into fifth and grabs my knee, then runs her hand along my jeans, going up my thigh till she reaches my crotch. I am anything but aroused. I look at her. I can see only her profile, focused on the road, but I think she's more focused on concealing her pleasure.

I see some red flashes in the distance, beyond Lili. I recognize the blinking lights, and can also perceive some white spotlights sweeping over the black fields. The distance between them and us seems enormous, and it takes me a while to understand that the strange texture of the terrain bordering the fields is actually the surface of the lake we were driving along earlier. He left her by the lake, I realize. Not along the road. I turn to look at Lili's face. I am imagining her as M.N.—imagining how her face and the bit of her body I explored would look after eleven days in the mud.

"What exactly is your friend's problem?" she tosses out abruptly, and with disdain, in a new voice, strong and clear. "Juanma," she adds, without taking her eyes off the road. If she's seen what I've just seen, she doesn't acknowledge it. I hear something damp in her diction, water in her mouth. Shamelessly, she delights in my surprise. "You might not realize it, but secrets like that spread quickly. Weren't you ever with an ex-girlfriend of his, or something like that? Most women realize it when they meet that type of guy. When Gordo started to tell me about this business… He's got a little one, I told him, or he's got a really bad problem with it, and that's how the discussion began. Because the way I see it, it's like this: if the guy's got that kind of problem, if out of frustration or pent-up hatred at not being able to get a chick to moan and scream he'd be capable of killing a girl when he *does* manage to fuck one, shooting him right there would almost be like solving his problem. Gordo says I don't understand anything. That for you guys there'd be nothing worse. But I want him to suffer for the rest of his life, and this way, there's always the risk that he'd learn to live with it. People can get used to anything. I don't know if I'm making myself clear. I don't have any doubts, but I'd like your opinion. If we do nothing, we know more or less how things will turn out. In principle, there's no reason for him to get caught, so the most likely thing is that he'll get off scot-free. By the time they find the body, too many days will have passed, and even if they look, they won't find any DNA in her, because it's obvious he didn't rape her. He was mean and desperate, right? And at a certain point the chick regretted coming with him. She felt uneasy, a woman somehow catches on, like I said, and she said no. And the sonofabitch, who'd already turned down a dirt road to get his rocks off with a quick screw, he sees how this slut wants to get away from him and then he gets really rough and wired. He starts to use force, squeeze her, and the poor girl can barely move inside the car, can't even kick him in the balls and that sonofabitch realizes how he can make her scream, and he doesn't stop. But there's no proof, just somebody who saw them together, that's all. And around here nobody's going to go around in the middle of the summer questioning these beautiful people. Not to mention all their connections, the family lawyers, the family friends and *their* lawyers, and the favors they're owed from judges and DAs... What might happen? Worst-case scenario: Central Prison for a little while until the judge makes a decision. And the judge can also be talked to. You know what Central Prison is like, don't you? A room downtown with Internet, cable TV, soccer, and pizza delivery. If you've got the money to pay for it, of course. One or two months, tops. And if things get very complicated, because it turns out the girl has some relative who's got some influence somewhere, they move him somewhere else. A prison somewhere out in the country, and a few months later, he's got weekend leave. Where does he go? Out dancing, and to pick up some other chick. A couple of years later, three at the most, he's back home. Like he's taken a long trip. By then, very few people will even remember the case, if the press doesn't get hold of it, but they won't mess with anybody from these parts, anyway. And for those who know her, it'll just be another flagrant failure of the political and judicial system. And there, that's where, you understand, that's where I want him to keep suffering. At least this way he'll be embarrassed even with a prison whore, even if she doesn't tell him so and lets out little moans of pleasure. He'll know. I want him to know nothing but shame and guilt to the end of his days. And fear. He should suffer, and he should shake in his boots every day, waiting for something else to strike when and where he least expects it. Maybe his sister will get into a terrible accident. Or his father, who did all the cover-up, gets a couple of bullets in each leg and one in the chest as he's leaving his club. All for a measly five thousand pesos. His mother... the poor old thing. Even though she does go to Mass every Sunday afternoon and helps her servants' families here and there... But you see how things are. There's no time for new ideas. Even thinking about it makes us anxious, and nobody has time to think about anything anyway. What would you do?"

We get back to the house. When we get out of the car, I let Lili go in ahead of me, and as I walk in behind her I work out a plan. Inside, raucous music is blasting, and in the kitchen and the main bathroom and next to the pool I see small groups of girls engaged in conversations that seem lively only from a distance. They drink, smoke anything they're offered, and shout and laugh out loud for no particular reason. I could list all their family names, their connections, the favors they've exchanged. The same old same old, and I wonder how long it would take them to exonerate the killer through a writ of indulgence if I suddenly told them about the swollen corpse Juanma dragged to the lake. Nobody here is judged for what he does, and never has been. The chalice of blood holds everybody united; they would all eat the brains of their dead if they were lost in the mountains and Daddy delayed a couple of weeks more than they expected before going to look for them. Only Bet, Dardo's beautiful sister, confuses me. She's smiling right now, and when I look at her I see that her eyes, secretly, and only her eyes, are calling to me.

I keep walking around looking for Dardo, smelling Gordo, the fat man who came in with Lili. Taking a measure of the tension in each room. I see weapons where before there was only arrogance, a thick fog of frivolity. I reach the very edge of the pool and look at the trembling bottom, afraid to find the naked corpse of M.N. with the greenish-blue bruises made by Juanma's hands. And there she is, half smiling with closed eyes.

All the male voices come from around the barbecue pit. This time he did it; that's what I'm going to say to Dardo. That he was just waiting for the sun and the lake fauna to erase all the evidence. That they've just found her. And that Gordo, and this girl: what do they smell of?

But, still, I have to stop to watch a truly grotesque pantomime. Dardo laughing and standing over Gordo, who is sitting at the poker table, a pile of chips and a few bills rolled into thin tubes in front of him. Juanma, who's also playing, shows signs of exaggerated disbelief at the hand of hearts laid out by the fat man, while Super and Fantastic, each wearing a gold cross around his neck with his shirt unbuttoned, impotently hold the losing hands Gordo has dealt out to them, shaking their paraffin-treated blond locks and looking thoroughly confused. Lili is already there, smoking, about five feet behind Dardo and Gordo. She looks at me and smiles.

"Okay, boys," Gordo says, clearing his throat and collecting his chips. "If you'll excuse me, I'm going to go change these."

"You're a champ, Gordo, but I'm going to kick your ass," Juanma says, nervously moving a family good-luck charm, completely wasted on him, from one hand to the other. "Someday soon."

Gordo, the sweat shining on his forehead as he gathers up his winnings, looks him straight in the eyes and makes a face. I look at Lili, at Dardo, and again at Juanma. The small crowd around the table starts to break up, and the losers get on their feet. Juanma stands up but stays where he is.

"Time to go?" he asks.

I look at Gordo, who finishes what he was doing before looking up at him, lifting his eyebrows. He grunts, in apathetic agreement.

Lili walks over to me, again with her false niceness, again playing her menacing game of seduction. While I was watching Gordo, I lost Dardo.

"Don't get in the way, darling," she whispers, her watery mouth pressed against me. "You see how they are. When things heat up, they simply snort more. That's just what they do."

I don't even look at her.

"I'd give you my number, but right now I need my space," she adds awkwardly.

I need a car. I retrace my steps and go back inside the house to look for Dardo. The same girls are there, as well as some others who look like they've just arrived from another party. The poker club unscrews liquor bottles and flips the caps off beer. Not a trace of my friend. I know I have very little time. One bathroom is occupied; so is the other. But no Dardo. I go upstairs and look into all the bedrooms, the game room, the three master bedrooms, finding less sex and more drugs than I would have guessed. Suddenly, I have a foreboding. I rush to one of the empty bedrooms facing the front and step out onto a terrace in shadows. I see Lili on the street, and Juanma and Gordo talking as they walk through the garden. A few feet behind—or maybe I'm delirious after this night—comes Dardo.

I fly down the stairs, pursued by the insults spewed at me by a girl whose chest I've just splashed with her own beer. My savior's name is Bet, Bet, Bet, Bet. Shit. Why are there so many people here? Excuse me. Sorry. Same to you, bitch. There she is.

"Bet. Bet. I need the keys to the Peugeot. Let me borrow the car. Please. Now."

I'm about to spill out the whole story just so she'll give me the keys. But no. All I can say is, they found her. No… I give her two whole seconds and she doesn't answer.

"Bet. It's for your brother."

Three seconds.

"Thank you."

The Mercedes is speeding away as I leave the house. I run as fast as I can, watching it go. No trace of Dardo. How could he have gotten into that car? The idiot will try to defend Juanma, or maybe he'll join in and end up complicating even further his family's hard-earned well-being.

I get in the Peugeot and drive through the resort town, looking for car lights down the darkened streets. I race past ten, twenty intersections until finally I see them, about two hundred yards into the field. I turn off my headlights and continue down a gravel road that I can just barely make out. I creep up on the Mercedes, which is driving slowly away from the coast.

The headlight of a scooter suddenly appears in front of me. It shudders as it drives over the rough road. I take my foot off the gas pedal. The headlight crosses the path of the Mercedes and raises a little dust, which disperses in the lights. I stop.

By the time I get out, two helmeted figures are violently pulling Juanma out of the backseat of the car. I try to approach without anybody noticing, aided by the darkness. There are shouts and the noise of a struggle, Gordo appears through the door on the passenger side and, without much convic-tion, yells for them to let him go. Juanma falls and one of the macrocephalics aims at his groin and shoots. His cry is heartrending. I'm about fifteen yards away, paralyzed, trying to think of what I should do without being able to think. Juanma lets out a desperate shriek, and then the flash of a gun out the back window of the Mercedes and the clipped sharp retort of a gunshot a millisecond later surprises everybody. One of the helmeted figures falls, and then there's a shout and seven or eight more shots like the last one. The second one falls. His helmet hits the ground and rolls. Juanma's shouts stop. The gunshots keep reverberating through the field, or so it seems. The shrieks of four or five lapwings break open the night as they take flight.

Gordo sticks his head back into the Mercedes. I hear his voice, now clear and strong.

"What the fuck have you done, you sonofabitch?" he yells. "Get out!"

The car churns up the dust and roars off into the distance. In the dark-ness of dawn, the lighter dirt of the road shimmers gently.

I carefully approach the dead. I stare at them. I'm shaking.

"Let's go," Dardo says, suddenly standing next to me, his hands empty, exhausted. We return to the Peugeot in silence. The lapwings keep shrieking in the dark western sky, the light of dawn already appearing over the sea. The wind has died down and I'm freezing.

"Have you gone crazy?" I ask. "Nobody's going to believe you."

"He deserved it," Dardo says. "So did I."

I see that my hands are trembling on the wheel.

"Just drive straight and we'll get to the road," he tells me when I'm about to turn.

I turn off my blinker and move forward slowly. We drive past the bodies, hugging the edge of the road. I look out the corner of my eye. Dardo doesn't seem to see them.

"And those other two?" I ask.

"Addicts. Crackheads, maybe. Gordo found them."

"How much did you pay them?"

"Two grand."

JEALOUSY

by BERNARDO CARVALHO

Translated by Alison Entrekin

Remember, if I'm talking, it's because you're not going to survive. I'm not crazy enough to leave a witness alive. That is to say, the more I talk, the more I'll compromise myself—and the smaller your chances will be. Every story is a countdown. You get what I'm saying, don't you? No one's ever going to know I was here. It wouldn't look good. I'm not in a position to allow that. I could leave right now, in fact—all you have to do is open your mouth, interrupt me, say something. But seeing as, from the look of things, you're not going to talk at all, I'm not going to have the chance. Could any meeting be more ridiculous than this? After all, why else would you make me come out here, if not to reveal something to me? Or are you going to say you didn't make me come out here? Fine, don't answer, but there's nothing to stop me asking, is there? Of course, for each new question that goes unanswered, your chances of survival get a bit smaller. What did you want? Did you actually think we didn't know he'd left here with a message? A secret message—in code, at that! Isn't it a laugh? Of course we knew. And you knew we were after him too, didn't you? Otherwise, why would you have decided to use him as a messenger? You wanted me to come here to ask you personally, is that it? You made me leave home to come out here and ask. Of course I was perplexed—if you decided to use him as a messenger, it must be serious. Isn't it serious? You've been pissed ever since they transferred you here, haven't you? And now you're even more pissed because they cut your cell-phone signal, am I right? What did you expect? Did you think you were going to have a signal here? You had no idea? Or did you think that the transfer would never happen, that he would prevent it? Now, what do you think would make a man like him defend a man like you? The basic principles of Law? That every man, no matter how vile, even the number-one representative of the scum of the earth, has the right to his defense? Is that it? Okay. But why would a lawyer like him stoop to working as a messenger boy for the scum of the earth? Of course, you'd probably tell me that he doesn't defend just anyone, that he isn't a messenger boy to just anyone. You think you're special, don't you? You must. As the number-one representative of the scum of the earth, you can't not be special, can you? You can't be just anyone, a normal guy, like everyone else. Nor can he. He's special, too. But did you know we knew each other before we went to law school? Yep, me and him. Teenagers. We were very close. You know how it is. Are you going to tell me you never did anything with a neighbor or a kid from school when you were in your teens? Of course it doesn't mean anything. Kids. My thing, for example, is women. I'm married with children. And I'm not here to compromise myself. You understand, don't you? Didn't I say that if I kept talking, you wouldn't get out of here alive? You heard me. Are you surprised? You had no idea? Of course you did. You had a background check run on me and him, I heard. You know I studied law; you know I was a public prosecutor before I became the secretary of public safety. But I bet you didn't know he was a shit stirrer at college. He used to interrupt classes to explain to the lecturers that justice has nothing to do with the truth. Deep down, it was all for my benefit, of course. Yep, it started back then. He enrolled in all the same courses I did. Justice has nothing to do with the truth. Isn't that what you think? You disagree? Do you think he decided to defend you because you're like-minded? Because he believes the same things you do? Do you think he decided to defend you the day he heard you talking about Kierkegaard and the need to believe in the unbelievable? Or was it when he heard you reciting Dante on YouTube? Isn't *Inferno* your bible? Isn't that what you've been blabbing to everyone, when you spout off about the unfairness of the correctional system? Isn't this your official photo, posing with Dante's *Inferno* on the nightstand in your cell? Dickhead. Do you mean to tell me you didn't know he was being followed? That we've been tailing him for a year, and that we followed him from here to the hotel, and from the hotel to the bus station the next day, and from the bus station to the airport? Did you really think we didn't know he'd left here with a message? And that the message, in a code that not even he could reveal, had to be delivered personally, and only after he'd lost the people who were tailing him? Are you going to tell me now that you didn't give him a message in code, which he'd have to pass on to your subordinates in person? Do you mean to say you didn't know I had a whole team working day and night to decipher your codes? But why did you decide to use him as a messenger, then, if not to get my attention? And why did you make me come out here, if not to reveal something to me? Of course it's hard for me to believe. How could he stoop to this? And, at the end of the day, what message is it that only he can carry? What? Of course I'm concerned. What's it going to be this time? What is it that only he can pass on, in code, without the faintest idea of what it's all about? Do you want to spread panic again? To paralyze the city? Don't tell me you're going to have an enemy faction's leader killed! No! You'd spark a new crime war! Or are you orchestrating another wave of kidnappings and massacres? Or something completely new? A surprise? Because so far everything's quiet and it's been three days since we lost track of him. Yep, we lost him. Do you think I'd be here if we'd brought him in? Now, tell me: do you think he took whatever it was you gave him to take, to buck himself up in the event that hesitation got the better of him? You too thought he might feel bad about being a messenger boy for the scum of the earth, didn't you? Smuggling unknown secret orders out of a maximum-security prison because the client—or does he already call you boss?—could no longer give them himself, by phone, because his cell-phone signal had been blocked. Did you think he might feel humiliated? You're a sensitive guy. Would you rather I called you a criminal genius? Do you think he chose to use public transport, instead of taking a taxi, to avoid a possible kidnapping? Do you think so, or do you know so? Weren't those your instructions? Isn't that odd, then? If those weren't your instructions, I'd say it's really quite peculiar, don't you think? And do you think that whatever you gave him to take to ward off a heavy conscience, humiliation, and fear might have something to do with the fact that he took the bus in the wrong direction, and instead of going straight to the airport, wound up in a neighborhood controlled by enemy factions? Don't you think it's strange? Up until then, we were tailing him. Look: I'm not insinuating anything. Do you think he made a mistake? Don't you think it's funny to follow someone who doesn't even know where he's going? A guy who wanders a city aimlessly? Or do you think it was deliberate? Otherwise, how do you explain the fact that he didn't take the bus back in the opposite direction as soon as he realized his mistake, instead choosing to ramble about an enemy neighborhood, putting his own safety at risk? The only explanation is that it was to confuse and disorient us, because he knew he was being followed, right? Or do you think he might be betraying your organization? Because if he isn't, what did he go there for? Do you think he might be working as an enemy faction's attorney as well? Working for both sides at once? On the quiet, just doing some consulting? Two faces. Have you thought about it? Would you rather not? Are there two criminal geniuses in this city? Do you think the effect of whatever you gave him to take—to deflect a heavy conscience, humiliation, and fear—explains his waltzing around an enemy neighborhood like that? As if he'd gone out to get a beer at the corner bar or take a stroll through the square? But with a secret message, in code at that! What makes you so sure he wouldn't defend the leader of an enemy faction? Is it Kierkegaard and Dante? What do you think he saw in you? The greatest example of the contradictions of society and justice? What did he tell you when he offered to defend you? Didn't he tell you that at college he always used to take the opposing side? All it took was for me to agree with someone, for him to take me to task! Didn't he tell you that he's been trying to convince me of the opposite of everything I thought was right from the moment we met? Even when what I was saying was just a matter of common sense. Didn't he tell you that he'd donned the cap of defender of the indefensible? And is there anyone more indefensible than you? Except that that was long before he'd ever heard of you. And long before he'd heard you talking about Dante and Kierkegaard. Which reduces you to an illustration of what he already thought before he met you, you see? Dickhead. You came a posteriori. I was already there, a priori. What? Didn't he tell you that even as a teenager he couldn't accept the unfairness of the world, that as a student he was always engaged in different causes? He no doubt told you that court is a stage where what counts is rhetoric and acting, didn't he? And didn't he tell you that, ever since we got in to law school, his life has been nothing more than an attempt to convince me of that? Didn't he tell you that there are, proportionally, more criminals at large and living with impunity among the powerful than there are among the convicted and incarcerated in our overcrowded prisons? Now there's a maxim you could adopt and repeat ad nauseam yourself, even though you read Kierkegaard and Dante and have a more sophisticated repertoire at your fingertips, no? You can imagine how we found his behavior rather odd, crossing a neighborhood controlled by enemy factions so boldly, as if there was no one in the street, unafraid of taking a bullet. Whatever it was you gave him not only relieved him of a heavy conscience, humiliation, and fear; it also relieved him of the common sense that he always fought against, in the name of contradiction and paradox. To him, I represented common sense. Now, is there any greater paradox than the secretary of public safety chatting with a criminal genius in a maximum-security prison because of a coded message that has yet to arrive at its destination? The secretary of public safety, no less, trying to convince the criminal genius to change his mind and stop the message from arriving! What's the matter? Is there any greater contradiction? Didn't he tell you that he enrolled in criminal law because I had, just so he could convince me of his ideas or talk me out of mine? And don't you know that, as a criminal lawyer, he won every case on which I was prosecutor? Just to prove that justice has nothing to do with the truth. That justice is just theatrics, rhetoric, and acting. To think that, with all that idealism, he ended up a mere messenger of crime! Don't you think he should've thought twice before offering his services like that? Because now he can't just turn down an order, can he? Or do you think he did it of his own free will? Do you think he didn't even need to take whatever it was you gave him to overcome a heavy conscience, humiliation, and fear? I wonder too. Why would he stoop to something like this? Was it just for the sake of provocation? Or did the power of walking about with a message capable of destroying the world go to his head? Is there any power greater than what you gave him with this message? What? Do you think that's it? Do you think power is enough to bring a man like him down to the level of the scum of the earth? Do you think power is enough to turn a lawyer into a messenger boy for organized crime? Is that what you want to prove? Is that why you made me come out here? Is that what you want to tell me? Well, I'm going to give you my point of view. Do you know what makes a man like him do what he did? You don't? Well, I'll tell you. What makes a man like him do what he did is what you failed to foresee when you trusted him as your lawyer. It's love. Right? And love is volatile. Isn't it? We followed him. We saw how he walked into a bar in that neighborhood as if it were just a succession of doors and empty rooms. Ignoring everything around him, as if he were the boldest man in the world. We saw how he moved through the streets as if he were dancing between bullets in the middle of a shoot-out. It's love, all right, but not love for you. No. Or do you really think it was just whatever you gave him to take? Or might he be betraying you? Didn't it cross your mind when you sent him off? Or do you still think you can trust him? Do you think a man like him could have been educated to defend the scum of the earth without ulterior motives? I'm asking. We followed him. I could tell you a bunch of other things about him, but the more I say, the smaller your chances of survival will be. You understand that, don't you? The more I talk, the more I compromise myself. And I'm not in a position to compromise myself. You could interrupt me and tell me something, anything at all about the message. The best thing would be if you interrupted me once and for all. Do you think he's already delivered it? That these questions are redundant and useless? It's just that he gave us the slip three days ago and nothing's happened yet. Yep, he lost us, somewhere along the way, like Dante. I know what you're thinking. I was thinking the same thing—maybe he's smarter than the two of us together. Because we should've felt the effects of the message by now, shouldn't we? Something should've happened. And if it hasn't, it's because he hasn't delivered the message. What? As long as he doesn't deliver it, it still makes some sense for me to keep on asking, doesn't it? Is there still a chance I might convince you to talk? We could strike a deal, even. Look: suppose the message falls into enemy hands. Isn't it better that we abort this whole business now? You think it's a silly question? But you understood what I said at the beginning, didn't you? You understood that when I run out of questions, you'll no longer have a reason to be alive? Do you think you'll be able to spread chaos if you're dead? No one would be to blame if, by coincidence or misfortune, men from other factions within this same maximum-security prison managed to corrupt the guards and come pay you a visit tonight. No one's incorruptible. So far, it's just conjecture, of course. I'll repeat myself to give you a little more time: I can see it's hard for you to swallow that he'd do all this just to provoke me, right? It's normal. It's a blow to your self-esteem. But don't you think it's more than a coincidence that he only offered to defend you after I was named secretary of public safety? You don't see a connection? Do you think I'm exaggerating? That I'm a narcissist? That I always want to be the center of attention? Is that it? It's what the media says. And what else? Do you really believe that, to him, you embody the paradox of an unjust country and a second-rate legal system? Is that it? Do you think that, to him, you're Robin Hood? But would Robin Hood send a message of retaliation, to terrorize the population of a city, just because he didn't have cell-phone reception? Do you think Robin Hood was vindictive like that? Don't you think we're prepared for the worst? I thought twice about coming out here to make this proposal to you. But all you have to do is open your mouth and tell me what the message says. What do you say? What if we let you make another call on your cell phone, or two—besides the one you'll have to make to cancel the message, of course? One or two calls to resolve the organization's most pressing matters? Doesn't that sound good? We abort the message before it reaches its destination. And no one finds out that you had a change of heart halfway through, not least because the Dante-reading criminal genius wouldn't be so volatile and indecisive as to send a message and then change his mind, would he? Nobody would buy that kind of contradiction. And aren't there a bunch of scapegoats out there for you to take your pick from? Starting with him, your attorney, whom you've made into a messenger boy? Surely you could ask him for just one more favor. He could pretend that he betrayed you, isn't it perfect? Isn't every man a potential traitor? Especially when we're talking about love. Didn't you think it was his love for what you represent that led him to defend you, after all? Wasn't it his belief that justice has nothing to do with the truth—that it's just theatrics, rhetoric, and acting? Wasn't it to convince me of it that he made me lose every case, when I was a prosecutor? Hasn't he been pursuing and provoking and challenging me ever since the first time he saw me? If that isn't love, then what do you call it? I'm not insinuating anything, nor do I want to disappoint you, but do you see now that he only decided to defend you because of me? To install chaos during my term in office. What did you think it was? Did you really think he's capable of falling in love with what you represent? A man with his education? Have you noticed that I keep putting off my final question a little more? And repeating myself. To give you another chance to change your mind and tell me once and for all what the fucking message is! Do you think, if we hadn't lost him, I'd be here appealing to you, putting myself in this ridiculous position, asking questions that go unanswered? So you see the situation I'm in. The secretary of public safety, appealing to the criminal genius! You do get that this is an irreversible situation, don't you? You get that it's unsustainable, right? That if I've had to stoop this low myself, it's because either I leave here with an answer or you don't leave here alive. Sorry if I'm repeating myself. It's just that I thought the criminal genius was smarter. And to think that, even under the effect of whatever you gave him to take to ward off a heavy conscience, humiliation, and fear, even so, with his altered awareness, he still managed to give us the slip! Can you believe it? How's that for cunning? Do you really mean to say it never occurred to you that someone like that could just up and abandon you in this shithole of a maximum-security prison? That he could betray you by going and defending the leader of an enemy faction who'd become a better representative of the paradoxes and contradictions of the justice system? Surely the criminal genius knows that love is fickle? And if it isn't love, how do you explain his pursuing me all these years, just to confront and challenge me in public? What do you call that? Weren't you just the tiniest bit suspicious when he lost the appeal to stop you being transferred here, to a maximum-security prison without any cell-phone reception? Such a simple appeal. He, of all people, who has never lost a single case? Surely it crossed your mind! Never, at any point? Didn't it ever occur to you that he could have other interests besides your well-being? Interest in the well-being of others, say? And that you might be just an instrument in his hands? Didn't it ever occur to you that he might just be using you to get to me? And that if there's one spectator in the world for whom he stages this whole act of love, it's me? Don't you see that he does everything he can to undermine what I do and what I think? I wouldn't like to be in your shoes. Being a criminal genius must be a pain in the ass, right? You can't trust anyone, can you? And it must be even worse, because you're farsighted, aren't you? You see from miles away when you're going to be duped, when a collaborator is going to turn on you. It's like living surrounded by people who say they love you. And love is volatile. It must be hell. Take this whole business of a message, for example. Just because I blocked all cell-phone reception? My question is: couldn't you have waited a bit? Don't you know these measures never last long? Do I have to come out here to explain to you, the criminal genius, that I too am under pressure? Don't you know there's the media, political parties, public opinion? You sit around reading Kierkegaard and Dante, or you say you do, taking photos with Dante's *Inferno* on your nightstand, but you don't understand the basics? Don't you get that everything he does is to test me? Are you okay with that—being at the mercy of his whims? What does the message say, then? What're you up to now? Or are you following his advice? Am I going to have to open your eyes for you? Of course he does it for love. But love for *me*, love for what I represent, not for what you represent! Think about it. Why did he wait until now? Now that I'm secretary of public safety and have taken a drastic measure like blocking all cell-phone reception in maximum-security prisons? Why? Is there any other explanation? All he thinks about is me. Or hadn't you noticed? Do you think my ego knows no bounds? That all I do is talk about myself? It's what they say. Now, why kick up such a big stink over a blocked phone signal? As if you didn't know these measures have to be taken from time to time, and that they're temporary, until the dust settles! He smooth-talked you. But all he thinks about is me, don't you see? He has problems with authority. And do you know what else? Do you really want me to tell you? He only defends you to make me jealous. I bet you'd never thought of that. Haven't you ever doubted him? Not even after he was unable to stop you from being transferred here? I've never seen him lose an appeal before. I don't mean to insinuate anything, keep you awake at night, but I was surprised. Of course you were suspicious. At some point. Because if you weren't, you wouldn't be a criminal genius. But you still leave yourself wide open? You still trust him to deliver a secret message, in code? That's what I don't get. What? You didn't know he was wandering about, making easy pickings of himself in a neighborhood controlled by enemy factions? Or do you really believe it was just to give the police the slip? Truth be told, you have every reason to be suspicious. Say, hypothetically, that he has in fact fallen in love with what you represent. Then it's more than likely that he's fallen in love with what the leaders of other criminal factions represent too, don't you see? Or do you think you're the only one who represents the paradox of this country's justice system? I'd be suspicious too, if I were you. No one's irreplaceable. Because he should have delivered the message by now, shouldn't he? And if he had, we'd already be feeling the consequences, no? Isn't that what happened the other times? If you're not going to say anything, why make me come out here? Of course you wanted to tell me something when you decided to make him a lowly messenger. It's been three days since we lost him. And if nothing's happened so far, no panic, no massacre, no wave of kidnappings, no violent retaliation for the blocking of cell-phone reception in the maximum-security prison, it's quite possible, probable even, that he hasn't delivered the message, wouldn't you agree? In other words, to be more precise, it's quite possible that he's betrayed you. Have you ever thought about what could happen if the message wound up in the hands of an enemy faction? If they deciphered the code? And if they then claimed responsibility for the calamity, instead of you? It's your authority being tested, not mine. Unless... Unless the message isn't exactly what we think it is, right? Unless you really don't have anything to tell me, and have been bluffing from the start. Don't tell me you made me leave home for nothing. In that case the message, in a code not even he can read, of course, and which he went to great lengths to deliver according to your instructions, overcoming all manner of danger and obstacles, managing to throw off the men I'd put on his tail, weaving his way through enemy neighborhoods to disorient us, is of no conse- quence whatsoever, nothing. Is that it? Don't tell me you've made a laughingstock of me. Have you made him stoop even lower, for nothing, to deliver a message that's nothing more than a whim, perhaps a settling of accounts, an internal matter? Is that it? Don't tell me you used him to send your verdict to one of those clandestine tribunals, the kangaroo courts you lot run out in the ghettos! I wouldn't be surprised if you'd subjected him to the humiliation of delivering that kind of sentence, to seal the fate of some poor collaborator, some wretch who's fallen into disgrace, in one of those mock trials you folks conduct out there. I wouldn't be surprised! Just to further humiliate the attorney who was unable to stop you from being transferred here, is that it? Just to rub it in his face? But what for? After all, what the fuck is this message that has no effects or consequences? You know your time's running out. What? What's so funny? Don't tell me you... What? No. You've got to be kidding! Out of jealousy? You didn't make him unwittingly deliver his own death sentence to one of those tribunals, did you?

SO MUCH WATER
SO FAR FROM HOME

by **RODRIGO HASBÚN**

Translated by Carolina de Robertis

Julia falls asleep in the backseat of the van while Ro and Carmencita chat with the driver. Far-fetched as it sounds, he insists that Brad Pitt and his other woman, the one before Angelina, came to Chapare a few years ago, and so did Leonardo DiCaprio, the guy from *Titanic*, and that other girl—what was her name?—the one who once played a sexy killer. Sharon Stone? offers Carmencita, who has deep bags under her eyes that age her by at least a decade. Such a pretty woman, says Ro. Among the friends, she was the last to cross that odious border into fifty, and she still keeps herself in enviable shape. Smoking hot, says the driver. The women wonder if they should say something to Tula, it's not right for him to address customers in such a familiar way, as if he's known them all his life. She came alone, the driver goes on, that's how the filthy rich like to travel, they spread the word and come one by one and, well, what better place than Bolivia to stay under the radar? Besides, there's nothing like Chapare anywhere else in the world, he adds a little later, and they still aren't sure whether to believe him, as far as they know their friend's hotel isn't all that luxurious and, also, Tula has never said anything about celebrities. Actually, it's been rumored that she's gone from bad to worse since finding out about Jaimito and that local country girl, one of the hotel maids, whom he'd gotten pregnant not long before Tula found him out and threw him out of her life and the hotel. Speaking of which, you'll never guess what I just found out, Julia said to Ro the night before, by phone, going on to tell her that the Indian girl was still working there—it seemed Tula hadn't wanted to fire her. Oh, darling, look, it's not like it's all her fault, Ro said in an attempt to defend her. What are you talking about? Julia said. If not hers, then whose?

Looking out the window at foliage that grew more lush with each mile, Carmencita distracts herself by thinking about the burst of affection she felt that morning for Jonás, when she saw him curled up asleep on his side of the bed. He usually woke up first, it had been years since she'd last seen him this way. He looked at peace, but he wasn't and he never would be again. Since the boys' accident he'd grown too accustomed to sadness, to getting lost in his own thoughts. What would he do with himself this weekend? What would those hours alone be like? Jonás asks himself those same questions as soon as he wakes up. Although he's been looking forward to them, the coming three days suddenly seem impossible to face. I'm only at the beginning, he thinks, in bed, and already I'm having a hard time getting up, moving half a meter, getting anywhere at all. He's still half asleep, the scent of the sheets brings to mind Carmencita the previous night, legs open but covering her torso with a towel, ashamed of her sagging breasts, her stretched nipples, her belly, as if he'd never seen them before. They'd fucked for the first time in months, it seemed the upcoming trip with her friends had revitalized them. What would these days far from home be like for her, after so long? Last night I slept like the dead, Ro is telling her in the van. Why was that, ma'am? the driver asks. I was incredibly tired, in addition to packing I had to take care of a thousand things, Ro answers and she recalls the fight with Hans, which is what really exhausted her, he'd been so thoughtless, approaching her every few minutes with some excuse to fondle her. There wasn't much to pack, though, Carmencita says. Yes, these three days are going to fly by, says Ro. Because Chapare is so beautiful, the driver says, and then he starts telling them about a town priest who has just been caught stealing decorations from a church. Carmencita returns to her memory of Jonás curled up on the bed. He's the man their sons will never become, she'd thought as she looked at him, and now in the van she thinks it again, he's the man our sons won't ever be, because they've stayed still forever, arrested in time. After several minutes of uncertainty, Jonás manages to get up and urinate and brush his teeth, but it all takes immense effort. How long since I've been home alone? he thinks. Twelve years? Eighteen? Twenty? He tries to remember, and can't. Half an hour later, when he arrives at the store, his employees are standing beside the metal gate and three clients are waiting. Good morning, Mr. Jonás, his employees say, and he greets the clients, Good morning, gentlemen, please excuse the delay. In the backseat of the van, Julia stretches dramatically, because she's just waking up but also to draw attention to herself. She says that she was dreaming about their arrival and, although no one asks, she adds that in her dream the hotel had a kind of convention going on, hundreds of men who, on seeing them arrive, clapped and whistled. Oh, darling, the things you dream, Ro says, and she laughs nervously, at her friend's dream but also at the way the driver has been staring at her for a while now in the rearview mirror. You're lucky you can sleep like that, Carmencita says to Julia, I wish I could. It's the secret to everything, Julia responds, the key to youth, beauty, absolutely everything. It's the best drug there is, Ro adds, and the driver says that, in fact, Chapare has gotten overrun with blow, it's not for nothing that you see so many foreigners there. He goes on to suggest that this is the real reason the celebrities visit Bolivia. Like in the eighties, says Julia, there was no singer who didn't want to come back then. I heard they even got paid in cocaine.

Someone had once insinuated that her sons were on drugs when they had the accident, Carmencita recalls, and to counteract this slander, she pictures the boys exercising: playing soccer with their high school team, or in the backyard throwing a Frisbee their father had given them, or, toward the end, returning from the gym in their sleeveless T-shirts, their arms more sculpted every day. Although she never mentions the accident anymore, not a day goes by, rarely even an hour, in which she doesn't think of her sons. Roque was still a child then, and it's hard for her to include him in most memories. He could have been in the car but his brothers said they wouldn't be coming back home, that their grandmother would worry, that he should stop bugging them and get on the school bus instead. They would have taken the bus themselves if they hadn't gotten their grandmother to let them drive the car that day, their first day in her care. Roque started to tear up and that's when one of his brothers slapped him on the back and the other one told him not to be a faggot, or at least that's the way Roque later told it and the way Carmencita now recalls it, as though she'd seen it with her own eyes. But in that moment she was on a plane that had left Río de Janeiro hours before, on the second leg of their journey. Those were happy hours, full of excitement, the first time going to Europe for her and Jonás, although, looking back, she could only remember them as horrific. The truly horrific hours, the worst of her life, came after they found out, when they called home from a pay phone as they arrived in Madrid. Her husband couldn't stop shaking, the telephone still in his hand. Mr. Jonás, one of his employees says to him now, a client wants to know if I can give him a discount without a receipt. You know you can, he answers, laconic as always. He's a good client, the employee tells him. Jonás asks what he's buying, and because it's a large purchase, he tells the employee to give him 20 percent off. He usually spends his day in the store, but right now he's in the back office. It's nine thirty in the morning and he's already tired, he just wants to go back to bed and stay there all day, doing nothing. He's doing nothing now, even though his computer is on. It's as if he isn't where he is, as if he's turned into a ghost. It's as if I've turned into a ghost, Roque also thinks sometimes, on the other side of the world, in Barcelona, but for him it's an agreeable sensation. He's just woken from a siesta, and he's ready to get back to work. He's developing a new series on dead animals in a range of settings: a cow with its throat slit at the entrance of a mall, four decapitated chickens hanging from a traffic light, bloody rabbits in a bag that a beggar drags down a church aisle. He has ideas for at least ten more pieces and, sometimes, now for example, as he brews a cup of coffee before getting back to work, he begins to feel like a ghost, a ghost or a dead animal or just an orphan. He hasn't done too badly for a Bolivian artist. That is, a Bolivian artist from a well-off family, because without that he couldn't even have gotten a ticket to Barcelona or been able to study at Pompeu. The studies were an excuse to leave, he knew it and his parents knew it, and now it's been exactly two years and five months since they last spoke. Of his twenty-three years, he hasn't been back in four. He looks out the window. He lives on the tenth floor of a relatively new building, there's a swimming pool downstairs. He imagines it full of drowned dogs, he sips his coffee.

The sound of Carmencita's cell phone returns her to the van, to her friends, to the driver who stops talking so she can take her call. It takes her a few seconds to realize what's going on. It's Tula, and she wants to know if something's happened to delay them. Carmencita seems confused, and the driver helps out, telling her they'll be at the hotel in fifteen minutes at most. We'll be there in fifteen, Carmencita says. Please tell Juancho I need cigarettes, Tula says, have him buy three packs, and then she suddenly hangs up. Hello, Carmencita says, hi, hello, and Ro says it must be the signal. Yes, ma'am, it's the signal, the driver confirms. Tula wants you to bring her cigarettes, she tells him. He says that they'll be there any minute. Carmencita looks out the window at all the luxuriance. Be there any minute, she repeats in her mind, be there any minute.

Dirty bathroom, Julia thinks, and she can't decide whether or not to sit down on the toilet. In the end, she decides to wait. Better to check the mirror for anything caught in her teeth, smooth her hair, and since she's here and can't help it, turn and examine her legs for a few seconds. She tells herself that the cellulite is almost unnoticeable, though yet again she feels a jab of rage when she recalls Rodolfo a few weeks ago, informing her of the new treatments at the German clinic. Last night she'd waited for hours for him to come home from his meeting with the bankers from who knows where (she channel-surfed like an idiot, packing and unpacking, not knowing who else to call) and when he finally arrived, at around four, he went directly to the guest room, supposedly to not wake her. But I'm not going to think about Rodolfo, Julia thinks, that will be my revenge, I won't spend another split second of this trip thinking of him.

In her room, Ro takes a shower more slowly than she thought she would and puts on a little black dress, the one that's most becoming to her figure. Delicious heat, she thinks as she heads to the dining room to meet her friends, delicious, delicious, delicious, but what's giving her even more joy is being far from Hans and his urges, and her daughter and her confusions, and the obligations of the house, which are not easy to fulfill these days, considering how uppity the servants have become. Julia and Tula are already at the table, gossiping about someone or other, but there's no one else in the dining room and Ro wonders if the other guests are sleeping or if, in fact, there are no other guests, or what. As soon as she sits down, a young Indian girl, sixteen or so, appears and asks whether the lady would like some coffee. Yes, Ro says, and she smiles, what a pretty young thing, she can't deny it. Darling, you've got to catch us up on your life, she says to Tula. The hotel is amazing, Julia says. Yes, Ro affirms, although she's starting to realize that things are going as badly as the rumors suggested. The girl brings her coffee and asks what else she'd like: there are *cuñapés*, *empanadas*, *masaco*, and fruit juice. Ro looks at the table and sees nothing on it. What about you? she asks her friends. We were waiting for you and Carmencita, Tula says, but if you want to start ordering, go ahead. No, I'll wait too, she says, although she's ravenous, those four hours in the van were no joke. Very well, ma'am, says the girl, heading back to the kitchen, and only then does Ro wonder whether she might be the one Jaimito was involved with, but it can't be, she's almost a child and, also, she has no belly. She looks at Julia and Julia returns the look and it seems that this girl is the one after all, her friend is making that face of displeasure Ro knows so well. You have no idea how much I've been looking forward to this, how many times I've imagined you here, says Tula. We were desperate to come, says Ro. It's just that there's nothing else to do here, says Tula, especially when there's a blackout, you start to imagine things, to think nonstop. That never does a person any good, says Julia. You're too much, Ro says, laughing, and Julia insists that she's serious, that it's not good to think too much, that's why she's always doing something. Then she complains about Carmencita, wondering aloud why she hasn't arrived. Maybe we should start ordering, says Ro. Tula claps twice and the girl appears again and this time Ro and Julia study her more carefully, her body, her hips, her breasts, she's very thin, maybe they're wrong about her. Bring us a little of everything, Teo, says Tula, so these ladies can experience a real breakfast. A few seconds after the girl leaves, Tula confirms that she's the one Jaime took advantage of. No one knows what to say and Tula lights a cigarette and Ro sips her coffee and Julia watches Carmencita approaching from the other side of the pool, she walks very slowly, poor thing, like an old woman. That's awful, Ro finally says. There's no point in being bitter, says Tula, I've mostly forgotten about it. For the best, Julia says, and then she asks if there's a bathroom nearby, because now she really can't hold it anymore. She gets up and says something to Carmencita and starts to walk, feeling that her friends are judging her cellulite, that they're celebrating her disgrace, but the truth is they're not even looking at her.

Two hours later, the four friends lie in the sun and the hotel sound system plays a stream of romantic songs, most of them hits that were popular long ago. A little like us, thinks Ro, covered in sweat, though she doesn't mind it because soon she'll go for a swim. Julia and I ruled in high school, she thinks. Her more than me, really, but she was a bit over the top, wasn't she? For years everyone thought of them as sisters, cousins at least, they passed as such sometimes, both of them on the thin side, tall by their city's standards, quick to laugh, intelligent. What more could you ask for? It's no wonder we were so sought after, she thinks, and she remembers, as she often does, when they were thirteen or fourteen, before either of them had kissed anyone, the way they sometimes practiced. My God, she blushes as she remembers how exciting those kisses were, we practiced with tongue and everything. How many men has Julia been with? Ro wonders, keen to think about something else. Fifteen, maybe twenty? After all that acting like a saint back in the day. And me with just my four, she thinks, taking stock: Pancho, who was good-looking but left after high school to study in Argentina (they only did it three times); Lucas, who was not the sharpest tack in the box but who took her to the finest restaurants in the city (they only did it once); Alvarito, the one she'd liked the most, no doubt about that, maybe he's the one she should have married (she doesn't want to think about how many times they did it, but definitely more than twenty); and Roberto, who was almost a consolation prize and with whom she shared fifteen useless years (in which they rarely did it), until they finally had the courage to divorce. Well, and Hans, Ro remembers, I forgot about Hans, and with how much energy he has, he wants it all the time. Five, then, she concludes, five in fifty years. Next to her, for a while now, Julia has been tapping the keys of her cell phone. Is there a signal here? she asks Tula, who is smoking at the edge of the pool. It's intermittent, Tula answers. Do you need to make a call? Maybe later, says Julia, and Ro asks who she needs to talk to. I forgot to ask Rodolfo to do something, Julia says. Oh, darling, Ro says, we just got here and you're already thinking about Rodolfo.

About thirty meters away, the driver is mowing the lawn. Juancho, Tula shouts, but he seems unable to hear her over the machine. Juancho! Tula shouts again, in vain. That piece of shit always pretends to be deaf, she complains, and before any of them can say a thing, about, for example, his overly familiar behavior on the way over, she asks Carmencita if everything is okay. It looks like she's sleeping, says Ro, and Julia remarks that she too feels like sleeping, that last night she barely slept a wink, but that dozing in the sun is bad for your skin. Carmencita hears them but doesn't want to say anything. The trip has been hard on her, it's brought back certain memories. She can't stop them, every so often they appear in her mind: Jonás or the boys or even Roque, it's been so long since she's thought of him and now, today, he's back, maybe because soon it'll be ten years since the accident. And in his little apartment in Barcelona, Roque thinks something similar, that soon it'll be ten years. A couple of hours have passed and he's waiting for water to boil so he can make another cup of coffee and he looks at the sketch for his new painting and smiles at the sight: a giraffe's head and neck strapped to the roof of a car. He has three months left before his first solo exhibit—it's in a small gallery, but that doesn't matter, you have to start somewhere—and he's progressing better than he ever could have hoped. He also works as a bartender in a gay club a few nights a week. Now that things are so unstable and so many of his friends have lost their jobs, he takes refuge in his art. Perhaps that's why the paintings keep coming, Roque thinks as he turns off the burner and pours boiling water into the coffeemaker, and his mind turns to his brothers and to his father and mother, his hatred of them, and the way that the hatred has faltered a little today. Jonás, meanwhile, closes the store and starts to walk. Like his wife, he was never able to overcome his guilt, or his shame, or the combination of both, because it's obscene for children to die before their parents and for the parents to have done nothing to prevent it, to not even have been there. Normally he goes home for lunch, now that he's alone he'll look for a place to eat. I'll take a step and then another and another until I arrive, he thinks, seeing it as a great feat. It's a little after one o'clock and it's as if I've been awake one hundred hours, he also thinks, and he wonders what Carmencita is doing in that moment. She's continuing to pretend to sleep in the sun with her friends, thinking that without a doubt this trip is doing her some sort of harm, it's stirring up a sensitivity that she'd long considered dormant, she even cried this morning as soon as she walked into the room she was assigned.

Ro stands up and adjusts her bathing suit before heading to the pool, but on a sudden impulse, instead of entering the water, she pushes Tula in. What the hell is wrong with you, Tula cries out a few seconds later and Ro won't stop laughing. With all the commotion, Carmencita and Julia become alert, though they're still hazy about what's going on. Tula barely keeps herself afloat as she protests. What the hell is wrong with you? she says again. This makes Ro laugh harder, and soon she's joined by Julia and Carmencita's laughter. At least help me get out, Tula says, and when Ro reaches out her hand, Tula pulls her into the pool and she falls in with a great crashing noise. Oh, darling, Ro says as she breaks the surface, and now the four of them are dying of laughter. It's as if they were in their early thirties again, that time when they all became friends. They were young mothers then, and happy wives or more or less happy wives. And no one had died yet, thinks Carmencita in the middle of her unexpected laughter. Now you, Julia says, wrestling with her. She lets herself go and they fall into the water together. How good it feels, they both think as their feet touch bottom.

I have to tell you something, Roque says to Jordi that night. They're already on their second bottle of wine and the pasta they're making smells incredible and Jordi turns serious and says, Don't scare me. It's something about my family, adds Roque, and he sees the relief on Jordi's face. That plaid shirt looks wonderful on him and he discovers, once again, that he's fallen hard for this guy, harder than any other time in his life. He fills their glasses and they toast, looking each other in the eyes, because otherwise it's seven years of bad sex, that is to say, hell itself, and Jordi says, You're making me nervous, tell me already.

They've been together eleven months. They met at a party and snorted who knows how much cocaine, and Jordi gave Roque a blow job on the street and it seemed to be a one-time deal, two or three times at most, which only proves that you never know. Jordi's a teller at a CaixaBank and knows little about art but supports Roque enormously and when he has to work at the bar, Jordi is almost always there, to the side, not out of jealousy but just to keep him company. An hour later, lying in bed, Roque tells Jordi it's not true that he's an only child or perhaps it is true but wasn't always, that he used to have two brothers. The room is dark, which helps him speak. He says that for years he was tormented by the idea that he could have saved them, that if he'd insisted on going with them they wouldn't have sped so much and the accident would have been avoided. I hated them that day, he says, because they didn't accept me as one of them, and then when my parents returned, they were so caught up in their grief that they didn't see me anymore, it was as if I had also disappeared. And then you left, Jordi dares to say. Yes, says Roque, as soon as I could, a few years later, and for them it must have been a relief, and when I disappeared in earnest, when I stopped returning their calls or emails, they accepted it without protest. In Bolivia no one wants a faggot son, he murmurs after a while. No one wants a faggot son anywhere, answers Jordi. He also has a secret: a friend of his father abused him when he was seven. But he shared this on the third or fourth date and they haven't mentioned it since. We deserve better memories, Roque thinks again and again, we deserve better families. A while later, nevertheless, he tells Jordi that he's going to call his parents, that he's not sure why he wants to but he does, that he needs to, that right now, after more than two years, he's going to do it.

I didn't want anyone else in the hotel this weekend, Tula says on the terrace, now truly sloshed, so we could have the place to ourselves and no one would bother us. Ro glances at Julia and sees, again, that telling face, full of skepticism. Carmencita, drunk for the first time in years, manages only to say that the mojitos Tula made are delicious. Wait until you try my daiquiris, Tula says, and to keep from losing her prior thread, adds that they're her clients' favorite, but that now she didn't want any of them around. She claps twice and the girl appears. It's as if she were just waiting for those claps to come out running. Is that all she does? Julia wonders. Wait and wait? Speaking of waiting, that thoughtless Rodolfo hasn't called her all day and she, out of pride, hasn't called him either. He must be with those bankers from who knows where or with his lovers or with his friends, the revenge of not thinking about him isn't working. What was her name again? Ro asks as soon as the girl leaves. We call her Teo, says Tula. Julia, for her part, would like to ask whether it's true that she's pregnant, but some topics are hard to broach, for example none of them has dared say a word about Jaimito. Time to work, says Tula, and she approaches the table where the girl is putting down fruit. How do country people live out here? Ro wonders. What are these coca growers' lives like without electricity? How do they manage in such precarious circumstances? She thinks about this for three seconds, just now registering the darkness of the surrounding land, and then she distracts herself by studying the girl, so delicate and angelic, maybe the pregnancy was creating that effect. Put some music on, Teo, Tula says. Yes, ma'am, answers the girl. It's as if the hotel were being run by the two of them and Juancho, who in addition to driving, also gardens and takes care of the grounds and repairs. Hans told me he's going out with Rodolfo, says Ro, and with Jonás if they can find him. He never answers the phone, says Carmencita. Rodolfo hasn't said anything to me, says Julia, and she can't wait any longer. I'm going to call him, she says.

She stammers a little and wonders whether her friends notice, then she steps away and begins to dial her husband's number. The lifeguard is asleep, careful you don't fall, Tula shouts, laughing, and Carmencita laughs too. At that moment the music finally starts. Thanks, Teo! Tula yells, she's almost got the daiquiris ready, the only thing left is to turn on the blender. A cumbia is playing, one that Ro likes, and she sings it to herself, looking across the distance at Julia, so beautiful in her white shorts and her light blue blouse. Tula hands her a daiquiri and another to Carmencita. Cheers, my friends, she says with a happiness they haven't seen in her all day, transformed by the alcohol and also, a little, perhaps, by a respite from her loneliness, even though earlier she told them you couldn't pay her to move back to the city. Louder, Teo, she shouts, and the volume goes up immediately, another cumbia starts, *no quiero saber nada más de ti, no tiene sentido, todo se acabó, el juego terminó, estamos perdidos*, and then she shouts for her to bring more ice. Julia returns extremely pissed off, Rodolfo won't even deign to answer her call. Oh, darling, Ro says to her, and strokes her hands. Tula says that men, if the ladies will pardon her language, are a bunch of fuckers, all of them without exception, and when the girl brings more ice Carmencita tells Tula that she should let the girl go to bed. Teo's a late sleeper, says Tula, she's not like Juancho, who's like a rooster. Isn't that right, Teo? she asks, and the girl nods, smiling for the first time. How could Jaimito have taken advantage of this girl, Ro wonders, how is it possible, how, and Julia would have been asking herself the same thing if she weren't so enraged at Rodolfo. Happiness, my friends, says the new, unrecognizable, drunk Tula, that's the slogan in this hotel. Happiness, for fuck's sake! And two drinks later she tells them out of the blue that Bolivia is being transformed, but not by people like us, we're a load of crap, we don't even care about our own asses. It's not our party, says Tula, and the truth is that no one really understands her, they're not even sure whether she's making an accusation or what. Solidarity and dedication aren't our thing, Tula continues. Just look at how many years it took you to come visit me.

An hour later they dance shamelessly, completely liberated. If you could see them from far away, let's say from the place where Juancho watches them as he lights a cigarette at the door of his room, they would look like four drunk teenage girls. If you saw them from slightly closer in, let's say from the place where Juancho watches them as he approaches to get a better look at the show, they would look like four wild women in their twenties. Up close, as he finally sees them, hidden a few meters from the terrace, they are four women in their fifties who've decided to spend a weekend together. None of them is thinking about anything anymore. They just dance, and sing with all their strength, and drink until none of them can think at all.

* * *

The next day Ro isn't sure whether it was a dream or what but the feeling is overwhelming and so many other things and she'll never mention it, not even in the police interrogations. In the dream or in reality she fell asleep in one of the folding chairs by the pool, absurdly drunk, as she'd been very few times in her life, and a while later she started to feel someone shaking her. She fell back asleep, thinking that the others must be asleep in the folding chairs around her, and a little later she started to feel someone stroke her legs. Hans, she murmured, I don't want to right now, and she heard a voice, the driver's voice, saying, I'll take you to your room, ma'am, if you stay here the mosquitoes will eat you alive. He carried her without difficulty, it was like flying, and then he was licking her down there, and it felt a little bit good but also it felt disgusting, and the next day, as soon as she opens her eyes, the first thing Ro feels is enormous confusion. The sheets are damp but that's not strange, it's so hot that they couldn't be otherwise. She's naked but that isn't odd either, she always sleeps that way. She touches herself down there and it's wet, although not wet enough to know with certainty what happened, at least not without more careful examination. Just the thought of it makes her panic and the only thing she can bring herself to do is take a shower. Later she'll convince herself that it was just a dream, that it couldn't be otherwise, and she'll be afraid to ask her friends what they remember about the end of the night, whether Juancho appeared at some point. And though she'd think about it many times throughout the years, she'd never mention the subject, not even during the interrogations.

Four hours of sleep were usually enough for Carmencita. At seven thirty she was already preparing herself a coffee in the hotel kitchen before heading out for her morning walk, if anything had given her relief over the years, it was precisely that. She'd spent too much of the previous day thinking about her sons and husband. The drinking had distracted her, lightened her. She felt even lighter as she walked by the edge of the highway. Only once in a while did a truck pass, bearing fruit, and she crossed paths with one or two foreigners, but in general it seemed like a deserted land. Jonás would never have imagined her this way, feeling all of a sudden a kind of magnanimity.

How had he been doing? Had Hans and Rodolfo succeeded in finding him in the end? They called the house several times, but Jonás didn't answer. Each second that passes, each minute, each hour, I feel them physically, he was thinking as he lay on the bed. If I concentrate, I hear time passing, the murmur of things that change surreptitiously, that transform, that stop being what they are to keep being what they are. My cells, my nails and hair, everything that's inside me moves and I can hear it, Jonás was thinking, and the house phone kept ringing, the sound of it one more part of the great orchestration. It rings and rings and no one answers, Roque says to Jordi, who says that maybe it's not their number anymore, or maybe they're not home. I called my mother's cell, Roque says, and Jordi strokes his face and says, It's late, we should go to sleep. I'm sorry, says Roque, I know all this is stupid. He also says that he won't call again, that there's no point in it, really, but an hour later he's on the phone again and two hours later he's on the phone again, and Jonás hears the flow of his blood, the beat of his heart, and hears also the ringing of the telephone, and he thinks what a pain in the neck his friends are, and in the end Roque gives up and takes his clothes off and lies down naked next to Jordi. Surrounded by the jungle, still walking, Carmencita tries to recall whether they ever came to Chapare as a family. She's trying to recover lost images, but instead others appear that she already knows well: a vacation in Santa Cruz, a visit to friends in Beni, a New Year in Iquique. There are photos of those visits, photos that often belie certain memories, with less blue skies and more washed-out colors, and Carmencita arrives at nothing, she can't remember whether or not her sons ever came to Chapare. It's almost ten, which means she's been walking for at least two hours, and she's all sweaty and decides to return, Tula has promised to take them to a national park full of marvelous rivers in which they can swim. So much water so far from home, thinks Carmencita, and she's thirsty and her headache is getting worse, but despite everything she's calm, the grandeur of nature easing her little miseries. They're little next to this, she tells herself, next to this they're almost too small to see.

Julia, meanwhile, wakes up very sad. She's the one for whom things have gone the best: she hasn't had to marry twice like Rocío, nor has she lost her children like Carmencita, nor has she turned into a drunk like Tula. So I don't have a reason to be very sad, she thinks in the wake of this encouraging list, I really don't, and she looks for her cell phone to see if Rodolfo has called and as she does she recalls that last night she got rid of it, in a fit of euphoria cheered on by her friends, she threw her phone on the ground and trampled it. Julia smiles incredulously, I'd better find it and stop being ridiculous and sad, she thinks, but the phone is nowhere to be found. A warm shower comforts her, this is how she eases the bad feelings. She soaps her body and washes and rinses her hair, and then she dries herself and applies lotion, and yes, little by little she starts to feel better.

Bring me coffee, Teo, shouts Tula from the edge of the pool, where she sits and smokes with her feet in the water. And because the girl doesn't respond, she says it again, loudly, Teo, bring me coffee! She likes hangovers almost as much as getting drunk. They make her feel suspended, a few seconds behind reality. You're here and not here, Tula thinks as she smokes at the edge of the pool, dipping her feet. Teo appears with a cup of coffee and leaves it near Tula. Would you like something for breakfast? the girl asks. *Masaco? Cuñapé?* Teo, Tula interrupts, do you like living here? The girl looks at her, taken aback, unsure of how to answer. I like it here, says Tula, I like it a lot. Yes, ma'am, says Teo and she stays still, watching water and ash mix in the cracks of tiles. She smells the scent of tobacco, sometimes she and Juancho filch Tula's cigarettes and smoke them at the door to their rooms. It's a strange moment, one of those moments in which the seconds lengthen, and she longs to run but she's forced to wait. Sometimes Juancho tells her that in the end the hotel will belong to them, that it's what they deserve considering how badly their boss Jaime treated her. That's the least of it, Juancho sometimes says, without us this thing wouldn't run. Just wait and see how we'll fix it up, he tells her, there'll even be a landing strip, so the filthy rich can fly right in on their planes. To hell with the van, we'll give them real luxury, and if they want blow, we'll give them blow, and if they want women, we'll give them women, and if the women need men,

men there'll be, we'll offer things to suit all tastes. And we'll take pictures of all the famous people before they leave, Juancho says, we'll see Brad Pitt and Angelina and that other one tanning themselves and having the time of their lives, that's what really draws new clientele. I have no idea what you're talking about, she says to him and says good-bye quickly, because she's bored or tired, but in her room she thinks about Juancho's words and also about all the things her boss Jaime made her do and about how she had to get rid of her baby, how horrible it was to see its little hands and feet, its body torn to pieces. Shall I bring you something to eat? she says now to Tula. Bring me more coffee, says Tula as she lights a new cigarette from the ember of the one before it, that's all I need to synchronize with reality, Teo, cigarettes and coffee. The girl leaves quickly and returns a few minutes later and leaves the second cup beside the first one, which is still untouched. Tell Juancho to go buy me three more packs, Tula says now. He's fixing the van's motor, the girl responds. Have him go anyway, Tula says, and you, start preparing breakfast for the ladies.

Three weeks later Tula will be found dead in the pool. The only two workers in the hotel will call the police and, because she was so inebriated at the time of death, it will be difficult to tell whether the drowning was accidental or malicious. Of course, the main suspects will be precisely those who reported the incident, Juan Carlos Meneses and Teodora Wilca, but as soon as arrest warrants are issued, the police will discover that the two have fled, either because they were guilty or because they weren't but knew they'd be accused of the crime if they stayed. Neither the investigation nor the interrogations will be of much use, and the police will never solve the case. As far as the hotel itself, no one will want to buy it from Jaimito, and over time, it will deteriorate into an unfathomable ruin in the middle of the jungle. Until their respective deaths (some gentler than others, some more painful than others, some lonelier than others), the friends will recall with gratitude that trip they took together to Chapare, in 2014. It was 2014, wasn't it? Or was it 2015? What they'll remember most will be the wild party the first night, although they'll also vividly recall the outing to the national park. The hangover made them sluggish and the only thing they did for hours was wade in the water, gossip about people they knew, doze intermittently. Back at the hotel, they dined on the terrace and that second night they stayed up late together, playing cards. The next day they returned to the city after lunch and the ride back was much quieter than the ride in, even the driver couldn't liven them up with his chatter (it was a dream, Ro thought dozens of times, it was just a dream). Although it seems incredible—oh, darling, it's so difficult to understand some things—all three of them missed their husbands.

Before they got into the van there were kisses and hugs and promises to return. There was also a photo that Tula insisted on taking. For posterity, she said, or to hang it up somewhere on the terrace, but it came out a little blurry. They took two more, and they came out the same. It wasn't that important, Tula said, you'll still be present. Now that you've been here, you'll always be here, she added as she watched them leave.

HORSES IN THE SMOKE

by **CAROL BENSIMON**

Translated by Clifford E. Landers

I have to come here to be with her. There's a mattress for a double bed thrown on the floor; from the window we can see the backs of the dirty buildings downtown, which are always dirtier than the fronts. We lean out that window a lot at night, drinking a mixture of cachaça and bergamot juice from camping mugs, a drink that for no apparent reason she's nicknamed Just a Latin American Lad, in reference to a 1976 Belchior song. Everybody in the building really likes 1976. Everybody likes the time before they were born.

That thing, the drink, Just a Latin American Lad, leaves viscous recollections on your tongue. I wake up thinking about her. She's redheaded, with hair that looks as if it's been shredded by a psychotic in the service of some cause of extreme complexity. A new design that will become a trend twenty-five years from now. Livia.

She's not interested in me the way I'm interested in her. Livia is like an abrupt descent whose end is pretty obvious from up above. I study architecture, I shook the hand of Oscar Niemeyer before he died, he was already over a hundred years old, he had even lent his signature to a line of sneakers. I don't know of any other internationally relevant guy who lived that long. I mean, people more than a hundred years old usually go down in history because living for more than a hundred years was all they did in life. They're surrounded by their children, grandchildren, great-grandchildren, sometimes their great-great-grandchildren, in small towns or villages in the middle of nowhere. *National Geographic* passes through at some point toward the end.

I'm talking about architecture because it says a lot about the impossibilities between Livia and me. I'm the guy who sometimes has to finish a maquette late at night, and I had to finish one *that* night, ten days ago. Looking back on it, I wouldn't have chosen to ruminate over a hypothetical housing project if I'd had the slightest suspicion that such an act, finishing the mock-up of a low-income housing development that would never be built, would come to seem senseless as soon as I became aware that other, more historically relevant things were going on at the same moment. And that's what happened: while I sat inside, two hundred soldiers of the Military Brigade were grabbing and dragging Livia and her friends out of the tents where they'd been sleeping for forty-seven nights.

I wasn't there. I can never be there. I think again about that scene and, every time it happens, it's one more time I'm not there.

Livia looks at me and doesn't say anything. When I'm in bed with her I feel calm, although I shouldn't. She leans on her side, her knees at a sharp angle, her hands clasped at her chin, which more or less lets her fit under the comforter on that cold June afternoon in Porto Alegre. Women feel the cold much more than men, which in no way kept Livia from sleeping forty-seven nights in a tent borrowed from a colleague who thought it better to stay home, Livia and the other guys and girls, though lots more guys than girls, all of them quite determined, righteous, and believing it was possible to reverse the absurd process of adding a lane to Avenida Edvaldo Pereira

Paiva, save the trees, and build a better city for us all.

She turns. She likes to admire the ceiling, which offers nothing beyond old details in plaster, fossils of a different downtown. I draw closer and purposely move the comforter a little, so that now I can see her shoulders, her breasts supported by the edge of the blanket, masterpieces more of design than of engineering, with two perfect observation points where the improbable curves end like in that church by Le Corbusier in Ronchamp. But something seems different. Some centimeters from her left breast I find a small scar. It resembles an arc, a waxing moon or a discarded nail clipping.

"Livia," I start by saying. Then I begin to have doubts about whether my tone of voice reveals a certain repulsion. "We still don't know each other very well, but I think I would have noticed that scar of yours." I laugh. "Did you *make* a scar?"

I've come off like I'm trying to play the funny guy I'm not, but Livia laughs in an almost childish way. "I had it done," she says, turning toward me again. "You know that tattoo artist on João Telles? The one who has an orange bicycle with handlebars like this?" She stirs in bed, simulating the handlebars, the type you hold with your arms spread wide. Apparently Livia is okay and we're okay and I shouldn't be so worried.

"You can't choose a scar in some goddamn catalog," I tell her.

Livia stares at me for a few seconds. It seems like she may be experiencing one of those very brief moments when we understand a million things. What earlier seemed a mystery is becoming as clear as treated water. Maybe it has to do with me, maybe not.

"How so?" she asks. "He doesn't have a catalog for that kind of thing." She tugs a little on the comforter, but the scar remains exposed. A part of me wants to embrace her, but another part wants to go on arguing. I tell her that by definition scars are random marks. The result of a fall, a blow, a distraction, the concrete part of stories that end badly, the unexpected both in time (when will it come?) and in form (the keloid brings with it possibilities of interpretation, similarities, a rabbit, a heart, a car, all the clouds there are), and therefore it doesn't seem logical, or rather, it seems *too* logical, to decide you want a scar—to decide what kind you want, and in what part of the body it suits best, when the "rule," after all, should be that of unsuitability.

Now Livia looks at the pinkish mark as if saying to herself that, between me and that small moon, she definitely needs to choose the moon. Then she looks back at me with rancor and says that part of what I said makes sense. She puts her finger over the new thing.

"But what if I had gone through that trauma," she says, "that fall, that blow, and it hadn't left any visible mark? Don't you think I have the right, the freedom, maybe the *duty*, to transform my pain into a definitive part of my body?"

At this point I don't know what to say. When women begin talking about the body, it's a clear sign that the conversation has taken a turn from the individual to the collective; feminism hovers in the air, repression, "being a woman," and you can't or shouldn't fight against it. Better to hope it passes. Livia gets up and, nude, leans on the window.

"Looks like the curfew worked," she says. "Have you ever seen—I mean, *heard* the city like this?" I answer no, I've never heard the city so quiet, and downtown the silence is no doubt greater than anywhere else. They're afraid the downtown will never be the same after tonight.

Which reminds me that I'm late. I get dressed quickly and grab my backpack, with the magic markers, the poster board, my red bandanna, the bottle of vinegar. In the corner where I left my things, I see the tent that Livia borrowed from her classmate. Livia was asleep when two hundred police arrived at four in the morning. She was dragged out by her hair. Some of the cops had blood in their eyes and 12-gauges in their hands. They called the girls sluts. The handcuff marks soon went away. I've made Livia promise that she'll stay inside tonight.

When I get to the street, I see that all the shops have their security shutters rolled down. The cars have disappeared, leaving me with the clear idea that the city would be better off without them. There's a vestige of very tenuous bluish light on the roofs of the old buildings. I make my way down the street as I button up my jean jacket, thinking that downtown is a fucking trap, that it'd be enough for the cops to decide to round us up, use some tricks, and we'd be surrounded on three sides by the waters of the Guaíba. I remember visiting my grandfather and listening to him talking about the flood of 1941. The war was far away from here, so the most palpable concern was with the water that in April started coming in under the door and then on all sides. Many people lost their homes. My grandfather went by canoe to the square across from the Public Market. It had never rained so hard in Porto Alegre and, according to experts, the combination of factors that led to the flood of 1941 should recur only once every 370 years. The year 2311 seems pretty far off even to me, but that didn't stop Thompson Flores, the sonofabitch mayor put in office by the military in the 1970s, from erecting a wall along part of the shoreline, creating a corridor devastated by intense traffic and tasteless graffiti. In urbanistic terms, a disaster, but it's still there.

I pass by the site of the Institute of Architects of Brazil. Verses by a popular poet decorate the boarding of an endless restoration. *I am part of those who believe the street is the principal part of the city.* That same building housed DOPS, the secret police, during one period of the military dictatorship, which means people were beaten and tortured where today we discuss urban mobility while no one listens to us or dares to change, exactly like in that time. I'm thinking about Livia, trying to get Livia straight in my head, when three guys more or less my age pass by on the opposite sidewalk. "In São Paulo it's gonna be a lot worse," one of them says to the others. All three have beards and they look at me, acknowledge me as an equal, and smile. I don't feel like smiling but I do, out of obligation, then continue on my way. Descending descending descending. Passing the barracks with nervous soldiers at the corners. Feeling that we can change the country today and then again on Thursday and then once again on Monday.

In the early morning, when the police invaded the encampment where Livia and the other idealists had slept for forty-seven nights, I was trimming a piece of poster board and very worried about the north facade of my low-income houses. But I lost concentration every time I thought about that trap, because the camp was nothing but a trap, a fiasco preordained from the very first night. There's no way to stop it when the asphalt tongue wants to come through, the contractor bankrolls political campaigns and you know what happens afterward. "Did you know that the engineering firm itself *offers* the municipal government the work project it's going to execute?" I told Livia and her friends at the encampment one night, and one of those guys who always carried a harmonica in his pocket looked at me with the smile of someone who unfortunately needed to speak sincerely with me.

"Then why are you doing architecture and *urban planning?*" he asked.

It does no good to say that the whole world is tearing down viaducts, that the car is the great villain of the decade; with luck, people here in Brazil will discover that fifty years from now. That morning, in any case, defeat seemed like something a day or two away, if the campers were going to respond peacefully to the repossession order, which gave them seventy-two hours starting that afternoon. Livia and the others would make the decision the next day, for now they were drinking wine and playing guitar: Bob Dylan, Belchior, and that song by Geraldo Vandré, "Don't Say I Didn't Speak of Flowers." So no one paid much attention when the Zapatista guy, at the foot of the campfire, started talking about defense tactics.

Someone there shouldn't have been there. The infiltrator, the P2 man, the traitor, informed the command that the people in the camp, kids of eighteen and twenty who no longer believe in political parties, along with some homeless people who had been taken into the group, were all drunk, high, weak, sleepy. It was time, therefore, to set the operation in motion. Three days later a guy known as Frank would tell me, banging his fist on the table in a bar, that practically the entire police operation had taken place outside the law. Frank is a government employee and knows what he's talking about. Trying to exercise discretion, after realizing that the blows on the table were drawing attention, he lowered his voice, moved closer to me, and began enumerating the things that constituted, in his words, the criminal posture of the public authority. 1) The repossession order should have been put into effect between eight in the morning and eight at night; 2) the Military Brigade had no reason to approach the protestors bearing firearms; 3) male soldiers were not supposed to search women; 4) it's illegal to cut down trees at five a.m.; 5) the suit that dealt with the felling of 114 trees along the Guaíba was, that very night, on the desk of an appeals judge, since the Public Ministry, though it had lost in the lower court, still had a period in which to appeal in favor of plant life and against road work.

But now nobody's going to replant the goddamn trees where they were.

When I get to the Praça da Alfândega, I can already hear the compact mass of drums, howls, and applause. I walk a bit farther and I'm in front of City Hall, passing through small openings in the crowd and being launched forward like a silver-plated pinball. I spend some time looking for familiar faces, but it's useless; I feel I'm leafing through an endless photo book of possible suspects for a crime that I have nothing to do with. I find a bit of breathing space, open my backpack, take out a piece of poster board and two magic markers. My poster is an immediate success with a short girl in dreadlocks and extravagantly printed clothes (I think it's spaceships on the jacket, which is made of some kind of waterproof material). "Cool phrase," she says. "Keep it," I answer. She's not sure I'm serious, so I smile to confirm the offer; she holds out both hands, grabs the poster, and leaves, joining a chant that's just beginning in the first rows. To my right, a young mixed-race kid wearing brass knuckles takes a picture of himself to post on the Internet. Then he disappears. I turn 360 degrees and get the impression that I've unwittingly fallen into the middle of a group of union activists. Their red flags flutter, and receive the immediate rejection of a good chunk of the protestors, who yell at the union men with great gusto, perhaps more gusto than when they yell against the plans for the World Cup or the rise in bus fares. *No parties! No parties! No parties!* An argument breaks out, and I decide to head for an area without so many idiots.

A camera is looking at me. It's attached to a lamppost and I'm probably the idiot standing closest to it. I suddenly remember what Frank told me. I feel a nasty worm crawling up my spine and think about the bandanna that I'm not using to cover my face, and about my crappy blue eyes, my pointed nose, and my World War I doughboy hair. Frank said, that night of the table-banging, that the cameras can do facial recognition. We don't even know if he's named Frank (probably not), but we believe everything he tells us. Frank had been caught on one of those cameras. The next day, he was called into his boss's office. Through the non-opening windows they could see the Guaíba down below, a sewage-filled parody of a tourist attraction.

"Did you participate in the protest yesterday?" "Yes, sir." "Why?" "Because I have certain ideals, sir." "What ideals are those, Frank? Do they have anything to do with breaking the windows of banks and motorcycle showrooms?" "I didn't do that, sir." "But you were there." "Yes." "If you were there, you agree with what they did."

At the end of the day, Frank received written notice that his transfer to São Luiz Gonzaga was being processed. There's only one thing that Frank detests more than right-wingers: shitty small towns six hours from the capital.

The crowd starts to move. At first it's confused and hesitant, recalling the behavior of some treacly liquid; Facebook democracy has made leaders irrelevant, so there's no one qualified to head the march. This worries me. How can we change the country if we can't even choose a direction, #comofas? The viscous liquid, devoid of all logic, flows toward Avenida Mauá. Everyone begins to follow the same rhythm. I'm walking for myself and those like me, very close to the cavalry that keeps pace alongside, their horses jostling us at times. I don't want to be crushed by a horse. I'm walking for my grandfather the traveling salesman and diabetic at eighteen. For my father who was in a file at DOPS, for my mother who had soft-rock LPs. And for Livia, the rosewood-and-forty-seven-nights girl.

The wind blows in from the Guaíba with the speed of a compact car. When we pass through a gate that leads to the docks, a single gust of cold air coming from the pampas, and before that from Patagonia and the South Pole, bends our handmade posters in half. Some fall to the ground and are trampled (the march can't stop). A kid blows a sweetish puff of marijuana into the muzzle of a horse. I see the girl in dreads again, but now her hands are free. Someone shouts that in Brasília a crowd has invaded the national Congress.

I don't want to be crushed by a horse that doesn't know what's going on.

Even so, I make a point of staying at the edge, in the space between the crowd and the forces of crowd suppression. I think about whether mounted police exist in other parts of the world and, in any case, whether it's advisable to use them for crowd control. It's fine if, in Canada, they want to send a guy and his horse to take care of a patch of forest and a waterfall—that seems like something civilized. Cavalry with swords in scabbards in the middle of a popular demonstration, on the other hand, signifies the triumph of barbarism. The underlined passage in a report on a third-world country. Could these guys be the same ones who, the night of the encampment invasion, were deployed to block the escape routes? I wasn't there, but the fact that I wasn't has made me want to know every detail about what happened. Now I've absorbed the sum of what is known by Livia, the Zapatista, the twins, João Francisco, Zeca, Duran, Alice, Pedro Moraes and Pedro Weinmann, Loló (the homeless man), Frank (who left an hour before the police arrived), Marina, and the guy on the bamboo bicycle. It doesn't all fit together, but a fragment of memory added to another fragment of memory added to another fragment forms a more complete picture than only one point of view would offer you.

There must be close to ten thousand people here. Drums and cries of *Fuck the World Cup*. Now we're passing in front of the gasworks, an old factory converted into a cultural center. The chimney goes up up up and sends word to the cold. From here it would be possible to see the waters of the Guaíba if it weren't night, or if the nighttime lighting were interested in offering us water and shoreline vegetation instead of that end-of-the-world sensation. I start walking a little faster, as if wanting to overtake the front of the march, and as I advance I feel the climate changing from the euphoria of a university celebration to the tension of an imminent battle. Here there are more people with balaclavas and bandannas. They seem like the type that would pick up anything pointed or heavy enough to cause damage. But this part of the city is lacking in urban furnishing; there's only the inhospitable street that will become even more inhospitable after the widening. I stop for an instant and am overtaken by hundreds, so that when I turn around I can again see the horses trotting off to the side. Then I run my eyes along the completely empty parking lot at the edge of the Guaíba and see a guy being struck down.

He's a long way off and very small, but he's all in black, and now he's become a crumpled mass on the ground while two other guys forget any sense of honor and justice and kick him again and again. Fucking shit. I wait about two seconds, perhaps believing that someone, someone other than me, is going to run over there and prevent a greater tragedy. The hero of the day. But no one from that entire multitude seems to have even noticed the shit going on in the empty lot. So it's me running in that direction. It's me frantically waving my arms in a way very similar to the instructions you get in national park pamphlets in the northern hemisphere about how to act if you find yourself face-to-face with a mountain lion or a brown bear. Fortunately, something about that wild choreography works; only twenty meters separate me from the brawl when the pair of aggressors decide to split off at a diagonal, heading, it appears, toward the place where the camp used to be.

The guy has his back to me, curled up, a pile of flesh. He coughs three times as I remove his red bloodstained bandanna. He tries to get up, achieving a relative sense of balance by supporting himself with his knees and his palms on the concrete. A Bordeaux-colored drop that seems like it could fill a kiddie pool drips from his nose. I hear the crowd in the distance like a whistle blowing very loudly in my ear. Then the guy turns his face toward me. It's Zeca, from the encampment. Fucking shit times a thousand.

"What's up, Lucas."

"Shit, man."

"There's alcohol in my backpack, get it for me."

I look around, having some difficulty finding the backpack, then locate it near a scrubby tree. I pull the flap on the largest pocket and find a bottle of rubbing alcohol. There are also two cans of spray paint, some dirty cloths whose use I can't fathom—but then I stop examining the pack because Zeca is calling me and asking if I've found it yet.

He opens the bottle, pours a little of the liquid onto his bandanna, and starts lightly dabbing his mouth and nose. His swollen face contracts from pain. I look at the street and have the impression that the demonstrators have stopped in front of the City Council building. Zeca continues to clean his face, but it's not looking much better.

I finally ask who those two were. Zeca coughs, sitting up on the ground now. He was good at imitating Bob Dylan during our nights around the campfire.

"There was a guy near me in the march taking pictures the whole time," he says, rubbing the bandanna forcefully on his upper lip. "He was P2 for sure."

"Was that one of the guys who attacked you?" I ask, and Zeca emits an inexplicable laugh and answers no, but the point is that all three, according to him, were P2, in other words, plainclothes military infiltrating the masses, probably with their eye on him, Zeca, and the other former members of the encampment, as well as on the anarchists, the student leaders, the participants in social movements—the subversives.

I don't know what to think. Since I started going out with Livia and, through her, meeting idealists of every type—people who used the term *bourgeois* and *capital* indiscriminately, anarchopunks living as squatters, students who can't imagine doing anything during their vacation other than hitchhiking through the poorest countries of South America—I had also come into contact with the highest and most anxious levels of paranoia I had ever experienced. Anyone who showed slightly discordant behavior, or who "undermined the movement" with some immature attitude, was labeled an *infiltrator*. Infiltrators numbered in the dozens, maybe in the hundreds, and were quite transmutable, meaning that yesterday's infiltrator could be a guy with good intentions tomorrow, although mistakes were never acknowledged and the necessary apologies never made. So when Zeca mentions P2—and he's one of the most paranoid of them all, seeing agents in deserted squares, at busy street corners, leaving the college—I again doubt, without saying anything, that our police are really that smart.

Zeca looks at the crowd. Everybody has definitely stopped right in front of the City Council building. Zeca gets up with my help, tests his legs, and realizes he can walk. He says he wants to go to where the others are, which at first strikes me as madness, then as an idiotic whim, but I don't want to seem like a coward, so I say nothing. I have a face without scratches and my legs are good.

"Why'd you bring rubbing alcohol, Zeca?"

He looks at me without answering.

There isn't time. The explosion comes too fast. Then a thick cloud of tear gas expands in all directions, and the group in the rear—which till now was singing jingles demanding better health and more education—surges back, coughs, asks for help, shouts, and then devolves into an uncontrolled wave in search of a piece of land. My throat starts to burn. I grope into my backpack, looking for the bottle of vinegar and the handkerchief. Zeca is covering his face with both hands.

"You got vinegar?" he asks.

"Hold on."

I find the small bottle, soak the two bandannas, and we breathe that smell of salads in the Italian colony in the mountains. Even though we're far away from the crowd, it's hard to keep our eyes open; I can't stop crying, and I feel like laughing at that whole clown show. I try opening my eyes again. Through a thick layer of tears, I manage to capture the general climate of the scene: a good part of the march has dispersed, probably heading toward downtown (assuming they don't get hemmed in by the cavalry). Meanwhile, the people on the front line, with more space now, perform a dizzy sort of choreography, enraged and hurt, feinting an approach but then drawing back at the last moment. Some have wrapped their T-shirts around their faces, despite how fucking cold it is; others still feel confident enough to yell, *Retreat, police, retreat, people power is in the street.*

The police don't retreat, of course. The Shock Troop has formed an isolation cordon a few meters from the barrier protecting the City Council building. With the wind coming off the Guaíba, the tear gas dissipates in a few minutes; we stop sniffing that horrible vinegar, the home remedy that all Brazil uses to reduce the effects of gas. I look at Zeca and feel really bad for him, an emotion I detest, but Zeca's shattered face doesn't leave me much alternative.

"Go home, man," I say. "You look terrible."

"You're crazy," he says. "I've never been so pretty." We burst out laughing. Then, sensing that it's inappropriate to laugh at a time like this, we start moving at the pace of the walking wounded, trying to skirt the field of battle near the City Council. Some protestors are throwing rocks now, and I can hear the brigade retaliating with rubber bullets. Over our heads I see the hanging structure of the aeromovel. That little car moldering up there, the tracks that end suddenly—I never found out why they stopped, why they changed their minds about light rail before *sustainable* became the word of the day—cause a colossal sadness in me. The setting is already semi-apocalyptic, but much more so tonight, with the tear gas and the noise of sirens and the sadistic authorities with their shields. Maybe not the apocalypse itself, but an artificial and modern apocalypse, an apocalypse out of an eighties film.

Something has started to catch fire. Where have the horses gone? I think about calling Livia to tell her what's happening here. Maybe she can supply me with news of the rest of the country, reports on whether the military police in Rio are more vicious than ours, whether anyone more from the press was attacked in São Paulo, how many bottles of vinegar were apprehended, how many bank windows broken, how many small businessmen lost everything, how many thousands of people are feeling that adrenaline, how the giant has awakened, blah blah blah, how the World Cup is going to dot Brazil with white-elephant stadiums—and is it true they invaded the national Congress? Which in fact is a work of Oscar Niemeyer's, like that entire city, the future of the past, the past with no future, something I don't know whether to love or hate. I give up trying to reach Livia.

In the meantime, the black smoke, still a bit distant, seems to have gotten thicker. A bunch of people are in the middle of the street. They ask one another what to do, where to go, how to get everyone together, or at least what's left of everyone, and maybe lead the remnants of the march to the Piratini Palace, the headquarters of the state government. After all, the excesses of the Military Brigade are the fault of the governor, not the mayor, and although the governor is a leftist and the mayor isn't and many people here sympathize with the ideas of the left, what happens is simply that the left comes to power and does everything very much like the right, forming spurious alliances with evangelical parties and having to say no to abortion, and even though you see in her eyes that President Dilma can't be against abortion she has to say so in public pronouncements to build a governing base, so that every time I think for very long about politics I feel like a barrel of shit is being poured over my head.

I'm thinking about all this when suddenly Zeca yells: "Look at Frank over there!"

I thought Frank had been transferred to São Luiz Gonzaga, but it looks like he's still here, or else he came to Porto Alegre just to take part in the demonstration. He recognizes us, smiles, then opens his mouth, amazed. "Holy shit, what happened to you?" he asks. The three of us walk toward the Lower City, which is also the direction of the fire, while Zeca explains the attack with an absurd wealth of detail. When he finishes describing the pair's clothing, their height, their hair (no hair), their noses, the shape of their faces and mouths, and the way their teeth sat, Frank puts his right hand on his forehead and says, "Man, I know exactly who you're talking about." Then he explains that those two are notorious skinheads, did Zeca somehow miss seeing the tattoos? The older one keeps two loaded, sawed-off shotguns in his apartment, along with a calf fetus in a jar of formaldehyde and a gray cat with sparse hair and a flattened face.

"How I know this is another story," continues Frank, "but the thing is, that guy is a nut job, stone crazy, driven by hatred and delusions of self-defense and military tactics. The guy talks about that stuff to anyone who'll listen every Thursday at Bambu's, at the last table on the left, chewing a burger with greasy fries." He also invariably eats three small pickled onions, Frank adds.

I would say Zeca is very disappointed to learn his attack was gratuitous, trivial, random, that he simply became an easy target when he wandered away a bit from the body of the crowd and ran into two assholes who thought he had the features of an Arab, a Jew, a Northeasterner, maybe some of the mannerisms of a homosexual—though he's not a Jew, or an Arab, a Northeasterner, or a homosexual. Zeca insists a while longer on the theory of infiltrators, but the idea won't stand up anymore.

A few particles of soot begin to fall. Besides black smoke, which rises solid as a mushroom cloud before us, we now see the flames. It's a bus. It's been tossed into the middle of the lane, and at this point seems more like the sketch of a hypothetical bus, as if the outlines were the last thing to disappear. There the horses are, lined up at a certain distance. Horses poisoned by the smoke, not knowing what the hell is going on. Frank and Zeca look at each other and smile like they're in a bank commercial.

I take out my cell phone and try to call Livia, but she doesn't answer. Once. Twice. Three times. Nothing. I start to cough a lot, and then a cop and his horse leave the line and come toward me. He looks down at me and asks me to leave. Politely. The horse is white, the only white horse of them all, which greatly impresses me. I back up a few steps and only then realize Frank and Zeca are no longer with me. Where can they have gone? Why didn't they let me know? After that, everything begins to feel very complicated. Like drinking eight shots of cachaça and trying to have a serious discussion about public transportation. People are taking photos of the burning bus with their cell phones. A television crew is filming the action from a distance. The arsonists, some five or six, scurry around the bus, not exactly dancing but seeming as if they are, as if a certain choreography existed in the chaos. All that smoke and the yellow of the flames make their silhouettes more languid, more dramatic, more self-assured. I am especially mesmerized by the one who has the look of a girl who cut all her ballet classes but never missed an opportunity to dance in the street, in her room, on the roof, mainly on the roof, inventing little leaps and twirls for no one and later thinking about how she'd never enjoyed herself as much as she had in those moments. Then that gorgeous fire-setter puts her hand in the rear pocket of her pants, looks at the display of her cell phone, and dials. She waits with the phone up to her ear for a moment, and then I hear my backpack vibrating. Before I can reach for it, something inside the bus explodes and collapses. That's when the cops rush in. No one is more startled than me.

DANIEL ALARCÓN is a novelist, journalist, and radio producer. His most recent novel is *At Night We Walk in Circles*.

CAROL BENSIMON was born in the southern Brazilian city of Porto Alegre, in 1982. She is the author of the story collection *Pó de parede* and two novels, *Sinuca embaixo d'água* and *Todos nós adorávamos caubóis*. In 2012 she was selected by *Granta* as one of the Best New Brazilian Novelists.

RODRIGO BLANCO CALDERÓN is the author of three collections of short stories: *Una larga fila de hombres*, *Los invencibles*, and most recently, *Las rayas*. Blanco Calderón participated in the 2007 Hay Festival Bogota as one of "Latin America's 39 Most Exciting Authors Under 39." He is the founder of the publishing house and bookstore Lugar Común, and he teaches literature at the Universidad Central de Venezuela.

NICK CAISTOR is a translator of more than forty books from Portuguese and Spanish, from authors such as José Saramago, Edney Silvestre, Roberto Arlt, Andrés Neuman, and César Aira. He is the editor and translator of *The Faber Book of Contemporary Latin American Short Stories*, and has contributed translations to many anthologies.

BERNARDO CARVALHO is a Brazilian novelist, journalist, and playwright, born in Rio de Janeiro in 1960. In addition to *Aberração*, a collection of short stories,

he has written ten novels, most recently *Reprodução*. His work has been translated into ten languages. His play *BR-3*, written for the experimental Teatro da Vertigem, was staged on the Tietê river, in São Paulo, and on boats in the bay of Rio. His latest play, *Dire ce qu'on ne pense pas dans des langues qu'on ne parle pas*, will have its world première at the Théâtre National in Brussels, in May 2014.

ANDRÉS RESSIA COLINO is the author of the novels *Palcante* and *Parir*, both of which were honored by the Uruguayan Ministry of Culture. In 2010 he was selected as one of The Best of Young Spanish Language Novelists by *Granta*. He lives in Montevideo, Uruguay.

MARIANA ENRIQUEZ was born in Buenos Aires, Argentina, in 1973. She has a degree in Journalism and Social Communication from Universidad Nacional de La Plata, and she is the editor of *Radar*, the arts and culture suplement for *Pagina/12*. She has published two novels, *Bajar es lo peor* and *Cómo desaparecer completamente*, a collection of short stories, *Los peligros de fumar en la cama*, a novella, *Chicos que vuelven*, and a collection of travel narratives.

ALISON ENTREKIN is a literary translator from Portuguese. Her translations include *City of God* by Paulo Lins; *The Eternal Son* by Cristovão Tezza; *Near to the Wild Heart* by Clarice Lispector; and *Budapest* and *Spilt Milk* by Chico

Buarque. She is a three-time finalist in the New South Wales Premier's Translation Prize & PEN Medallion.

LAIA JUFRESA is a Mexican writer based in Madrid, Spain. She just finished writing her first novel, *Umami*.

DANIEL GALERA is a writer and translator born in 1979. The most recent of his four novels, *Blood-Drenched Beard*, will be published in the U.S., in 2015, by Penguin Press. He has translated works by Zadie Smith, David Foster Wallace, and John Cheever, among others. He lives in Porto Alegre, Brazil.

FRANCISCO GOLDMAN's next book, *The Interior Circuit: A Mexico City Chronicle*, will be published this July. He lives in Mexico City and Brooklyn, and teaches one semester a year at Trinity College in Hartford, Connecticut.

JEFFREY GRAY is a professor of English at Seton Hall University. He is author of *Mastery's End: Travel and Postwar American Poetry* and of many articles on poetry and American culture. He is editor of the five-volume *Greenwood Encyclopedia of American Poets and Poetry*; co-editor (with Ann Keniston) of the recent *The New American Poetry of Engagement: A 21st Century Anthology*; and translator of Guatemalan novelist Rodrigo Rey Rosa's *The African Shore*. He was born and raised in Seattle, Washington, and has lived in Asia, the South Pacific, Europe, and Latin America.

DANIEL GUMBINER is the managing editor of this quarterly. He lives in Berkeley, California.

Born in Cochabamba, Bolivia, in 1981, **RODRIGO HASBÚN** has published two books of short stories, *Cinco* and *Los días más felices*, and a novel, *El lugar del cuerpo*. He was awarded the Latin Union Prize, and his stories have been adapted into the films *Rojo* and *Los viejos*, for which he co-wrote the screenplays. In 2010 he was selected as one of the Best of Young Spanish Language Novelists by *Granta*. He currently lives in Toronto, Canada.

YURI HERRERA is a Mexican writer. His novel *Trabajos del reino* won the Premio Binacional de Novela Joven 2003 and received the Otras Voces, Otros Ámbitos prize. His second novel, *Señales que precederán al fin del mundo*, was a finalist for the Rómulo Gallegos Prize. Most recently, he published the novel *La transmigración de los cuerpos*. His work has been translated into several languages. He is currently an associate professor at the University of Tulane.

ANNA KUSHNER was born in Philadelphia and first traveled to Cuba in 1999. She has translated the novels of Leonardo Padura, Guillermo Rosales, Norberto Fuentes, and Gonçalo M. Tavares.

JORGE ENRIQUE LAGE is a writer and editor from Havana, Cuba. He has published five collections of stories, *Yo fui* *un adolescente ladrón de tumbas*, *Fragmentos encontrados en La Rampa*, *Los ojos de fuego verde*, *El color de la sangre diluida*, and *Vultureffect*. He is also the author of the novel *Carbono 14, una novela de culto*. His most recent work, *La autopista, the movie*, is forthcoming in 2014.

CLIFFORD E. LANDERS has translated more than two dozen book-length works from Portuguese, including novels by Rubem Fonseca, João Ubaldo Ribeiro, Jorge Amado, Patrícia Melo, Jô Soares, Chico Buarque, Ignácio de Loyola Brandão, Nélida Piñon, Paulo Coelho, Marcos Rey, and José de Alencar. He is a recipient of the Mario Ferreira award and author of *Literary Translation: A Practical Guide*. A professor emeritus at New Jersey City University, he resides in Naples, Florida.

VALERIA LUISELLI was born in Mexico City and grew up in South Africa. She is the author of the novel *Faces in the Crowd* and the book of essays *Sidewalks*, which have been translated into more than ten languages. Her nonfiction pieces have appeared in the *New York Times*, *Granta*, and *Letras Libres*, and she has worked as a ballet librettist for the New York City Ballet. Her most recent novel, *The Story of My Teeth*, is forthcoming from Coffee House Press. She lives in New York City.

MEGAN McDOWELL is a literary translator from Richmond, Kentucky. Her translations have appeared in *Words Without Borders*, *Mandorla*, the *Los Angeles*

Review of Books, and *Granta*. She has translated books by Alejandro Zambra, Arturo Fontaine, Carlos Busqued, and Juan Emar. She is also a managing editor of *Asymptote* journal. She lives in Zurich, Switzerland.

KATHERINE SILVER is an award-winning translator of literature from Spanish and also the codirector of the Banff International Literary Translation Centre (BILTC) in Alberta, Canada. Her most recent translations include works by Martín Adán, Daniel Sada, Horacio Castellanos Moya, César Aira, Rafael Bernal, Jorge Luis Borges, and Marcos Giralt Torrente.

RODRIGO REY ROSA was born in Guatemala in 1958. After finishing his studies in his country, he lived in New York, and later in Tangier, Morocco. Rey Rosa has translated several books by Paul Bowles into Spanish, as well as the works of other authors such as Norman Lewis, Paul Léauteaud, and François Augiéras. He is the author of several novels and short story collections, including *The Beggar's Knife*, *The Pelicari Project*, *The Good Cripple*, *Severina*, and most recently, *The Deaf*.

CAROLINA DE ROBERTIS is the internationally best-selling author of the novels *Perla* and *The Invisible Mountain*. Her work has been translated into sixteen languages. She is also the translator of two Latin American novels: *The Neruda Case*, by Roberto Ampuero, and *Bonsai*, by Alejandro Zambra. Her writings and literary translations have appeared in *Granta*, *Zoetrope: All-Story*, *The Virginia Quarterly Review*, and elsewhere. De Robertis teaches creative writing at the Latin America MFA through Queens University. She lives with her wife and two small children in Oakland, California, and Montevideo, Uruguay.

SANTIAGO RONCAGLIOLO is the author of *Abril rojo*, winner of the Premio Alfaguara de Novela and the Independent Foreign Fiction Prize. He is also the author of a book of short stories, *Crecer es un oficio triste*; a journalistic research book, *La cuarta espada*; a literary biography, *El amante uruguayo*; and a children's book, *Matías y los imposibles*. His works have been translated into more than fifteen languages. His most recent novel is *Tan cerca de la vida*.

ANDRÉS FELIPE SOLANO is the author of the novels *Sálvame, Joe Louis*, and *Los hermanos Cuervo*. His work has appeared in the *New York Times Magazine*, *Words Without Borders*, and *Anew*. He was selected as one of the Best of Young Spanish Language Novelists by *Granta*. He currently lives in Seoul, South Korea.

JOEL STREICKER's translations of Latin American authors have appeared in *A Public Space*, *Subtropics*, *Words Without Borders*, *Zyzzyva*, and *Epiphany*. He received a 2011 PEN American Center

Translation Fund Grant to translate Samanta Schweblin's collection of short stories, *Pájaros en la boca*. Streicker holds a B.A. in Latin American studies from the University of Michigan and a PhD in cultural anthropology from Stanford University.

JOCA REINERS TERRON is a novelist, poet, and Brazilian playwright. He was born in Cuiabá, Mato Grosso, and now lives in São Paulo. He started the Ministry of Disaster, an independent publishing house that galvanized the Brazilian literary scene in the nineties. His novels include *São Não Há Nada Lá*, *Hotel Hell*, *Do Fundo do Poço se Vê a Lua* (awarded the Machado de Assis Prize for Best Novel of 2010 by the Brazilian National Library), and *A Tristeza Extraordinária do Leopardo-das-Neves*. He has also released the graphic novel *Guia de Ruas Sem Saída*, illustrated by André Ducci. He writes reviews for the newspaper *Folha de S. Paulo*, among others.

STEFAN TOBLER is a literary translator from Portuguese and German, and the publisher at And Other Stories, a young publishing house that features literature in translation. Tobler's most recent translations include *All Dogs Are Blue*, by Rodrigo de Souza Leão, and *Água Viva*, by Clarice Lispector.

JUAN PABLO VILLALOBOS is the author of *Down the Rabbit Hole* and *Quesadillas*. His work has been translated into fifteen languages. He was born in Mexico and currently lives in Brazil.

NATASHA WIMMER is the translator of Roberto Bolaño's *The Savage Detectives* and *2666*, among other books. She lives in New York City.

ALEJANDRO ZAMBRA is a Chilean writer, poet, and critic. He currently teaches literature at the Diego Portales University in Santiago. His first novel, *Bonsai*, was awarded Chile's Literary Critics' Award for Best Novel, and the English translation by Carolina De Robertis was a finalist for the Best Translated Book Award. The novel was adapted for film by Cristián Jiménez and released at Cannes. Zambra has also published two poetry collections, *Bahía inútil* and *Mudanza*, and a book of essays called *No leer*. He was selected in 2010 as one of the Best of Young Spanish Language Novelists by *Granta*.

ALSO AVAILABLE FROM McSWEENEY'S

store.mcsweeneys.net

FICTION

ALL THIS AND MORE

store.mcsweeneys.net

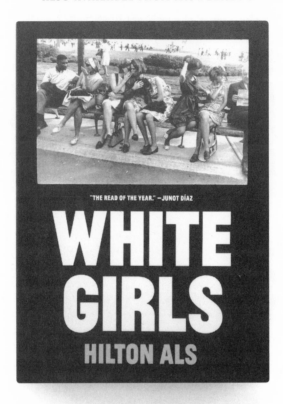

WHITE GIRLS
by Hilton Als

"The read of the year." —Junot Diaz

White Girls, Hilton Als's first book since *The Women* seventeen years ago, finds one of the *New Yorker*'s boldest cultural critics deftly weaving together his brilliant analyses of literature, art, and music with fearless insights on race, gender, and history. The result is an extraordinary, complex portrait of "white girls," as Als dubs them—an expansive but precise category that encompasses figures as diverse as Truman Capote and Louise Brooks, Malcolm X and Flannery O'Connor. In pieces that hairpin between critique and meditation, fiction and nonfiction, high culture and low, the theoretical and the deeply personal, Als presents a stunning portrait of a writer by way of his subjects, and an invaluable guide to the culture of our time.

THE PORTLANDIA ACTIVITY BOOK
by Fred Armisen, Carrie Brownstein, and Jonathan Krisel

This is *The Portlandia Activity Book*—a compendium of guaranteed enrichment for the Pacific Northwestern part of your psyche. Like a cool high school that prefers a sweat lodge to the traditional classroom, this book will expand your mind through participation, dehydrate you to a state of emotional rawness, then linger in the corners of your bare soul.

Here you will find enough activities to get you through a year's worth of rainy days, including: *How to Crowdfund Your Baby*, *Punk Paint by Numbers*, *Terrarium Foraging*, and so much more. With pages unlike any you've seen before, this is the kind of book that you can be yourself around. Shed the trappings of normalcy, let down your glorious mane, and take the deepest breath of your life. Portlandia is beckoning your arrival.

THE PARALLEL APARTMENTS
by Bill Cotter

Justine Moppett is thirty-four, pregnant, and fleeing an abusive relationship in New York to dig up an even more traumatic childhood in Austin. Waiting for her there is a cast of more than a dozen misfits—a hemophobic aspiring serial killer, a deranged soprano opera singer, a debt-addicted entrepreneur-cum-madam, a matchmaking hermaphrodite—all hurtling toward their own calamities, and, ultimately, toward each other.

A Texan Gabriel García Márquez who writes tragicomic twists reminiscent of John Kennedy Toole, Bill Cotter produces some of the most visceral, absurd, and downright hilarious sentences to be found in fiction today. *The Parallel Apartments* is a bold leap forward for a writer whose protean talents, and sheer exuberance for language and what a novel can do, mark him as one of the most exciting stylists in America.

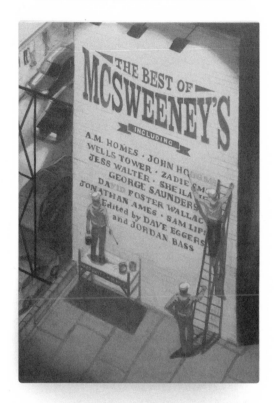

THE BEST OF McSWEENEY'S
Featuring more than forty of your favorite writers

To commemorate the fifteenth anniversary of the journal called "a key barometer of the literary climate" by the *New York Times* and twice honored with a National Magazine Award for fiction, here is *The Best of McSweeney's*—a comprehensive collection of the most remarkable work from a remarkable magazine. Drawing on the full range of the journal thus far—from the very earliest volumes to our groundbreaking, Chris Ware–edited graphic novel issue to our most popular project yet, the full-on Sunday-newspaper issue known as *San Francisco Panorama*—*The Best of McSweeney's* is an essential retrospective of recent literary history. With full-color contributions from some of the pioneering artists and illustrators featured in our pages over the years and a breathtaking array of first-rate fiction (and some incredible nonfiction, too), this is a book to be pored over, and lasting proof that the contemporary short story is as vital as ever.

NEXT ISSUE

Stories by
MONA SIMPSON
KAWAI WASHBURN
JUSTIN BIGOS
LYNN COADY
BILL COTTER
JOSEPHINE ROWE
THOMAS McGUANE

An entire mini-book of new humor by
BOB ODENKIRK

Two unearthed, never-before-seen stories by
SHIRLEY JACKSON

Subscribe at store.mcsweeneys.net